Oct 5/07

FOREIGN
AFFAIRS

NICK WILKSHIRE

a novel

FOREIGN AFFAIRS

NICK WILKSHIRE

JESPERSON PUBLISHING

JESPERSON PUBLISHING
100 Water Street
P. O. Box 2188
St. John's, NL
A1C 6E6
www.jespersonpublishing.nf.net

Library and Archives Canada Cataloguing in Publication

Wilkshire, Nicholas, 1968-
    Foreign Affairs / Nick Wilkshire

ISBN 978-1-894377-24-9
I. Title.
PS8645.I44F67 2007   C813'.6   C2007-904733-5
©2007 Nicholas Wilkshire

We acknowledge the financial support of
The Canada Council for the Arts for our
publishing activities.

We acknowledge the support of the Department of Tourism,
Culture and Recreation for our publishing activities.

Printed in Canada

For my parents

acknowledgements

Thanks to Rebecca Rose and everyone at Jesperson, especially Annamarie Beckel for your excellent work in editing. Special thanks also to Constable Cory Hoehn of the RCMP for your invaluable advice.

Thanks, as always, to Tanya and the three amigos...for everything.

one

It was still early May, but the mid-morning sun was already hot. The streets of Aix-en-Provence were filled with the usual mix of locals and students, all making their way to the city's central artery, the tree-lined Cours Mirabeau – home to a vast array of sidewalk cafés and boulangeries. Jean-Christophe Malle tossed a two-franc piece at the newsstand proprietor and flashed him a smile.

"Bonjour, Gaston, ça va ce matin?"

"B'jour, M'sieur Malle. Quel beau temps," the man replied in a thick Provençal accent, his weather-beaten face creased in a smile.

Malle glanced at the cover of the paper as he continued on his way towards the Cours. He looked at his watch to confirm he had time for a quick coffee before his meeting, then skipped across the gridlocked traffic on the Cours and sat at a table outside one of the many sidewalk cafés, this one named La Belle Époque. Within seconds, a young waiter was hovering over him with a tray full of empty coffee cups.

"Café au lait."

"Oui, monsieur," the waiter replied, disappearing inside.

"Bonjour, mesd'moiselles," Malle said, noticing a group of pretty young Scandinavian students at an adjacent table. The closest one smiled awkwardly and replied in broken French before turning towards her friends and giggling something in Swedish.

Malle smiled and returned to his paper. He was old enough to be their father, but he took care of himself and his good looks kept him in constant supply of younger women. A career bureaucrat from Paris, Malle had taken early retirement and recently bought a spacious one-bedroom apartment just minutes from the Cours. Not content to live off his generous pension, he had applied to teach some political science courses at a local school for foreign students. With any luck, he thought to himself, he would end up with a class full of young Scandinavians like the ones at the next table. There were worse things he could be doing with his twilight years, he decided.

As his coffee arrived, Malle put down his paper and lit a Gauloise, exhaling a satisfying line of blue smoke that spread up towards the bright spring sky. He noticed a slight sway in the tops of the trees along the Cours and wondered if the Mistral was blowing down on the coast. He would be in Nice tonight, and he hoped to get some windsurfing in on the weekend before returning to Aix on Sunday. He was suddenly reminded to confirm his reservation and reached for his cell phone, eyeing the group of students as they got up and donned their backpacks. More shy smiles in his direction – he really didn't find the young ones much of a challenge any more. Not like his date for the weekend, he thought as he waited to be connected to the front desk of the Negresco Hotel.

Malle had met Annie Renaud at a cocktail party a few months prior and had sensed fireworks from the moment he saw her. Strong of will and exuding self-confidence, she was unlike any of the women he had dated in recent memory. Annie knew exactly what she wanted and had no reservations about getting it. For his part, Malle was quite prepared to accept his role as the other man – merely a temporary diversion for her. But he was no less content to be used for sexual purposes, while fulfilling his own in the process. With his reservation confirmed, he sat back and leisurely finished his coffee, watching the passing drivers honk and shout at each other out on the Cours. And though he tried to concentrate on his newspaper, Malle's mind was occupied with thoughts of the two nights he would spend this weekend in Nice. His reverie was broken by the appearance of the waiter, who tucked a small bill under Malle's saucer. Settling up, he gathered his things and made his way up the cobblestone streets into the heart of the old city, and to his meeting with the school's director.

Jean-Christophe Malle skilfully maneuvered his Audi up the narrow Rue des Quatre Dauphins and pulled into the reserved parking spot a few doors down from his building. He smiled and let out a contented sigh as he shut off the engine and pulled the key from the ignition. The two-hour drive from Nice had been well worth it. He'd spent a large part of the weekend in bed with the insatiable Annie. Her fiancé was one lucky bastard, Malle thought as visions of the past two nights returned in vivid detail. He shook his head and looked at his watch. It was late and he was teaching his first class tomorrow, and he really shouldn't have had all that wine with dinner. Together, they had polished off a couple of bottles before he had hit the autoroute. He got out of the car and went around to the rear, releasing the trunk and retrieving his suit bag. Making his way towards his apartment, he smiled as he listened to the sound of singing voices carried by the warm evening air from the cafés on the Cours. Crossing the entrance to a nearby alley, Malle was plucked clean off his feet and pulled back into the alley by a force around his neck so powerful he could hardly breathe. As his bag fell to the ground, Malle tried to shout but couldn't get out a sound as what he realized now was a forearm tightened around his neck, unmoved by his flailing attempts to loosen its grip. Malle kicked his legs desperately as he was backed into the shadows and he felt hot breath on his ear.

"Don't make a sound," Malle's assailant said gruffly, in an accent that Malle had heard before but couldn't quite place. His eyes grew wide as he saw the glint of a knife blade in front of him.

"Take my wallet...my watch," Malle managed to whisper, his heart pounding. He felt the hot breath in his ear again.

"I don't want your money. I want to watch you die."

Malle tried to squirm out of the chokehold, but it was pointless. He kicked frantically as he felt the cold steel plunge into his neck, tearing its way across. He tried to scream but could only manage a gurgle as his life drained out of him. As he slumped forward and fell to the ground, he heard again the gruff voice that uttered the last words he would ever hear: "That's for Annie."

Malle's assailant folded up the knife and tucked it into his waistband, then dragged the body to the side of the darkened alley. He glanced around quickly before disappearing into the shadows along the Rue des Quatre Dauphins. As the echo of his footsteps on the cobblestones faded into the distance, a shadow emerged from a doorway twenty feet down the alley, and a form shuffled cautiously forward. Approaching the lifeless body, the man recoiled at the ghastly sight of Malle's shredded neck and his hollow, ghostly stare. The man paused for a moment, fighting an urge to vomit, then collected himself and moved off towards the lights and sounds coming from the Cours Mirabeau.

two

Karl Roy cursed as he swerved to avoid being run off the road by a merging car. Unfazed by the near miss, he hopped the front wheel of his bike up onto the sidewalk and carried on peddling along the Portage Bridge through the morning rush. Once on the Ottawa side of the river, he headed east down Wellington Street, past the Parliament buildings, their gothic towers glinting in the morning sunlight. At the Chateau Laurier, he turned onto Sussex Drive and passed the American Embassy and the Byward Market before arriving several minutes later at the sprawling building that housed the Department of Foreign Affairs and International Trade. As he locked up his bike outside, he glanced at his watch. All in all, the ride from his apartment on the Quebec side of the river had taken less than fifteen minutes – not at all bad for rush hour.

Roy took a long sip of the cold water in his bike bottle before joining the steady flow of people entering the building. It was going to be another muggy spring day, projected to hit the mid-30's, and by the looks of it, the sun would be out for his uphill ride home. Roy waved his security badge under the guard's nose and made his way to the basement locker rooms, where he stowed his helmet and unloaded his backpack. Although he held a mid-level position as a foreign policy advisor, Roy was not much of a clothes-horse, preferring to spend his money on travel and sports gear. Still in his early thirties, he was also a product of the casual dress movement, which reserved a tie for only the most formal of meetings. With none on the radar today, he quickly changed out of his cycling gear into wrinkle-free khakis, loafers and a polo shirt and made his way to the elevators.

Arriving on the fifth floor, he passed more security and stopped into the little kitchen to fill his cup with coffee before unlocking the door to his office and settling behind his desk. He usually arrived an hour ahead of the rest of his unit and took advantage of the quiet to organize his day. It also allowed him to beat the worst of the rush hour on the bridges most days. Firing up his computer, he went through the list of e-mails that had accumulated since the previous day. He deleted the half that were junk and selected the rest to be printed. Noticing the flashing light on his phone, he checked his messages and discovered one from a real estate agent with a line on an apartment in the Glebe. He called back and, getting the answering service, left a message suggesting a lunchtime showing. He had been back in Canada for only three weeks but he was already getting tired of the cramped little basement apartment he had rented on a month-to-month basis. He was also keen to try living on the Ottawa side for a change, having grown up in Gatineau. In fact, after the month he had just had, he was intent on starting a whole new life.

"Karl, over here."

Roy spun around and caught sight of John Brewer sitting under an umbrella at the far end of an outdoor café in the Byward Market. With the largest concentration of restaurants in the downtown core, the Market's proximity was one of the perks of working at Foreign Affairs.

"I got here a little early and bagged us a table – it's crazy here at lunchtime."

"Good work. Too bad you can't find me an apartment too." Roy smiled.

"You just can't please some people."

"So the Glebe apartment didn't last long."

"Like I said, it was too good of a deal to last. By the time I called to get us a showing, it was gone. But we'll get you out of that dungeon before the end of the month – don't worry."

Brewer had been Roy's best friend in high school and though he had spent a couple of semesters at the University of Ottawa majoring in keg parties, he had soon had enough of academic life and moved on to real estate. The two had remained in touch and in the time Roy had spent getting his master's in political science, Brewer had made a small fortune in the ballooning Ottawa residential real estate market. Based on this initial success, he had entered the commercial market and made quite a name for himself. And though he enjoyed the perks of financial success, including a swanky condo near the Market, a shiny sports car and a chalet in Mont Tremblant, Brewer remained down to earth with his friends.

"So how's the new job?" he said as the waitress handed them their menus.

"Not bad. I know some of the people from a few years back. And the rest seem like a decent group so far."

"Can't interest you in some real work?" Brewer said with a wink.

"No thanks." Before deciding to do his master's, Roy had worked in marketing with a Toronto firm and spent a couple of frantic years chasing the clock until he realized he just wasn't cut out for life in the fast lane.

"The money my clients spend on these big-shots, and for what? I could send a shitload of business your way – you wouldn't have to take it all, you know," Brewer said.

"Yeah, I'm sure you punch out every day at five." Roy smiled, shaking his head.

"You're right – there's more to life. Traveling around and expe-riencing other cultures, meeting..." Brewer trailed off. "Sorry man."

"Don't worry about it, better to find out now than later."

"You got that right. Besides, plenty of fish in the sea." Brewer was cursing himself for bringing it up. He knew Roy had returned from a three-year posting abroad only after discovering his fiancée was sleeping around.

"I think I'm just going to steer clear of the fairer sex altogether for a while," Roy said.

"Yeah, I know what you mean," Brewer said, sipping his water. "Not that it matters, but did you ever find out who the guy was?"

"No idea. All I know is I came home early from a conference in Paris hoping to surprise her and...Well, I guess I'm the one that got the surprise. While she was running around half-naked, some guy was taking off out the back door."

"That really sucks. How long were you together?"

"About eighteen months. She really had me fooled."

"Listen, I know just what you need," Brewer said.

"Oh yeah, what's that?"

"She's a real estate agent I met just the other day. She's new in town and unattached. Lots of fun and very attractive."

"Thanks but I'm not really looking–"

"I know you're not looking, but neither is she – that's why it's perfect."

"I don't know," Roy said, shaking his head.

"You can double with me and Jane. Dinner at Fortino's Friday night – don't say no."

Roy smiled. He knew his friend meant well. He also knew Brewer would drive him crazy until he gave in, so he chose the path of least resistance. "Sure, why not?"

"Attaboy. I'll set it up today."

The two chatted and laughed through lunch, and before he knew it, Roy was looking at his watch in alarm. "Wow, is that the right time? I've got to get back."

"What's on the agenda – installing a puppet regime in some rebel outpost in the southern hemisphere?" Brewer asked, waving to the waitress and mouthing a request for the cheque.

"Hey, we're the good guys, remember?" Roy replied, reaching for his wallet.

"Put that away." Brewer frowned, snatching the bill and giving the waitress his plastic.

"What am I, a charity case now?"

"No, but I get to write it off."

"Did we discuss business? I didn't notice."

"Well, listen up. I've got a line on two very nice pads – one's just around the corner from here and the other's on the canal. How's your afternoon looking for tomorrow?"

"Clear, I think. I'll give you a call if it's not."

"Good, I'll call you later with the times."

Brewer signed the receipt and they made their way to the door and said goodbye. Walking back along Sussex Drive in the sunshine, Roy felt much better than he had in days. Brewer was always good for his spirits. And why shouldn't he start dating again? He had felt sorry for himself for long enough and it was time to move on. He had just changed jobs and in a couple of weeks he would have a new place to live, so why not jump back into the dating pool? Glancing at his watch, he quickened his pace. He had a lot of work to get through before the end of the day.

Roy sat behind his computer composing an e-mail to a colleague in another policy unit. An impromptu meeting had gone on longer than expected – it was almost five o'clock – and had raised some interesting questions that he could use some help resolving.

As he finished the message, an assistant poked her head around the door. "There's someone here to see you," she said tentatively. "Were you expecting the police?"

Roy looked up from his computer. "Police? I wasn't expecting them, but tell them I'll be out in a second."

She disappeared and he returned his attention to finishing his e-mail. A few minutes later, he was out at the reception area. "Karl Roy," he said, extending his hand to the first of the two cops, neither of whom was in uniform.

"Detective Francis Granger," said the first, getting up and enveloping Roy's hand in a bone-crushing grip. "And this is Inspector Morris," he said, motioning to his younger colleague.

"What can I do for you?" Roy said.

"We'd like to have a word with you regarding an incident in France."

"France? That's no longer my file."

"Perhaps we could discuss this in your office," Granger said, looking at the puzzled receptionist.

"Sure." Roy shrugged his shoulders and led them back to his office. "Have a seat," he said, closing the door behind them.

"Thank you," Granger said as he and his partner sat.

"So what's this all about?" Roy asked, leaning back in his chair. Although he didn't feel threatened by the two men sitting across from him, he was more than a little curious as to why they were here.

"We're investigating a recent incident that occurred in Aix-en-Provence," Granger began.

"Like I said, that's no longer my area. I've been assigned to the Americas file."

"Actually, this incident occurred during your posting in Nice, and we were hoping you could provide us with some details," Granger continued with an easy smile.

"Well, I'll certainly help you if I can."

"Do you know a Jean-Christophe Malle?" the younger officer asked.

"Malle?" After considering the question for a moment, Roy shook his head. "I don't know that name."

"How about Annie Renaud?" Granger asked.

Roy recoiled slightly, stung by the sound of her name. "Yes, I know her," he said.

"How do you know her?" Morris asked.

"Can I ask what this is all about? I'm not sure I like–"

"She was your fiancée, wasn't she?" Granger continued casually.

Roy felt his cheeks colouring. "I really think I'm entitled to know what this is all about," he said, trying to control his anger.

"Jean-Christophe Malle was murdered three weeks ago in Aix," Granger said, watching Roy intently.

"I already told you, I've never heard of him. And what does that have to do with Annie anyway?"

"Mr. Malle was last seen alive in the company of Annie Renaud in Nice, where they shared a suite at the Negresco Hotel for the weekend." Granger paused to let it sink in before adding, "I believe it was the weekend before you returned to Ottawa."

Though Roy was frozen in his chair, his mind was quickly assessing the danger he was in. The break-up of his relationship was known to plenty of people in the Canadian consular office in Nice, as was his sudden request not to renew his posting in France for the two-year rotation he had been planning. It was obvious the police had already talked to a number of people before arriving at his door. As he tried to regain his composure, his survival instincts began to kick in. "I'd like to speak to a lawyer before I say anything else."

"Sure." Granger nodded and Roy felt a rush of relief. But it was short-lived.

"You can contact a lawyer from the station," said Granger. "We'd like you to come there with us, to answer some more questions."

"Am I being charged with something?"

"You're being detained under the authority of this warrant," Morris said, retrieving a document from his briefcase and passing it to Granger, who slid it across the desk.

"I'd like to make a call first," Roy said as he scanned the document and reached for his phone.

"You can make your call from Elgin Street, Mr. Roy."

It was "Mr. Roy" now, and the friendly tone was noticeably absent. Roy hesitated, the receiver in his hand.

"Come on, Mr. Roy," the younger officer said in a lighter tone. "We don't want to embarrass you here. You'll be given every opportunity to contact counsel, don't worry."

Hearing the footsteps of colleagues outside his door, Roy decided to go quietly. As he left his office between the two cops, he noticed a puzzled look on the face of a junior analyst down the hall.

"Everything all right, Karl?" his assistant asked, appearing from the photocopying room.

"Yeah, just some information-sharing," he said, giving her a smile. Passing the front desk, he stopped long enough to give a furtive glance to the receptionist, who returned it with a look of concern.

"Are you sure everything's all right?"

"Get the number for Peter Verdun out of my day-timer and call him," he said quickly, as Granger grasped him by the arm.

"Come on, Mr. Roy."

"Tell him I'm at the Elgin Street police station and it's urgent he get hold of me ASAP," Roy added over his shoulder before he was tugged out the front door.

three

Peter Verdun locked his car door and looked at his watch. He was late again. Cursing to himself, he tucked his keys in his pocket and hurried towards the entrance to the police station. His pre-trial conference had run twenty minutes over and by the time he finished here, there was no way he was going to make his lunch date. Still, when he thought of Karl Roy and what he must be going through right now, a missed lunch was pretty insignificant.

Verdun and Roy had been undergraduate classmates and had kept in touch over the years, despite Roy's extended absences abroad and the fact that they had gone down very different career paths. After law school, Verdun had started out in a big firm but had soon become bored with commercial paperwork and had switched to criminal defence. In the past five years, he had developed into an experienced advocate for a wide range of clients, charged with everything from impaired driving and petty theft to robbery and murder. He had seen some pretty unusual things in his line of work, but nothing had surprised him more than the call he had received the previous afternoon from Roy's frantic secretary. By the time he had made some inquiries and determined what he was up against, it had been too late to see Roy, though he had spoken with him by phone long enough to tell him to say nothing until they had been given an opportunity to meet. He knew Roy well enough to know that there had to be a mistake – he was incapable of murder – and Verdun was keen to right this wrong as soon as possible.

Entering the building and presenting himself at the front desk, he pulled out his agenda and scratched out the lunch date. His secretary had already gotten into his afternoon so it was unlikely the lunch would have survived anyway. As he sat there waiting, he tried to remember the last time he had seen Roy. It must have been three years ago, at a U of O alumni party. Roy had been on his way to the South of France at the time. Verdun recalled being envious, to the point of questioning his own career choice at a time when he was particularly busy and beginning to feel the effects of burning the candle at both ends for months on end. He pictured them having a drink and discussing the advantages of a diplomatic posting on the French Riviera.

His thoughts were interrupted by the approach of a young woman in uniform.

"Mr. Verdun?" she said.

"Yes." Verdun stood up to greet her.

"You can see your client now. Please follow me."

He followed her down the hall to an elevator.

"Another beautiful morning," she said as they boarded the elevator and she pressed the button for the basement.

"Yes, it is," he replied with a smile. "I didn't catch your name."

"Corporal Green."

"What's the 'S' for?" Verdun asked, pointing at a badge pinned to her chest.

"Stacy," she said.

They exchanged smiles during the awkward silence before the elevator doors opened onto the detention floor. He followed as she led them to another secured area and she spoke through an intercom to a uniformed officer behind a locked door.

"Corporal Benoit will escort you to the meeting room," she said as the door buzzed and a burly officer brought him back into the detention area. Verdun followed him down a hall and waited as the guard unlocked a door and led him into a small, stark meeting room furnished only with a metal table and chairs. It featured another door on the opposite side, next to what looked like a one-way window.

"Have a seat if you like," the guard said. "Your client will be here in a minute."

"Thanks," Verdun said, preferring to stand. He set his brief-case on the table and took out a legal pad. A few seconds later, the door on the other side of the room opened and Roy was led in by a guard and seated at the table.

"Karl, how are you doing?" Verdun said, shaking Roy's hand as the guard left the room and closed the second door, presumably to take his post on the other side of the window.

"I've been better," Roy said with a sigh. "What's it been, four years?"

"Something like that."

"Bet you never thought you'd be representing a former classmate," Roy said.

Verdun laughed. "I've been doing defence work long enough to know it doesn't take much to get tangled up in the system, other than being in the wrong place at the wrong time. Obviously there's been some misunderstanding."

Roy nodded his head slowly.

"Don't worry, Karl, we'll get it straightened out."

"I hope you're right. What have they told you?"

"All I know is they're holding you on some kind of international warrant I'm not familiar with. But they can't keep you for long without facing a *habeus corpus* application."

"So where do we start?"

"Tell me what happened. Starting yesterday afternoon with the visit from the police."

Roy described the arrival of Granger and Morris, and their inquiries about the murdered Frenchman and Roy's relationship with his ex-fiancée.

"And you don't know this...what's his name again?" Verdun interjected.

"Malle, Jean-Christophe Malle. No, I've never heard of him."

"All right, go on," Verdun said as he scribbled the name on his pad.

Roy continued the narrative, explaining his posting to Nice – one of Foreign Affairs' consular posts – how he met Annie and how he discovered her affair.

"So you saw the man she was sleeping with?" Verdun said quickly, before catching himself and looking up from his notes. "I'm sorry, I know this must be painful."

"It's all right, I'm not that worried about my feelings right now," Roy said. "And I didn't really see him. It was dark and he was already out the back door by the time I knew what was happening. I just caught a glimpse of his back before he disappeared into the shadows."

"Did you catch his hair colour or height?" Verdun asked, looking up from the notepad.

"He had dark hair – I'm pretty sure of that. As for his height, I've never been good at judging people's height, but I'd say he was average."

"What about Annie?" Verdun said, putting down his pen. "You said you met at a wine and cheese or something. What did she do?"

"She was a policy analyst with French Immigration Services – specializing in North Africa."

"What was her background?"

"Born in Marseille, went to university in Paris and worked there for a couple of years in another government department before returning to Marseille."

"And when did you meet?" There was a brief silence, following which Verdun looked up from his notes to see Roy staring at his hands. "Are you all right?" Verdun asked.

"What? Yeah, sure." Roy tried a half-hearted smile. He had been thinking about Annie, daydreaming about her smoothly tanned skin and long blond hair – the way she had looked that early spring day they had taken the train to Cassis, a little seaside town east of the Côte d'Azur. Leaving their towels and empty picnic basket on the beach, they had swum around the little peninsula that sheltered it and come ashore on the rocks. He had clambered eagerly after her as she led the way up into the cliffs, until she stopped in a little alcove protected from the wind, and from prying eyes. They had made love and dozed in each other's arms, in the glow of the afternoon sun.

It was hard to believe now that this dream world had still been real just a few short months ago. That it had come apart so quickly made it all the more difficult to bear. But worst of all was the heartache, a numbing pain that invaded his chest and then made its way through his whole body whenever he allowed his mind to wander. Like an addict waking from a sweet dream to find the stark reality of withdrawal gnawing at his very soul, Roy was brought back to the present by Verdun's question.

"We met almost a year ago – around Easter," Roy said, feeling a sudden urge to smoke, though he had quit several years before. "We saw each other on weekends for several months, then she moved to Nice last Christmas. We got engaged on Valentine's Day."

Verdun continued along the same line of questioning for a little while longer before changing tack. "What was the nature of your work in Nice?"

"Trade PR for the most part. There was some policy work, but the focus was developing new areas of trade."

"Did you deal with a lot of secret material?"

"Some of it was, but the majority of it was just routine."

"Did Annie have access to any of the more sensitive material?"

"I rarely took work home, and if I did, it wouldn't have been the secret stuff," Roy said, letting out a small sigh. He wondered what Verdun must think of him and the sorry state in which he now found himself. For the time being though, he was content just to answer the questions without trying to guess what was going through his friend's mind.

"What about your relationship with colleagues, friends? Any trouble?"

Roy shook his head. "None."

"Is there any reason, financial or other, why someone would want to frame you?" Verdun asked.

"I haven't come into any money since my university days, if that's what you mean," Roy said. "And not many people are going to take the trouble to try and extort money from someone whose only income is from a government pay cheque."

They continued until after noon, when Verdun finished his scribbling and looked up at his friend. "Well, I think I've got enough for now. I'll get disclosure from the Crown this afternoon and we'll have another sit down to go through it – perhaps this evening."

"What about your retainer?" Roy asked. "How much do you need up front?"

"We can talk about that later. For now, let's concentrate on trying to convince them they're on a wild goose chase. We'll know more soon."

Verdun packed his things in his briefcase and got up to shake Roy's hand as the guard came in. "Try not to worry. I'm sure we'll get it straightened out."

"Thanks, Peter," Roy said, shaking his hand.

Verdun sighed, dropped the affidavit on his desk and ran his hands through his hair. The more he read, the more he began to realize how much trouble Karl Roy was in. "Wendy," he called to the paralegal who was walking by his office.

"Yes?" she said, poking her head around the door.

"Could you find me a copy of the Extradition Act please?"

"Sure," she said with a nod. "Is that federal?"

"Yes," he said, looking at his watch as she disappeared again. He had less than two hours before his meeting with Roy, so he would have to ignore the grumbling from his stomach.

The package that had been couriered from the federal prosecution service was not that large, so Verdun had thought its review and his consequent preparation for the meeting with Roy wouldn't take that long. But he had not fully appreciated the fact that extraditions were outside his usual area of practice, and in order to know what he was up against, he had additional background reading to do. From what he had gathered so far from reading the materials, the process had been set in motion by a request from the French government for a provisional warrant for Roy's detention. And while there were several affidavits in support of the request that set out the basic facts, it was far from the complete picture. Since the motion had been heard on an *ex parte* basis – in other words without anyone representing Roy's interests – there was no way to know what, if any, other evidence the judge had considered in deciding to issue the warrant. To make things worse, it seemed that extraditions were handled by prosecutors from the International Assistance Group of Justice Canada, as opposed to the prosecutors Verdun was used to dealing with, and with whom he had developed a good working relationship for the most part. He would have to talk to someone on the defence side who was familiar with extraditions eventually, but for now he was on his own.

From reading the affidavits, Verdun determined that Jean-Christophe Malle, a fifty-one-year-old French civil servant, had been murdered on the night of May 21 in a side street in Aix-en-Provence, France. The victim had bled to death from a single knife wound to his neck, which had severed the carotid artery. The affidavit went on to state that on the night in question, Malle had been returning from a weekend with one Annie Renaud. Her broken engagement to Karl Roy was soon discovered by the French police, though not before Roy had abruptly cut short his posting in France and returned to Canada, only days after the murder.

While the affidavits went on to ensure procedural requirements were met, the relationship between Annie Renaud and Roy, combined with his swift departure from the country in the week following the murder, seemed to be the main foundation for the warrant. And though the timing of Roy's departure was certainly troubling, everything was still circumstantial. Verdun was much more concerned, however, with a particular paragraph, buried deep in one of the affidavits, which alluded to additional evidence linking Roy to the crime. If this was a reference to physical evidence, the implications were much more ominous, as physical evidence was always much harder to defend against. As he got up to stretch his legs and walk over to the window, it occurred to him that the evidence referred to could be DNA. Renaud's interaction with both Roy and the victim within a relatively short period of time raised the possibility that Roy's DNA could have made its way into the crime scene, whether on an article of clothing or a strand of hair. And while it seemed unlikely, DNA had an unnerving habit of devastating even the best of defences, and it was becoming more and more the rule rather than the exception in criminal courts.

But he was getting ahead of himself. Until the evidence was tendered, there was nothing Verdun could do and little point in worrying about what-ifs at this point. He abandoned his speculation as the young paralegal appeared at his door with a photocopied document in her hand.

"Here it is," she said. "No amendments and no regulations, you'll be happy to know." She was an experienced researcher and knew the perils of relying on anything but the current version of a piece of legislation.

"Thanks, Wendy. Sorry to keep you," he added, noticing it was after six.

"That's ok, I've got a dinner date downtown tonight."

"Well have fun," he said, taking the document from her.

"I'll lock up on my way out," she called out from the landing.

"Thanks," he yelled back. He hadn't realized everyone else had left. Jim Smythe, Verdun's sole partner in the firm of Verdun, Smythe was in Toronto on a file, but their two associate lawyers had been buzzing around all afternoon. Then he remembered Smythe had gotten them tickets to the Senators' hockey game. They had both joined the firm two years before and had been excellent additions. Bright and hard working, they were also versatile enough to handle whatever came through the door of the small firm. Though Verdun had begun his practice in a large firm and had learned a lot from the senior lawyers he had worked with, he had craved more control over his own career, and his life. Now, whether to take on a new file was a decision he made on his own, much like the decision to work nights or weekends. And while the hours had not decreased by much, his ability to choose them made all the difference. His partner shared a similar background, and philosophy on work, which went a long way in making their little firm a good place to work.

Returning to his desk, Verdun settled in with the photocopied Extradition Act and began reading. Karl Roy would be waiting for good news and as yet, Verdun had little to offer.

four

"What's the word, Peter?" Roy asked as his lawyer was escorted into the same meeting room they had shared only hours earlier. His words were more tentative and his manner more anxious since the morning's meeting, Verdun noticed. The incarceration was having a visible effect on his client.

"First things first, we're going to make an application for bail – tomorrow," Verdun said, deciding to start with the best of the news he would be sharing this evening. Roy's chest and shoulders lowered slightly as the prospect of freedom was mentioned for the first time in concrete terms.

"It's not a given though, you need to know there's a chance it will be denied."

"What are the odds?" Roy tensed again.

"Let's just concentrate on making them the best they can be."

Roy nodded.

"This," Verdun said, pulling a file folder out of his briefcase and putting it on the table between them, "is the request for extradition by the French government. It says that Annie Renaud's business card was found in Malle's pocket, and when they questioned her, she revealed your recent–"

"She's responsible for this? You've got to be kidding me," Roy exploded. To hear that Annie was responsible for his predicament was more than he could bear.

"There's more, Karl. When the French police tried to question you, they discovered that you had already left the country." He paused. "Just days after the murder."

"I told you already–"

"Hang on." Verdun held up his hand. "Let me finish and then you can take me through all of it. The French police say they were advised by the consular office in Nice that you had recently decided to return to Canada for personal reasons. So the recent break-up, combined with the timing–"

"Is enough to arrest me?"

"It was enough for a Canadian judge to sign a provisional warrant, which is what they're holding you under. But you have a right to interim release – bail – if we can establish that you're not going to bolt."

"Where the hell do they think I'm going to go?"

"Precisely. We need to make it clear to the judge that there is no reason to detain you until the hearing. In other words, we establish that you're a fine, upstanding Canadian citizen with no criminal record and every intention of showing up to clear your name."

"And how do we do that?"

"Ever had any trouble with the law?"

Roy shook his head. "No, not so much as a speeding ticket."

"I had to ask. Can you get someone on short notice to testify about your character?"

"I got a call from my old boss earlier today, offering whatever help he could give."

"When did you last work for him?"

"He was the head of mission in Nice for my first year and a half there. He was promoted to something at the ADM level back here six months ago."

"That's good. I'll need his name and number before I leave."

"No problem."

Verdun scribbled some notes while Roy looked on in silence. When he had finished writing, Verdun looked up at Roy's haggard face. He seemed to have aged a decade since this morning. He was obviously distraught and afraid, and Verdun felt an urge to cheer him up.

"Look, Karl, I don't want to understate the implications here – you're being accused of murder. But without a criminal record and with only circumstantial evidence against you, I think your prospects of bail are good."

Roy's face lightened a little.

"But I've got a lot of work to do tonight, so we need to go over a few more things before I go."

Over the course of the next thirty minutes, Verdun extracted the information he needed from his client and provided him with a brief outline of the procedural aspects of a bail hearing. He offered as much reassurance as he dared before leaving to begin a long night of work. Returning to his car in the warm evening air, he couldn't help wondering about the untendered evidence referred to in the affidavit. He had not wanted to alarm Roy any more than necessary since it would not be raised in the bail hearing, but he didn't like it; it made him uneasy. As he fumbled in his pocket for his car keys, he decided to focus his attention on tomorrow's hearing. One step at a time, he thought.

Packing the last of his papers into his briefcase, Verdun took a last swig of coffee before heading out of his office, down the flight of stairs two at a time, and out through the front door. As he made his way out onto Elgin Street, he was greeted by a warm breeze carrying the usual cocktail of exhaust fumes mixed with coffee and bread from the bakery next door. He squinted in the bright morning sunlight and looked for an opening in the traffic as he made his way north to Place Bell, in front of which several of his black-robed colleagues had gathered, waiting for the lights to change. As they began to cross en masse, Verdun dashed across the southbound lanes and cut a diagonal path through the idling cars on the other side of the road divider. He caught up with the group just as it reached the curb in front of the courthouse.

"There goes the neighbourhood," said a white-haired prosecutor.

"Morning, Tom. We need to talk about that theft-under," Verdun replied as they approached the courthouse. Tom McIntosh was a veteran Verdun dealt with on an almost daily basis, and though he was a dogged adversary and a worthy representative of Her Majesty, Verdun also considered him to be eminently reasonable in the vast majority of cases.

"I told you I plan to proceed. What choice do I have?" McIntosh waved a hand.

"Come on, he's a nineteen-year-old kid. Why ruin his life over a twenty-dollar CD?"

"It's more than that. He resisted arrest and–"

"Come on, Tom, it's wrong and you know it. He'll make full restitution and throw in an apology too if you like." He held open the door as the prosecutor followed him inside.

"We'll see. Anyway, that matter's not on this morning, is it?"

"No, I'm here on an extradition."

"So you're the reason the IAG is here this morning." McIntosh stopped to lay down his briefcase.

"Who?"

"International Assistance Group – they're the ones who handle extraditions."

"I forgot, you guys have acronyms for everything."

"Well, duty calls. Have fun," McIntosh said, looking at his watch as Verdun made his way to courtroom #3. He entered the room and went to the counsel table, nodding silently at the three lawyers seated at the Crown's table.

"Mr. Verdun, I presume," said the elder of the three and the obvious leader of the group. He approached and extended his hand. "Myles Benton."

"Peter Verdun."

Verdun took his seat and began emptying the contents of his briefcase onto the table. The small courtroom was relatively quiet, with only a half-dozen people seated behind the counsel tables.

"So when do I get a look at this mysterious evidence?" Verdun asked as the two junior lawyers whispered together.

"All in due time, Peter – may I call you Peter?"

"Sure, Myles."

"I'm not sure how familiar you are with these international matters – they can be quite cumbersome." Benton chuckled. "It's hard enough to get our hands on statements taken by the local police, let alone evidence from across the pond."

Verdun couldn't help bristling at Benton's condescending

tone. "Well, until you do, I wouldn't expect much luck in this courtroom," he replied, tossing his book of authorities on the table. He had managed to assemble a decent list of cases that a paralegal had delivered just an hour before at the court registry. He also knew Judge Robert Hughes was not a man who took the presumption of innocence lightly. Verdun had been heartened to learn upon the return of his paralegal that Hughes would be presiding over the bail hearing.

"I don't know, it's a rather serious offence." Benton frowned.

"I just hope you didn't come down here for nothing, that's all," Verdun said.

"I don't think the French government takes murder any less seriously than we do."

Having established the rules of engagement, the two lawyers returned to shuffling their respective papers as the clerk arrived and announced the arrival of His Honour Robert Hughes, a giant of a man with bushy white eyebrows atop thick bifocals that partially obscured his eyes.

"Good morning, gentleman," he said as they all took their seats and the clerk picked up the phone and whispered something into the receiver and then called the courtroom to order. A few seconds later, a side door opened and Karl Roy was led into the docket off to the side. Verdun had not had time to speak with him again this morning, but gave him a smile as his client sat nervously, apparently unsure what to do with his hands.

"Who's here for the Crown?" Hughes said gruffly.

"Myles Benton, Q.C., Your Honour." Benton rose to his feet. "With James Murchison and Paul Ouellet, students-at-law," he said, gesturing to the two men seated next to him.

"Are you all making submissions this morning?" the judge asked, peering over his glasses.

"No, Your Honour, I alone will be making representations on behalf of the Crown."

"Very well, proceed, Mr. Benton."

As Benton began to lay out the facts alleged in the provisional warrant, it was clear that he was a man who enjoyed the opportunity his profession afforded him to speak. It was also clear that Hughes was not going to waste time.

"I can read, Mr. Benton," he interrupted. "I see no need to repeat the contents of your written submissions."

"Of course not, Your Honour," Benton said, undaunted. "As I was saying, the crime alleged in this matter is particularly heinous, striking down a respected member of the French civil service in his prime."

"No one's saying it's not a serious crime, Mr. Benton," Hughes said, looking over the counsel tables at the area behind Benton. "But as you are well aware, there has to be evidence of a risk of flight, or danger to the public – neither of which is borne out in your written materials. Do you have anything to add to them? On those specific points that is."

Verdun couldn't help thinking this was going too well. He glanced casually at the area where Hughes had been looking, noticing for the first time a well-dressed and somewhat European-looking man sitting behind Benton. He also caught a glimpse of a very attractive woman farther back who was scribbling furiously into a notepad.

"Well, Your Honour," Benton began, trying to continue his speech.

"Feel free to jump in, Mr. Verdun," Hughes said as Verdun's head snapped back around and he rose to his feet.

"Mr. Roy is a respected member of the Canadian Foreign Service, Your Honour, with an impeccable employment record, as attested to by the affidavit from his former supervisor. He lives in Gatineau, as does his entire family. He has no history of crime whatsoever and cooperated willingly with the Ottawa police before being taken into custody. Add to that, the fact that there is not so much as a shred of hard evidence to connect him to this crime – heinous as it surely was – and I can see no grounds for his further detention."

Benton looked on silently as Hughes wrote some notes.

"Mr. Benton?"

"Your Honour, I can only reiterate the severity of the crime and–"

"Yes, I know, Mr. Benton. You'll have ample opportunity to prove that at the extradition hearing. Until then, Mr. Roy will be free to go about his business with a few conditions."

"Your Honour, if Mr. Roy is to be released pending the hearing, the minimum security ought to be at least one hundred thousand–"

"There will be no security to be posted, Mr. Benton," Hughes interrupted. "There's nothing to indicate Mr. Roy is a flight risk, and a financial surety is therefore unnecessary in this case."

Hughes ignored Benton's protests and peered behind the Crown's bench again, before returning his gaze to the counsel tables, and then the prisoner's docket.

"I will order that you contact the Crown if you should plan on leaving the National Capital Region, Mr. Roy. Other than that you are free to go."

As Roy emitted a visible sigh of relief, Verdun quickly rose to his feet. "Thank you, Your Honour."

"Yes, thank you," Benton added, less enthusiastically, as the clerk called the room to order and Hughes left by the door behind the bench.

Roy remained standing as Verdun approached the docket. "So I'm really free to go?" asked Roy.

"Yeah, they'll process you and give you your things back and then you're out of here."

"Thank God. I don't know how to thank you, Peter."

"It's just the first battle you know. It's not over by any means."

"When's the hearing?"

"Just under a month from now. We'll have lots of time to prepare for it, but for the moment, you could probably use a break. Take a few days and then give me a call."

"I will – thanks, Peter."

"Don't mention it."

As Roy was led out the side door, Verdun returned to the table to collect his things, and noticed Benton engaged in a lively exchange with the well-dressed man behind the Crown's table. There was no sign of the alluring brunette though, and he returned his attention to packing up his briefcase. When Benton returned to his table to do the same, they exchanged glances.

"Savour the victory, Peter, I assure you it won't be this easy next time around."

Although Verdun had been the winner this morning, the almost mischievous expression on Benton's face was not one of defeat, but rather of a man who knew something his adversary did not. Whether that was the case didn't matter now, and Verdun decided to follow Benton's advice, heaving his briefcase off the table and making his way out the door. Outside the courthouse, he was approached by a small group of reporters wanting his comments on the case, which he gave in sparing detail.

Making his way back across Elgin Street, Verdun felt a smile cross his face for the first time in days. The sun was shining, there was a pleasant breeze and he had just won the freedom of his client. He knew the case was far from over, but he had so little occasion to smile lately that he decided he was overdue. For the rest of his walk back to the office, he even whistled.

Karl Roy sat on a big rock on a hill overlooking Pink Lake, watching the sun go down. The trail that encircled the lake was one of the most popular in Gatineau Park, and though he was sharing its beautiful scenery with plenty of other hikers on this warm spring evening, he was too preoccupied to notice anyone else. After his release that morning, he had gone to his parents' house in Hull for a good meal and some rest. After the initial euphoria, he had been preoccupied with a mixture of anger and confusion over his current predicament. But with all of the conflicting emotions rushing through his head, one haunting image dominated everything else. No matter what happened from here on in, or how much he tried to fool himself, he was not over Annie Renaud, and he was beginning to wonder whether he ever would be. He tossed a pebble into the lake and watched the ripples cross the surface as a group of tourists paused below him to take pictures. Annie had entered his quiet, ordered world and turned everything upside down, and he had loved her all the more for it. Even now, with the havoc she had caused, she was all he could think of. As for Malle, as Roy watched the tourists move on and tossed another pebble into the water, he felt no regret whatsoever. After all, it was an eye for an eye.

five

Verdun entered the coffee shop down the street from his office for his usual mid-morning fix. As he searched in his pockets for some change, he spotted someone at the head of the line. His instincts screamed at him to retreat, but it was too late. She had paid for her coffee and, upon turning away, had spotted him.

"Peter," she said, a smile appearing on her face as the real one disappeared from his, replaced by an anxious facsimile.

"Heather, how are you?"

"I'm fine. Nice to see you."

"What brings you here?" he asked, careful to maintain his place in the line, lest he be stuck in an awkward conversation with no pretext for escape.

"I had a job interview at Bell."

"How interesting," he said, trying desperately to remember whether she was in communications or marketing. It all sounded the same to him anyway.

"Yes, they do a fair bit of their marketing in-house," she added.

"I see." He nodded, glad to have his answer. "So how did it go?"

"It was great. I think the job's mine if I want it."

"Congratulations." He tried to sound genuinely enthusiastic even though the prospect of her invading his personal coffee shop on a daily basis filled his heart with dread. He had been on one blind date with this woman a few weeks ago, and though it had been pleasant enough, he hadn't felt anything special. Now, he was trying to remember what their rules of disengagement had been. Had he agreed to call her? Or had they made a more vague promise to keep in touch. Whatever the case, there had been no such contact, and as he placed his order to go, he wondered if she was moving on or waiting for him to sit with her.

"Your office is near here, isn't it?" she said, sipping her latté.

"Just up the street." He fumbled for his money.

"Well, I've got to run. It was nice to see you."

"Yes. Likewise," he said as he took his tray of coffee over to where the cream and sugar were laid out and watched her leave. When she was a safe distance in the other direction, Verdun regained the street and headed south towards the office. Pausing to deposit a coffee on the receptionist's desk as she fielded a hostile call, Verdun made his way to his partner's office.

"Just bumped into Heather," he said, depositing the tray on Jim Smythe's desk and retrieving his own coffee.

"Heather?" Smythe said, looking up from his desk. Unlike Verdun, who was fastidious about his workspace, Smythe's office looked like a paper bomb had gone off. No portion of his desk or side table was visible under the unruly mess of file folders, papers and used coffee cups. A large part of the floor was also occupied with filing boxes and stacks of paper.

"You know? *Heather*."

"Oh her. Did I tell you Margaret is still pissed off at you for not marrying her?" Smythe grinned. His wife Margaret was a self-declared matchmaker for Verdun. "Least you could have done was go out for a second date. Margaret needs some reward for all her hard work, you know."

"Sorry, she just wasn't my type."

"She didn't put out, huh?" Smythe sipped his coffee. Verdun's single status was an ongoing joke between the two, who had been friends before founding the firm together four years earlier. A jolly, easy-going sort, Smythe also enjoyed mocking Verdun's anal-retentive tendencies, and though he protested dutifully, Verdun couldn't help enjoying the good-natured abuse.

"God, this place is a pigsty," Verdun laughed.

"Why don't you give it a once-over for me? Make it look like your office."

"Very funny. How's the factum coming?" Verdun glanced on Smythe's desk.

"Jones did a pretty good first cut." Smythe looked around to make sure the associate wasn't outside before adding, "That kid's worth his weight in gold."

"Yeah, we were lucky to get him."

"I think I heard the courier while you were out. Don't know if your extradition stuff came."

"Thanks, I'll check. I've been waiting for that stuff for almost two weeks."

"Margaret wants to give you one more chance," Smythe said as Verdun turned to leave.

"Oh no."

"Oh yes. Friday night at our place. Bring a nice red – and none of that Merlot either."

"Who is she?"

"All in good time, my boy, all in good time."

Verdun laughed as he returned to the reception desk. He liked Margaret and he had to admire her persistence. But he just didn't seem to be able to connect with members of the opposite sex lately. He had dated regularly, even seriously on a couple of occasions, but between work and a series of failed relationships, he was beginning to wonder whether he would ever find the right person. He envied Jim and Margaret and the kind of bond they shared, but he was also familiar with enough divorced or miserably married peers to be wary of rushing into anything. And here was another example of the risks, he thought, as he noticed the thick envelope on the receptionist's desk from the International Assistance Group of the Department of Justice. This had to be the Crown's disclosure file on Karl Roy's extradition hearing. Now there was a man who was paying the ultimate price for love. He opened the envelope and emptied the contents neatly onto his desk, carefully discarding the envelope in the recycling bin under his desk.

Verdun skimmed the cover letter and then began reading the enclosed affidavits and witness transcripts. When he got halfway through the first one, he ran his index finger over his top lip and sighed. Spotting his secretary returning from her coffee break, he called out. "Julie, could you set up a meeting with Karl Roy as soon as possible please?"

"The extradition case?"

"Yes. Thanks." He returned to his reading and a frown gradually clouded his face. "Jesus," he said quietly, shaking his head.

Karl Roy sat in his lawyer's waiting area, trying to concentrate on an article on U.S. foreign policy, but it was no use. He tossed the magazine back on the table and sighed. The call from Verdun's secretary had rattled him more than he thought. He knew it was coming at some point, but he had enjoyed being blissfully ignorant for the past two weeks and had gone about business as usual. He had returned to work with the full support of his boss and against the advice of his parents, who thought he should take the time off. One thing he had not done was to get a new place at the end of the month. He told himself that it was because he didn't like any of the half-dozen places John Brewer had found for him, but he knew deep down that the uncertainty of his future had something to do with it too. Even if everything went smoothly from here on in, the legal bill would be considerable. At least he had enough in the bank that he wasn't too concerned about the immediate financial implications. Today's meeting was presumably to go over the disclosure evidence that would be used against him at the extradition hearing to be held in ten days' time, and he was anxious to find out what it was.

"You can go in now, Mr. Roy. Second door on your left."

"Sorry to keep you waiting, Karl," Verdun said, meeting him at the door. He showed Roy into the office and closed the door behind them.

"That's ok," Roy said and took a seat. He glanced at the neat pile of documents on Verdun's desk blotter and smiled. "So what are they saying in there – that I plotted to kill Jacques Chirac?" Despite his attempt at humour, Roy's stiff posture in the chair betrayed his true state of mind.

"No," Verdun said with a smile. "But what they are saying isn't much better, I'm afraid."

"All right, let's hear it."

"They have several new statements, for starters. One from a Mr. Fatou. Do you know him?"

"He was a neighbour. Why, what's he got to say?"

"Says he overheard a fight between you and Annie a few weeks before the murder."

Roy nodded. "That would have been about the affair," he said with a sigh.

"You mean the night you discovered it?"

"No, a day or two later. Our final confrontation, I guess. She came to see me – to explain."

"I see." Verdun nodded, taking notes.

"I was angry, and still shocked, I guess. I didn't know what the hell was happening. She came to apologize and I guess we had it out."

"So what are we talking here? Yelling or–"

"I didn't lay a hand on her, if that's what you mean."

"I meant, was it loud? You know, is it reasonable to believe a neighbour could have heard what you were saying? That sort of thing."

"Yeah, it was pretty loud, I guess, and it was a warm evening so the windows were probably open."

"Do you remember what was said?"

"I don't know. I told her what I thought of her and that I never wanted to see her again and she could go to hell and all that." Roy shrugged.

"Ok." Verdun looked up from his notes. "I'm going to give you a copy of all of this so you can review it in detail, but his statement says you threatened her."

"Bullshit."

"He says he heard you say: 'Don't ever come back here or I'll wring your neck' – that's the translation anyway."

Roy shook his head and sighed. "It's possible I said something like that. I was pretty angry with her, but that doesn't mean anything."

"I know. But they are obviously trying to paint a picture of someone who was in a murderous rage."

Verdun continued to summarize the evidence against his client over the next forty-five minutes, asking questions along the way, and the two agreed to meet again after Roy had reviewed the disclosure evidence in detail. "Thursday afternoon then?" Verdun said, getting up from his chair.

"So, I guess things are not looking good," Roy said, almost to himself. He remained seated.

"It's not great," Verdun said, sitting back down. "But it never is. And don't forget extradition's a two-part process. All the hearing does is give the judge an opportunity to decide whether there's enough evidence to convict you after a trial. The decision of whether to actually hand you over to the French is made by the Minister of Justice. And that's a much more political process."

"On that note, have you heard from Malcolm recently?" Roy asked, referring to his former boss.

"I'm going to meet with him tomorrow," Verdun said. "He has assured me he will do everything possible to exercise political pressure to keep you in Canada."

"I'm sure he'll do whatever he can," Roy said, heartened by the mention of Malcolm McGavin, now an assistant deputy minister at Foreign Affairs.

"He seems a very resourceful man."

"See you on Thursday then," Roy said as he got up to leave. "Try not to worry, Karl."

Verdun took off his jacket and slung it over his shoulder as he walked along the busy Sparks Street Mall, past one of the crowded outdoor eateries located in the centre of the pedestrian walkway that runs the length of the downtown core. The noon sun was hotter than he had anticipated when he set out on foot from his office fifteen minutes earlier. As he neared the restaurant McGavin had chosen for their meeting, a soft breeze blew down the mall and came to his rescue. He adjusted his sunglasses and took in the scenery all around him, from the street musicians to the attractive, professional women who seemed to be particularly abundant on this fine summer's day. The sight of so many couples enjoying an outdoor lunch together dampened his spirits a little. It had been a couple of weeks since his last date, courtesy of Margaret Smythe, which had been an absolute disaster. After that evening, Verdun had told the Smythes in no uncertain terms that it would be his last blind date ever, but with his current lifestyle, the traditional dating process didn't seem to offer much hope either. Perhaps he was destined to go through life alone. It wouldn't be so bad after all. He enjoyed his work, even though from time to time the constant adversity got to him. But while he occasionally longed for someone with whom he could let down his guard, he knew such trust was rare even among his married friends.

Arriving at the cozy little restaurant tucked between a men's wear store and a souvenir shop, Verdun adjusted his eyes to the dim light and made out McGavin's distinctive features seated at a table in the rear corner. As he made his way to the table, McGavin rose and extended his hand. "Hello, Peter."

"Malcolm," Verdun replied, taking his seat. Although he was accustomed to calling people by their first name, it had sounded odd in the presence of such a distinguished-looking man. He had first met McGavin just after Roy's bail hearing and had been impressed with his presence then as well. Verdun guessed he was in his late fifties and he was always impeccably dressed. He had spent his entire career on various diplomatic postings around the world before landing a position as an assistant deputy minister back in Ottawa six months ago. Fluent in four languages, he was the poster boy for Foreign Affairs and was sure to make an excellent ambassador some day.

"Hope I didn't drag you too far out of your way," McGavin said as the waitress filled their water glasses. "I'm in between meetings at Justice and haven't got much time."

Verdun nodded, remembering that the building that housed Justice's headquarters was just around the corner. "This is fine. I need the exercise," he fibbed, being in excellent shape thanks to regular visits to the gym.

The waitress recited a long list of specials from which each man made his selection.

"So how is Karl?" McGavin said as she left with their order.

"He's trying to stay positive."

"What an unimaginable nightmare." McGavin shook his head. "First Annie, now this."

"Did you know her?"

"Yes, I met her on several occasions. It was clear Karl was quite smitten with her. And for good reason. She was exquisitely beautiful, and very bright. It's such a shame."

"Yes, it's been a tough couple of months for him, but I'm hoping you can help."

"I'm at your disposal. Whatever I can do."

"Well, your testimony would be very helpful at the hearing. The length of time you've known Karl professionally, combined with your own credibility, will go a long way to describing Karl's character."

"I've prepared some notes, as you asked, to flesh out the affidavit I gave at the bail hearing. I can get his performance reviews as well if that would help. They're all exemplary. Karl has a bright future ahead of him when this blows over, I can assure you of that."

"That would be great," Verdun said, skimming the notes.

"On the political side, I can also say that Karl has the full support of the department in this matter. And Foreign Affairs is not without influence over Justice. Just this morning, I was discussing this case – informally of course – with a colleague in the prosecution service. He gave me every assurance, off the record, that the International Assistance Group won't push too hard at the bail hearing."

"I have a hard time believing Myles Benton would back off easily," Verdun said.

"Benton's known as somewhat of a showman. Though in this case, he was playing to the French Embassy's attaché rather than the judge."

Verdun remembered the well-dressed man seated behind Benton at the hearing, the one the judge seemed to be paying particular attention to.

"That might also explain why he was assisted by two articling clerks," Verdun mused.

"Precisely. Extra bodies to fill out the playbill for the French government. Justice can't be seen to be ignoring their request."

"And are we to expect the same at the extradition hearing?"

"It hardly matters. From what I hear, the Minister of Justice is extremely uncomfortable with granting an order to extradite at this point."

Verdun tried not to smile. This was the information he had been looking for – some insight into how the minister would exercise his discretion in the all-important second stage of the extradition process.

"You mean because of the circumstantial nature of the evidence?"

"Perhaps there are legal reasons for his reservations, but I only know of the political ones."

"I'm not sure I follow." Verdun sipped his drink.

"Justice and Foreign Affairs have been cozying up lately. They think they can get more from Treasury Board if they help each other out. Foreign Affairs has just been to bat for Justice over the proceeds of crime program. Are you familiar with it?"

"A little." Verdun vaguely remembered hearing something about the government program on the radio recently – that it was awash in red ink.

"Foreign Affairs actually did a first-rate job of supporting Justice's request for bail-out funding. So Justice is looking for something to reciprocate with. I'm told the minister's office is very interested in considering Karl's case as just that opportunity – provided Justice is reassured with a reasonable case for his innocence, of course. There are limits you know." McGavin smiled.

"Of course. And what about your department? How does it feel about Karl?"

"I wasn't embellishing in my affidavit at all. He really does have a stellar record. His reputation is well known within Foreign Affairs and I've made a point of conveying it to the minister personally. Karl is intelligent, well liked and generally thought to be a rising star."

"Well that's good news."

"Naturally, we're hoping you'll see to it that no committal order will be granted at the hearing and it never comes to a political decision."

"Naturally." Verdun smiled. "But if it *is* granted?"

"Foreign Affairs is willing to cash in its favour on Karl. And Justice seems amenable as well. It's actually not a bad deal for them."

Their meals arrived, and they continued their discussion of Roy's case, and McGavin's role as a witness, before moving on to more casual conversation over coffee. After Verdun had described his own background, McGavin went on to offer him a colourful description of his own career in far-away hotspots. Among other places, McGavin had served in the Berlin office during the Cold War and it occurred to Verdun that he might have made an excellent spy at some point in his career. Enthralled as he was by McGavin's stories, Verdun lost track of the time, until McGavin glanced at his watch. "Good God, is that the time?"

"Oh," Verdun said, waving to the waiter. "I'm due in court this afternoon."

"And I'll be keeping a roomful of your colleagues waiting if I'm not careful," McGavin said with a smile. "Lunch is on me – I insist."

"No, really, I'm the one–"

"I won't hear of it," McGavin said with authority, handing the waitress his credit card. It was clear the matter was closed.

"Thank you."

"The pleasure was all mine. So we'll meet briefly a few days before the hearing to go over my testimony?"

"Yes, I'll call your office to set up a time."

"Very well then. Please give my regards to Karl."

"I will, thanks again."

It had been a very productive lunch, Verdun decided, as they parted company at the door to the restaurant. The news about Justice's instructions to Benton had been particularly interesting. At first, Verdun had felt a bit deflated knowing that Benton may have had his hands somewhat tied at the bail hearing. That would explain his less than stellar performance compared to Verdun's. Ego issues aside though, it did bode well for the upcoming hearing, even if it wouldn't mean changing Verdun's preparation.

six

"All rise," the clerk said as silence fell over the courtroom.

"Here we go," Verdun whispered, as Roy stood beside him at the counsel table and the judge took her seat on high.

"Please be seated."

Madam Justice Eleanor Crane was a stern-looking woman in her fifties. Her black hair was tied up in a tight bun that seemed to stretch the skin of her pallid face at eye level, giving her a look of permanent discomfort – or perhaps displeasure. She was a relatively new appointment to the Ontario Superior Court, but, facial features aside, she gave every indication that she was very comfortable with her position on the bench. After a formal greeting in the direction of Myles Benton Q.C. and his trio of juniors – she had obviously had the pleasure of his counsel before – the faint smile on her lips evaporated and she gazed down severely in Verdun's direction. "And you are?" she said, gathering up her pen.

"Peter Verdun, Your Honour."

"I prefer 'My Lady,' Mr. Verdun, if you don't mind. I, for one, believe in the time-honoured traditions of the bar." Her disdain for the trend towards more informality in the legal process was obvious.

"Of course, My Lady," he said, sitting back down, as a reporter chuckled behind him.

"M'Lady," Benton began, "the Crown would like to begin by adding an exhibit to its file for the record."

Verdun started to object. "Can I ask why this was not provided–"

"Let the Crown tell us what it is before you object, Mr. Verdun," Crane said sharply. "I will not have a shouting match in my courtroom."

"Well, Your Hon…My Lady. I simply wanted to know why this exhibit did not form part of the Crown's disclosure file."

"This is not a trial, My Lady," Benton said quickly. "The Crown is not subject to the same rules of disclosure. In any event, this is new evidence – unavailable until now."

"Objection overruled." Judge Crane waved dismissively in Verdun's direction as Benton passed him a copy of the affidavit on his way to the bench.

"As you will see, M'Lady, this latest affidavit sheds important light on the offence for which the accused's extradition is being sought."

Verdun flipped over the cover page and began reading, freezing momentarily at paragraph three and looking up at Benton.

"In fact, it is crucial, since it is the evidence of an eyewitness to the murder of Mr. Jean-Christophe Malle."

"My Lady–" Verdun began, as Roy leaned over to read the affidavit, but didn't get far before Crane had cut him off again.

"Perhaps you can explain why this evidence is only now being disclosed, Mr. Benton."

"It arrived by diplomatic bag this morning, My Lady. There is a representative of the French Embassy in this courtroom who can testify to that effect if need be. I realize this is somewhat irregular and I would have liked to provide my learned friend with more notice, but this really is the first opportunity to tender it."

Verdun was racking his brain for some procedural rule to exclude the evidence, but he knew it was hopeless.

"Would you like some time to review this evidence, Mr. Verdun?"

"Yes, My Lady. I think an adjournment until–"

"We'll resume at one. That will give you ample time to confer with your client."

"But My Lady, that's hardly enough–"

"I'm sure you're well aware of the procedural rules applicable to extradition hearings, Mr. Verdun. It's not as though you have to prepare a cross-examination. I think I'm being generous in the circumstances. Any objections, Mr. Benton?"

"None, My Lady."

Verdun felt like slapping Benton's smiling face.

"Thank you, My Lady," he said without enthusiasm as Crane left the bench and excited chatter broke out in the courtroom. Verdun packed up his things quickly as Roy sat, still reading and shaking his head.

"This is bullshit," he muttered.

"Come on," Verdun said, taking him by the arm and leading him out of the courtroom and through the crush of spectators gathering towards the rear of the room.

Behind the counsel tables, listening to the excited chatter of Myles Benton's juniors, Malcolm McGavin remained seated, his face clouded with a look of grave concern.

Verdun shut the door to the small conference room and took a seat at the table opposite his client. "So," he began, as Roy looked on with a puzzled expression. "What do you make of it, Karl?"

"What do you mean, what do I make of it?"

"I mean, how do you react to this?" He waved at the affidavit on the table in front of them. "It appears there was a witness to Malle's murder," Verdun added, watching Roy's face for a reaction.

Roy's expression changed slightly as his brow furrowed. "Since I didn't do it," he began, "the fact that someone witnessed the real killer should be good for me, don't you think?"

"Have you read the affidavit?"

"You haven't given me a chance to get past the first page."

"He says he saw the whole thing from a doorway twenty yards away. Malle had his throat slit by a man who fits your general description."

"I'm five-ten with dark hair and average build. There's an awful lot of people out there who fit my general description."

Verdun nodded, but said nothing, preferring to let Roy continue.

"Maybe he's lying. You don't find it odd that this is the first we've heard of him?"

"I do," Verdun agreed. "But as you know, we don't get the chance to cross-examine their witnesses at this stage, so I have no way of finding out if this guy is for real. What really concerns me is on the second page. Here, why don't you finish reading?" He turned the affidavit around and Roy picked it up.

About halfway through the page, he stopped reading and looked up. "But this is…This is crazy."

"You mean the part where he remembers distinctly hearing the murderer say 'That's for Annie' before he left?"

As Roy sat there wide-eyed, the first hint of doubt about his client's innocence entered Verdun's mind.

"This is unbelievable," Roy said. "What am I even supposed to say to that? Other than it's bullshit. Or that the cops bribed some homeless person to help them frame me."

"I'm just telling you what we're up against, that's all."

"So how do we counter that?"

"I can take another run at the unusual timing, but the damage is done. The evidence is already in."

"So you think she'll grant the order?"

"It doesn't look good, Karl. I have to be straight with you."

"This is unreal."

"But the minister's still on side, and you're not going anywhere unless he changes his mind, no matter what the court does today. Besides, we're not done here. We can cast some doubt over the affidavit evidence. I'm thinking about a Charter argument as well."

"Cast doubt how?"

"Well, not many people see very well from twenty feet away in the dark. And like you said, the physical description is pretty vague – meaningless really."

Roy did not seem convinced. "And what about the mention of her name? How are you going to deal with that?"

Verdun looked at his client for a moment and then tried his best to smile. "I don't know, Karl. But I'd better think of something. And fast."

seven

"Beer?" Jim Smythe thrust a cold one into Verdun's hand and took a seat in the lounger next to him.

"Cheers." Verdun peered out from under the brim of his baseball hat and took a sip. The cold liquid was a welcome relief in the late afternoon sun. He had accepted Smythe's invitation to come to his family's cottage on Lake Bennett for Canada Day weekend only after being repeatedly assured that there would be no blind date awaiting him when he got there. In fact, Verdun had been pleasantly surprised by a truly relaxing weekend. After arriving to a late dinner on Friday night, he had spent the early morning hours fishing the other side of the lake from Smythe's canoe. They had taken shelter from the midday sun by browsing the quaint little shops of the nearby town before returning for a late afternoon swim. Although the lake was densely populated with cottages, it had maintained an aura of peace about it, and as he sat there on the shore with a cold beer and a light breeze to cool him off, he had to admit he was enjoying himself immensely.

"I'm going to need a chef soon," Margaret called from the cottage. "The steaks are almost ready for the grill."

"You want to do the honours?" Smythe asked.

"Sure, why not? About time I did something useful."

"You can say that again."

Lighting the barbecue, Verdun returned to his seat as Smythe pointed to a boat towing a water skier out in the middle of the lake. "Now that's the life."

"Are you kidding? You'd break your neck."

"No, no, the boat," said Smythe. "It's one of those Sea-Doos. Lots of power, but it can turn on a dime."

"Set you back a few grand too, I bet," Verdun commented.

"They're not so bad second-hand. The guy over at the marina's got a used one for less than ten."

"I never really pegged you as a boat guy, Jim, I have to say."

"So now you're going to insult me too. I'm offended."

Verdun laughed and they both let out a groan as the skier crossed the wake, lost his balance and did a face-plant in the waves.

"That's why you want to be the driver," Verdun said.

They sat, sipping their beers, and watched as the boat swung around and the skier was pulled back out of the water to try his luck again.

"So any news on the extradition?" Smythe asked.

"Nothing. It's starting to concern me actually."

"I thought you said the minister was in the bag."

"He was, originally. But I get the sense from McGavin that something's wrong."

"Down again!" Smythe laughed, pointing out at the hapless water skier. "You think the eyewitness evidence may have had an impact on him?"

"I don't know what to think. I get the feeling there's something McGavin's not telling me."

"And Karl. What does he think?"

"He's definitely noticed a change in McGavin as well, but doesn't have any better idea of why." Verdun sighed, taking a sip of beer.

"And if the minister decides to hand him over to the French?"

"We have the option of a judicial review, but you know what our chances of success there are."

"Not good." Smythe shook his head. "And you say there's no Charter argument to be made?" He had been involved in an extradition only once, and it was several years before and under very different circumstances.

"You know how it works, Jim. The Charter applies, but it doesn't. The theory goes something like this: On the one hand, as a Canadian citizen, Karl has Charter rights. But on the other, because the extradition is an international matter, the international treaty with France takes precedence. To argue otherwise is to argue that France is incapable of conducting a fair trial on its own soil."

"What a mess," Smythe sighed.

"Yup."

Their discussion was interrupted by a loud clang from the cottage.

"You all right in there, Margaret?"

"Fine. Time to cook the steaks. And open the wine, will you, Jim?"

"Well, enough about this extradition stuff," Smythe said, getting up and patting his colleague on the shoulder. "We have important matters to attend to back there."

"Are the bugs out?" Margaret asked, pulling up a chair in front of the fire pit.

"No, they're not too bad," her husband replied, poking at an errant log with a stick and pushing it back into the fire.

"That was a wonderful meal, Margaret," Verdun said.

"Well, you did the steaks," she replied.

"Ah yes, the barbecue. My one form of culinary expression."

Smythe laughed as the sound of a boat's outboard sputtered to life somewhere in the distance. Though the night sky was clear, there was little to light the dark waters, other than a sliver of moon and the odd campfire on the other side.

"How can he see anything out there?" Margaret asked.

"Probably some old-timer who knows every nook and cranny," Smythe said, pulling a thin case out of his shirt pocket.

"Or some drunken teenagers," Verdun remarked, as Smythe thrust the case at him.

"Cigar?"

"Sure, why not?" Verdun took one as Smythe's lighter roared to life under his nose. He puffed at the flame for a few seconds, until the tip of his cigar glowed red.

"Thanks, Jim."

"Mmblh" came the reply, as Smythe worked on his own.

"You're a healthy pair," Margaret said in mock rebuke, adjusting her chair slightly away from the path of the rich smoke.

"Where did you get these?" Verdun asked, blowing a thick stream of the fragrant smoke above their heads.

"Duke's. You know, the new place just around the corner from the office."

Verdun nodded.

"Cubans. So I was led to believe by the proprietor anyway," Smythe added.

"Cubans, eh? Very nice. So what's the occasion?"

"Who says we need an occasion?" Smythe said with a sly grin on his face. "Though since you ask, Margaret's pregnant."

Verdun was taken aback. He knew they both wanted kids but had no idea they were trying. "That's wonderful. Congratulations!" he said, getting up to shake Smythe's hand. He stooped over and gave Margaret a kiss on the cheek. "I'm so happy for you both. You'll make amazing parents."

"Thanks, Peter," Margaret said as he noticed the look on her face. It was true joy.

"So that's why you didn't have any wine. I was wondering whether I'd made a bad choice!" They all laughed. "So when are you due?"

"Valentine's Day. We're calling him Cupid," Smythe said.

"No, we are not," Margaret scolded him. "And who says *it's* a boy?"

"The psychic told me," Smythe chuckled.

"Don't listen to him, Peter. It's a girl, and we're going to name her Emily."

For a long time, the three friends sat around the fire talking and laughing as a light breeze blew in off the lake and fanned the flames. At around eleven, Margaret said goodnight and retired, followed shortly by her husband. Sitting there by the fire, with only the sounds of its embers settling and hissing and the water lapping gently at the dock, Verdun's mind wandered. He thought of his friends' good fortune. They made each other so obviously happy that it was hard not to be envious. Together they were building something real, something beyond the shallow and meaningless things that held such prominence in his single world. He was tired of the facade he felt obliged to put up most of the time, whether it was on the job or on a date. He was good-looking and successful, and he could get sex when he wanted to, but he was tired of jumping from person to person and longed for something lasting. As a loon cried out in the distance, Verdun looked at the empty chairs beside him and wondered whether he would ever find someone he could relax with, and give up the race. Then he thought of Karl Roy, and his heart hardened a little at the thought of a fallen brother. He wondered when McGavin would be in touch and worried about the implications of his recent silence. Verdun had an uneasy feeling that it was a sign of bad news to come.

It was after midnight when Verdun filled a bucket with lake water and doused the glowing embers. He would be driving back tomorrow and spending the afternoon at the office in preparation for a trial on Tuesday. He took a last deep breath of the warm night air before making his way to the darkened cottage and the lonely bunk awaiting him there.

Verdun had just passed through Perth, heading east on Highway 7, when the shrill cry of his cellular pierced the smooth jazz wafting through the air-conditioned cocoon of his SUV.

"Peter Verdun," he said, pausing the music.

"It's Malcolm McGavin."

Verdun analyzed the voice for any sign of what was to come. "Yes, Malcolm. How are you?"

"I'm afraid I have bad news."

Verdun's heart sank. "What is it?"

"It doesn't look good for Karl. I've spent the past week talking to everyone I can think of, trying to find out what's going on, but it wasn't until this morning that I got word."

"Word of what?"

"The Minister of Justice is going to order Karl's surrender to the French authorities tomorrow."

"But why? I thought there were political reasons why he wouldn't."

"I know. I'm still not sure what happened, but there seems to have been a fundamental shift in policy. I'm sure the eyewitness evidence at the hearing didn't help."

There was silence at the other end as Verdun had to slow down behind a transport truck doing eighty. "You think there's some other reason?"

"Well, maybe. My sources tell me the Justice Minister is being pressured from within."

"You mean within Justice?"

"Yes. But no one I talked to in Justice thinks an untested affidavit is enough to warrant handing over a respected member of the federal public service, particularly now, given it's the French."

"Why does it matter that it's the French?"

"There's been a bit of a flap over the weekend. A diplomatic incident in Paris that has left some fairly important noses out of joint at the Canadian Embassy."

"But surely that's got nothing to do with Karl."

"Maybe not directly, but you'd be surprised at the games that are played. I just think that, given all of the circumstances, it's odd for Justice to be behaving this way. Unfortunately, I don't know why and it doesn't really matter for Karl. The fact is, he will be extradited."

"Shit," Verdun sighed as he pulled out into the passing lane. "Can you appeal the minister's decision?"

McGavin's voice wasn't hopeful. "In a manner of speaking, yes. But the chances are very slim. I was really hoping it wouldn't get to that point."

"I see. Well, I'm going to keep digging and see what I can find. There has to be more to it." Verdun sighed. "Well, I'd better get hold of Karl. Listen, I want to thank you for all you've done. I know you've really tried."

"I just hope the minister will come to his senses before it's too late. Best of luck, Peter."

"Thanks." Verdun fumbled on the passenger seat for his day-timer and flipped through the back for Roy's number. He sighed as he pressed the numbers into his cell phone. He hated being the bearer of bad news.

Karl Roy took a seat on a bench and watched as people strolled, ran and biked past him on the well-used trail at the edge of Gatineau Park. Within walking distance of the house his parents had owned for over thirty years, the park provoked many fond memories of the area. On this warm late-summer evening, it was a place of peace and tranquility, a shelter from the storm brewing in his mind, and in his heart.

Roy had taken Peter Verdun's call and the news it brought quite well. He had spoken in a calm, measured voice, thanking his lawyer for everything he had done and promising to think carefully about what he wanted to do next. It was not as though Roy had been surprised and, as the day wore on, his initial resignation had given way to relief. He was tired of his life being held hostage while he waited for one decision after another. In fact, he was so tired of the whole, interminable process that he just wanted it over with. Verdun had already laid out the option of a judicial review weeks ago and it seemed hopeless to Roy anyway. As he sat there enjoying the last of the sun's warmth as it disappeared in the leafy treetops, Roy knew the die was cast and that he would be returning to France. He felt an uneasy pang cross his heart as he realized that, if nothing else, he would at least get a chance to see Annie Renaud one last time.

eight

Verdun swung his SUV into a tight spot in the long-term parking and popped the hatch. He glanced at his watch before jumping out and pulling his suitcase from the back. He slung his carry-on bag over his shoulder and pulled out the handle of his suitcase before rolling it across the parking lot towards the terminal. It was unusually hot and muggy, even for early September in Ottawa, and by the time he reached the doors, a trickle of sweat was making its way down the middle of his back. He breathed a sigh of relief as he entered the terminal building and was met by a rush of cool air. He made his way to the appropriate line and fumbled for his ticket. He patted his jacket pocket to confirm he had brought his wallet and passport as well, before beginning a mental checklist. He had locked up the house and given a spare key to Jim Smythe, who had promised to look in on things. With any luck, he would bring Margaret along and she would think of watering the plants. As the line advanced slowly and he contented himself that his personal affairs were in relatively good order, Verdun turned his mind to work. Jim would be covering for him at a sentencing on Monday, and the rest of his court appearances had been divided up among the two associates. He reached for his cell phone when he remembered a meeting he was supposed to re-schedule. He quickly dialed the office and left a message on his secretary's voice mail. With only a handful of people in front of him and plenty of time before the flight, he decided to relax. Everything was under control.

After Karl Roy made the decision not to try and appeal the Justice Minister's decision to extradite him to France to face trial, Verdun had set about trying to find him French counsel to defend him. He called some contacts in the Canadian Bar Association and was given a few names. As it turned out though, it was Malcolm McGavin who had put him onto Pierre Larousse, the son of a diplomat McGavin had come to know well during one of his postings in Paris. The younger Larousse was in his thirties but had spent his entire career on his feet in the French criminal courts and seemed a good choice. Verdun had already briefed him extensively over the phone, but with the preliminary court proceedings set to begin in a few days, he decided to cash in some air miles and make the trip to France to lend whatever support he could. He also happened to be in desperate need of a break from the office, and the fact that Roy's case was being heard in Nice was, he had to admit, another reason for the trip.

Larousse had a number of preliminary motions that would delay the actual trial for a month or two, but he anticipated that it would go ahead at some point in the fall. As for Roy, he had managed to maintain a stiff upper lip in the days before leaving Canada, but it was clear to Verdun that he was under a lot of stress. The one bright spot was that, with Malcolm McGavin's considerable help, Verdun and Larousse had managed to arrange for Roy's pre-trial detention in staff quarters owned by the Canadian government in Nice instead of a French jail.

Before he knew it, Verdun was at the gate listening to the boarding call. After a short hop over to Toronto, he would have just enough time to have a quick drink in the departure lounge before catching the red-eye to Paris. As Roy's first appearance was not until Monday, Verdun had arranged to stay one night in Paris before heading down to the coast on Sunday afternoon. He had no concrete plans for the weekend, other than to go to the Louvre and Notre Dame, and to find a good restaurant for Saturday night. He knew an old girlfriend from his law school days who was living there now, practicing international law in a big firm. Verdun had considered calling her but decided against it. She was probably married anyway. As the advance-boarding announcement came over the P.A. system, he decided he would be quite content to relax and take in the City of Lights on his own. He chuckled to himself as he made his way to the gate. He was sure Margaret Smythe would be working overtime to arrange his marriage while he was away.

Verdun folded up *The International Herald Tribune* and put it on the table, leaned back and folded his arms over his chest. Without his even noticing it, a faint smile had appeared at the corners of his mouth. He didn't want to look at his watch, or move, or even think, for that matter. All he wanted was for this state of contentment to continue for as long as possible. Sitting there in the late morning sun, the crumbs from his pain au chocolat still fresh on the plate and just the slightest buzz from his café au lait pumping through his bloodstream, he was truly happy. He had arrived somewhat jet-lagged on the previous morning, despite his best efforts to sleep on the plane. But he had managed a two-hour nap right after checking into his hotel, and when he awoke, he was ready to take on the brilliant fall day that awaited him outside. He started with a breakfast at a café down the street and then took a cab to the Latin quarter, where he strolled for hours, taking in the cathedral and the rest of the Rive Gauche. After a late lunch, he made his way to the Louvre, where he spent the rest of his afternoon strolling leisurely among its vast collection.

When he could walk no longer, he had returned to his hotel for a brief rest before changing into a jacket and tie and heading for the restaurant recommended to him by the hotel doorman. Verdun would be giving him a big tip when he checked out today, that was for sure. He had been sipping an aperitif at the bar while his table was being prepared when he met a group of German lawyers in town for a conference. He was invited to join their table, and had enjoyed a wonderful meal and been regaled with colourful courtroom stories. He reciprocated with his dinner-party classic of the time he appeared in court on behalf of a colleague and ended up representing the wrong client, albeit successfully. After a sumptuous dinner complemented by a series of burgundies the likes of which he had never tasted – most notably a 1985 Gevray-Chambertin – they all descended to the jazz club located in the basement for a nightcap, which turned into several. Before he knew it, it was after two. He had bid his friends farewell as they piled into a cab headed for another club, who knew where. Verdun chuckled as he remembered some of the stories.

From his vantage point outside the café, he watched a small boat cruising up the Seine, an old man in a beret at the wheel, a pipe sticking out of his mouth. The warm sun on his face, Verdun watched the little craft disappear around a bend in the river before he looked reluctantly at his watch and confirmed that his time in Paris was indeed drawing to a close. He was flying to Nice in the early afternoon and would soon have to get back to the hotel to get his things packed up.

A few hours later, Verdun was going through security at Charles De Gaulle Airport in preparation for the short flight down to Nice. By the time he made it to his gate, they had already begun boarding so he didn't even get a chance to pull out the paperback he had bought in Ottawa. He hoped for a chance to hit chapter four once he was settled in his seat. As he boarded the plane and looked for his seat number, he was pleasantly surprised to find that fate had been kind to him this day, as a very attractive brunette was stowing a laptop case under the aisle seat next to his. He put his jacket and carry-on, with the paperback still in the pocket, in the overhead bin and waited for her to look up.

"Je m'excuse," he said. As she smiled and got up to let him in, it occurred to him that she looked familiar.

"Aren't you Peter Verdun?" she asked.

"Yes," he said, trying desperately to remember where he had seen her before.

"You're Karl Roy's lawyer," she added, and it finally came to him. She was the reporter he had seen at Roy's bail hearing.

"Isabelle Jacob," she said, offering her hand. "I'm a court reporter with *The Citizen*."

"We're a long way from Elgin Street." He smiled, taking his seat and shaking her hand.

"I remember you now. You were at Karl's bail hearing."

"That's right. Small world, isn't it?"

"Sure is. Are you here on Karl's case?"

"Sort of. I was working on another story in Paris, and I knew his case was starting this week so I thought I'd come down and do a little piece. I assume that's why you're here."

"Yes. I'm going to see Karl and meet with his lawyer here."

"Were you in Paris long?"

"Just for the weekend. How about you?"

"I've been here for a week. I'm hoping Nice will be a bit of a working holiday. It's really quite a beautiful area. Have you been before?"

"No, never had the pleasure," he said, imagining them exploring it together, frolicking on the beach. He snapped back to reality, realizing she was asking him something. "I'm sorry," he said as the captain came on and gave them the pre-flight spiel.

"So you're not representing Mr. Roy in Nice?"

"Oh no. We've retained French counsel for him. Very experienced. I'm just here to brief him and lend Karl whatever moral support I can. To be honest, it's a bit of a holiday for me too – I'm overdue."

"I know what you mean."

They taxied into take-off position and were soon hurtling down the runway and up in the air. After they became accustomed to the change in noise level, they continued their conversation. Although he found her quite charming, Verdun was mindful of the fact that she was a reporter and kept any discussions about Roy's case very general.

"So I have to ask," she said after the flight attendant had delivered their drinks, "do you really believe he's innocent? I mean, I know it's not supposed to matter but…"

"Sure it matters. And yes, I do believe he's innocent."

"You have to admit though," she said, "the eyewitness evidence was pretty damaging – assuming it's true, of course."

Verdun looked at her and smiled. He wasn't sure if she was fishing for a story or just making conversation. The fact was he didn't care anymore, he just didn't want this flight to end.

"It's all right, I'm not taking notes." She smiled at him coyly. "I promise not to print any of this. I'm just asking. And what are you grinning about?" She tossed her long brown hair back and began playing with it.

"I'm always amazed at how quickly a little mud will stick, that's all."

"The eyewitness you mean?"

"This so-called eyewitness has yet to see the light of a courtroom and already his word is the Gospel. You said so yourself – 'assuming it's true' is how you put it, and all of a sudden it's up to Karl to prove him wrong. It's supposed to be the other way around, you know. Whatever happened to the presumption of innocence?"

"But that's where you come in, right?" she said, sipping her wine. Verdun couldn't tell if she was being serious or sarcastic. The slight curl at the corner of her mouth gave her away.

"Do I sense a little cynicism? Or is there a lawyer joke coming?"

She threw back her head and laughed. "All right, you got me. But it's not what you think. I've actually got a soft spot for lawyers – my dad's fault."

"Your father's a lawyer?"

"Retired. He was a trial lawyer in Montreal."

"Really. So is that why you're covering the courts?"

"In a way, I guess. He took me to court with him when I was a kid and showed me around."

"That must have been fun," Verdun said, as a flight attendant offered newspapers, which they both refused.

"Yeah, it was. I thought I had the coolest dad in the whole world." She smiled. "But I got to see the flipside when my parents got divorced. That was enough to turn me from the life of a litigator. I made it as far as law school, but I knew when I graduated that I didn't want to practice, so I got into journalism."

"I've always thought journalism would be a great career."

"It's got its advantages. How about you, what led you into the courts?"

"I don't know really. I articled in a commercial firm and stayed long enough to discover I didn't like it much and just sort of gravitated towards criminal work."

"You did that murder trial a couple of years ago – the banker who killed his wife."

"He was acquitted, actually."

"That's right. You got him off, didn't you?"

"I prefer to say he was acquitted."

"Touché. You got a lot of press as I recall. Not bad."

She had been doing her homework, he thought as a warm feeling flowed to his cheeks. They talked about their respective professions, Ottawa and Paris, and before they knew it, they were beginning the descent into Nice. Thirty minutes later, they were in the terminal.

"Share a cab?" Isabelle asked as she started towards the exit.

Verdun looked at her compact carry-on suitcase and realized it was her only luggage. "I guess I should have packed light. I've got to wait for my bag. I don't want to hold you up."

"Maybe next time." She smiled. "It was nice to meet you."

"Likewise. I'll see you in court tomorrow." He watched her disappear through the sliding doors and cursed himself for lugging that big suitcase around with him. The carousel hadn't even started turning, so there was no hope of catching up with her outside. But as he recalled the pleasant flight and the warmth of her parting smile, his frustration was soon overtaken by another emotion – one he hadn't felt in far too long.

nine

Verdun had just enough time to drop his bags at the hotel and freshen up before his meeting with Karl Roy and Pierre Larousse. The sun was setting and a warm breeze was blowing as he set off from his hotel on the short walk to the Canadian mission in Nice. On his way, he passed a series of outdoor cafés and the sound of whistling waiters clinking glassware and dishes before entering a residential area that grew more and more affluent the farther he went. Roy had mentioned that the government always tried to locate their missions in good areas. Verdun spotted the Canadian flag atop a two-storey villa and made his way up to the wrought-iron gate that surrounded almost all of the houses on the street. He pressed the buzzer and, in response to a voice over the intercom, announced himself. A few seconds later, a security guard appeared and examined his passport before opening the gate. Verdun followed the guard up the path towards the well-kept villa and, as he got to the steps, the front door opened and a suntanned young man stepped out to greet him.

"Mr. Verdun, I'm Matthew Coté. I'm the trade officer here. Welcome to Nice."

"Thanks, Matthew. Call me Peter."

"Mr. Larousse and Mr. Roy are inside. Come on in." He led Verdun to a large room off the main foyer, where Roy and Larousse were sitting at a table covered in papers.

"Glad you could make it, Peter. How was the trip?" Larousse said as he got up to greet him.

Verdun shook his hand. "You must be Pierre."

"Bienvenue à Nice."

"Merci," Verdun said in his best French accent, which wasn't great. "Hello, Karl," he said as Roy made his way around the table to shake hands.

"Thanks for coming, Peter."

As Verdun took a seat and looked around him, he smiled and turned to Roy. "So, the accommodation's all right then?"

"It's a pretty gilded cage actually," Roy whispered, motioning towards a man seated in a chair just beyond the doorway at the far end of the room. "And I have you to thank for that."

"You can thank Malcolm McGavin and Pierre for this arrangement," Verdun said, looking to Larousse. "Still, I'm glad to see you're comfortable."

"Not as comfortable as he'll be when this is over," Larousse said.

Verdun nodded as they settled in around the table to get down to business. "So," he began, "have there been any developments on the eyewitness?"

"None," Larousse replied. "As we discussed on the telephone, I will be filing a demande...a petition before the court tomorrow to examine this witness in advance of the trial."

"But they don't have to let you, is that right?" Roy asked.

"Correct." Larousse nodded, explaining the procedure for criminal prosecutions in France. Although they featured the same principal elements, they differed in many ways from proceedings in Canada. The extradition process added some wrinkles and, as Larousse had explained to Verdun before, could provide them with a little more leeway than usual.

"We will be asking the court to make several advance rulings tomorrow to get a better look at the case of the Procureur. I expect some of them will be successful."

"What do you make of this eyewitness, Pierre?" Verdun asked.

"It is difficult to know." Larousse furrowed his brow. "But I know there is something unusual about this witness. I could sense it when I spoke to the Procureur last week."

"Have you considered hiring someone to look into his background?" Verdun asked.

"Yes, but these individuals are very expensive in France, and I thought it best to wait until after these initial matters are dealt with. It may be that the court will help us without the need for such expense."

Verdun nodded. Larousse seemed very self-assured and knowledgeable, to the point that Verdun wondered what else he could offer at this point, not being familiar with the French civil law system and its procedural intricacies. Still, he was relieved that Roy was in such good hands. For his part, Roy seemed more relaxed than he had been in Canada, and whether it was due to the comfort of his surroundings or Larousse's reassuring manner, it was good to see him relieved, at least temporarily, of some of the stress that had been eating at him in recent months.

Verdun went over the key elements of the extradition evidence and filled in a few gaps that Larousse had not already memorized from the file and, feeling he had offered whatever assistance he could, he was content to sit back and listen as Larousse prepared his client for what lay ahead. Just after 9 p.m., Larousse concluded the briefing and the two lawyers suggested Roy get a good night's rest.

"Thanks again for coming, Peter," Roy said as they got up from the table. "It's nice to see a face from home."

"My pleasure."

"And make sure you get out and see the area before you go back," Roy added. "It's truly beautiful."

"I'm going to try," Verdun said, shaking Roy's hand.

Verdun and Larousse walked down the flagstone path to the villa's front gate. "He seems like a good man," Larousse said.

"Yes," Verdun said. "I've known him since university and I can tell you, they've got the wrong guy."

"Let me give you a ride to your hotel," Larousse offered, motioning to a sleek, midnight blue Mercedes parked across the street.

"Thanks, but it's such a beautiful night, I think I'll walk. I'll see you in court tomorrow."

"A demain alors."

Verdun walked towards the downtown area, admiring the lush gardens and ornate villas nestled among them. He felt good knowing that Roy's defence would be properly handled. But as he strolled along, and an involuntary smile crossed his face, he knew there was another reason. He was looking forward to the next morning's proceedings.

The sun was shining as Verdun stepped out onto the steps of the Palais de Justice behind Pierre Larousse, who took out a pack of Gauloises and offered it to him.

"No thanks, I quit."

"Ah." Larousse lit one of the short cigarettes and exhaled a pungent, blue cloud. "You poor man."

Verdun laughed. "So, it seems to be going well."

"The judge seems sympathetic," Larousse said, taking a long puff. "I'm thinking of arguing for Karl's release. What do you think?"

The two had discussed the issue of Roy's pre-trial detention before, and normally it would have been automatic for Larousse to seek to have him released until the trial. But Larousse had been reluctant to draw undue attention to Roy's less-than-institutional detention arrangement at the consulate, fearing that if the motion were denied, Roy could end up in a French jail for a month.

"I don't know." Verdun shook his head. "I guess it's Karl's call, but it would be pretty hard to find better accommodation than what he has now."

"The press are sure to make an issue of it," Larousse added, exhaling another blue stream. As if on cue, Isabelle Jacob appeared at the top of the courthouse steps and made her way down to where the two men were standing.

"Good morning," Verdun said, suddenly lightened by her presence. He had been disappointed by her absence from the earlier part of the morning's session. "I didn't see you in there."

"I was scribbling in the back row."

"Oh, Isabelle Jacob," he said, remembering his manners. "This is Pierre Larousse."

"Enchanté." Larousse gave her a charming smile and Verdun suddenly felt as though he had just opened the henhouse to a fox.

"Isabelle is a reporter from Ottawa," he added, nervously noticing the way Larousse was appraising her.

"It's all right, I'm not looking for a statement," she said, mistaking Verdun's anxiety for concern over Karl Roy's best interests. "Though I would be interested in talking to your client, in your presence, of course."

"We might be able to arrange something. I'll have to ask him, of course," Larousse said coolly, as the court clerk appeared at the top of the steps and made eye contact with Larousse to indicate that court was about to resume.

"Well, I'm here for a couple of days. Here's my number at the hotel," she said, offering Larousse a piece of hotel stationery with a number scribbled across the top. "I've got to go make a phone call to Paris. I'll see you gentlemen inside."

As she climbed the steps and disappeared inside, Larousse tossed his cigarette to the ground and crushed it under his shoe. "Are all your reporters so lovely?"

"Unfortunately not." Verdun grinned.

"You should change your accommodation to Le Soleil." He looked at the letterhead on the sheet of paper.

"You're the one with her number, Pierre."

"Alas, but my wife would not be happy," he said with a mock sigh as they made their way up the steps. "Besides, anyone can see she has eyes only for you, my friend."

"I'm sorry, what did you say?" Verdun said, watching a conversation on the other side of the courtroom break up.

"You must come for dinner before you leave," Larousse said, turning to follow his colleague's gaze. "Or perhaps you have other plans?" he said with a smile as he followed Verdun's line of sight. "I'll give you a call tomorrow."

"Dinner would be nice. Thank you, Pierre."

"De rien," Larousse said, patting him on the shoulder. "Et bonne chance."

As Larousse took his leave, Verdun made his way to the scene of the conversation he had been watching between Isabelle Jacob and a French reporter, waiting for an opportunity to present itself. As he approached her, he took a deep breath and summoned up his confidence. "So it looks like you're going to get your interview. Well done."

"Thank you, but I get the feeling Pierre's going to have a long list of topics I'm not allowed to ask about."

So it was Pierre now, he thought. "Well, that's to be expected. You can't blame him for protecting his client."

She nodded, as the slightest hint of an awkward silence came over them. Verdun waded in. "Listen, I was going to check out one of the cafés in the old part of town for lunch. Would you like to join me?"

His heart sank when she replied, "I can't. I've rented a car for the day to go to Monaco."

"Oh really, that sounds nice," he said, wishing the ground would open up and swallow him right there and then. It had been a while since he had been on the wrong end of a brush off. But did she really have to rub it in by smiling at him that way?

"Funny thing is," she said. "I'm terrible with cars. I don't suppose you'd like to help me out with the driving? We could have lunch there."

"I'd love to," he said. There truly was a God after all.

She looked at her watch. "I was going to leave straight from here, but we can swing by your hotel if you'd like."

"Let's go then," he said as they headed out the door of the courthouse and down the steps.

ten

"Isn't it beautiful?" Isabelle shouted over the roar of the wind as the little Peugeot convertible crested a steep hill and the deep blue of the Mediterranean came into full view below them.

Verdun smiled in return. It was difficult to imagine a more scenic drive than the forty-minute stretch of winding road cut into the rocky cliffs between Nice and Monaco. The prospect of lunch in Monte Carlo with Isabelle made his smile even wider.

"Beats the hell out the office, doesn't it!"

"Look at that," she said, pointing down to a tile-roofed villa seemingly built into the hills, just above the water line. A large yacht was moored at the end of a little dock. "From there, you could hop on your yacht and take a spin down to St. Tropez or Cannes for lunch and be back in Monte Carlo for dinner."

"I'm wondering if they're short of lawyers here," he yelled back, eliciting a laugh from his beautiful passenger.

Within minutes they were in a long tunnel leading into Monaco. At the other end they began their descent into Monte Carlo itself. "There's the palace and the casino." Isabelle motioned to the hills above the far end of the marina where row upon row of enormous yachts were moored. "Let's park over there."

Verdun maneuvered the Peugeot into a parking spot, and they got out and strolled along the marina, marveling at the scenery. "This is unbelievable." Verdun shook his head as they passed a shiny Rolls Royce Phantom parked on the dock next to a large yacht.

"Would you like to go up to the palace?" she said.

"As long as we stop at a restaurant and you let me buy you lunch."

They walked up the steep and winding streets that led to the pink-walled palace overlooking the harbour. About three-quarters of the way up they decided to stop for lunch at one of the many restaurants and were soon sitting on a terrace, with a view of the marina below and the sprawling azure waters of the Mediterranean beyond.

"So what do you think of Karl's chances?" Isabelle asked, as a waiter arrived with their wine.

"I think he's in good hands with Pierre. I just hope the truth will come through at trial."

"Yes." Isabelle nodded, a slight smile on the edge of her lips.

"So that's it. You've duped me into coming to Monte Carlo so you can squeeze me for details about Karl's case."

"What did you think you were coming for?" she said in mock surprise.

"The beautiful scenery, of course," he replied, not taking his eyes off her.

She returned his look for a few seconds, then let out a little laugh. "All right, all right." She threw up her hands. "I know Karl's your client and you can't talk about the case."

"To his eventual acquittal then," he said, raising his glass.

She clinked her glass off his and took a sip. "What if I told you I'd been doing some research on the victim while I was in Paris?" she said as the crisp white wine slid down his throat. He didn't really know much about the victim at all, having spent the majority of his time on Roy's case researching and arguing procedural issues related to the extradition. Larousse had done some background work and discovered Jean-Christophe Malle had been through several wives in his time, but not much else of note.

"I'd be interested in knowing what you discovered, since you seem intent on keeping your reporter hat on."

"Did you know he worked for the French foreign service at one time?"

"I knew he was retired from the government."

"Or that he was posted in Ottawa?"

"Really?" Verdun was genuinely surprised.

"Yes, it was about twenty years ago. Malle was a trade officer, on his first foreign posting. His last, as it turned out." She sipped her wine as Verdun waited patiently for the rest. "Yes, his posting was revoked and he was recalled to France."

"Why?"

"I'll tell you if you help me do a little piece on Karl."

"You don't give up easily, do you?"

"What's with the attitude? I've got some information you're going to want to hear. All I want is a little quid pro quo."

"I told you on the plane–"

"I'm not going to ask about the details of the case," she said, shaking her head. "Or anything that might incriminate Karl. I just need a little help with the procedural stuff. I'm a little rusty on my Napoleonic Code."

"I'm a common law lawyer, remember – not much help in that department, I'm afraid. Why don't you ask Pierre?"

She shook her head. "Because he doesn't have the same perspective as you. You've been involved from the start and you can give me a better overall view for my readers' benefit."

Verdun shrugged.

"Look, I'll give you an outline of the scope of the interview beforehand, so you don't compromise your client in any way," she offered.

"Let's hear what you've got first."

"Promise me you'll consider it seriously?"

He looked at her plaintive expression and found himself fighting the urge to jump right onto the record. "Look, I'll think about it, but that's the best I can do."

"All right then," she said. She leaned closer in an almost onspiratorial pose before continuing. "It turns out Malle was recalled for killing someone in a car accident – a young girl."

"What?" Verdun was shocked, and leaned forward himself to hear the rest, catching a whiff of her delicate perfume as he did.

"Apparently he was in Montreal for the weekend and struck a young girl in a residential area. He had just left a consular reception and was on his way across town to another function, and he was drunk."

"Was he charged?"

"No, he was released before they could get a breath sample. The French government claimed immunity and had him shipped back home before the lawyers had a chance to get the case in front of a judge."

"And that's it? We didn't go after him?"

"Apparently not. A colleague is checking the archives for me, but so far all she's turned up is a few minor articles in the Montreal papers. There were different attitudes towards impaired driving back then too."

"And what did the French do with him?"

"Not much. Put him out to pasture in Strasbourg for a couple of years, until he could make his way back to Paris, where he worked towards a full pension."

Verdun sat back and sighed. "I can't believe it! This guy kills an innocent girl and his government bails him out without blinking an eye. Meanwhile, ours hands Karl over without a second thought – based on someone's hunch."

"It is somewhat ironic, don't you think?"

"It's sickening. I assume Karl doesn't know about this."

"No. At least I don't think so."

Verdun's mind was spinning. He wanted to call Malcolm McGavin right away. McGavin would surely make use of it to shame someone at Foreign Affairs into standing up for Roy.

"Got you thinking, huh?"

When she smiled, he noticed, it was always with her eyes. He found it intoxicating.

"Hmm. What? Yes, yes you did."

"Glad you came?"

As he contemplated her question, Verdun found himself captivated by the twinkle in those dark, sultry eyes, set as they were against the backdrop of her olive skin and long chestnut hair. In an instant, the importance of the information she had just provided melted away and he was seized with only one thought. He did not want this day to come to an end.

Verdun sat expectantly at a conference room table in Pierre Larousse's law offices, waiting for Annie Renaud. He had returned from Monaco the previous evening to find a message from Larousse to the effect that Annie Renaud had contacted him and expressed a desire to meet. She had requested that Roy not be present, which Verdun supposed was reasonable in the circumstances, though he felt little sympathy for the woman who was at least partly responsible for Roy's predicament.

He heard Larousse's voice in the hall and turned to see him come through the door, followed by a woman he assumed was Annie Renaud. She nodded in acknowledgement and extended her hand as Larousse introduced her and inquired whether she would like something to drink. Verdun shook her hand as she declined Larousse's offer, and as he watched her sit, he could understand why Roy might have fallen under her spell.

Tall, athletic and lightly tanned, with long blonde hair and steel-blue eyes, she was quite striking. She wore a conservative blue ensemble with matching suede shoes, and while it was clear she took fashion seriously, it was just as clear that she would look no less attractive in a burlap sack.

"Thank you for meeting me on such short notice," she said, in flawless English. Verdun remembered Roy mentioning she had spent several years in England as a student, which had obviously served her well.

"I wanted you to tell Karl how sorry I am for what has happened. He must be very angry with me." She looked at her hands. "Very angry."

"He's in a very difficult situation, Ms. Renaud," Verdun said as gently as he could, preferring to hear what she had to say next before mentioning the damning affidavit she had supplied to help land him here.

She nodded and looked at him, as if reading his thoughts. "The police were very…dishonest. They took a statement from me right after the murder, but when they found out about my relationship with Karl, they seemed angry with me." She wrung her hands and looked down at them again as she gathered herself to continue.

"Ca va bien, Mlle Renaud?" Pierre asked.

She nodded and looked up again. "They said they did not look kindly on my not telling them about our engagement and that they were considering charges against me."

"Unless?" Larousse interjected.

"They made me sign a second statement, acknowledging the argument Karl and I had just before the...death."

"You mean the shouting match at your apartment that was overheard by your neighbour?"

"Yes. I didn't want to sign it, and even then I had no idea what kind of trouble Karl was in. And they twisted my words."

Larousse looked up from his notes. "What do you mean, twisted?"

"You know what I mean. I told them something and then they put a statement in front of me and it was different. Not totally false, but different."

"We'll get into the details later, but we need your assurance that you will testify about this at Karl's trial," Larousse said, offering her a box of tissues. She took one and wiped her eyes.

"Yes, I will testify. I came here to tell you that I will help any way I can. Karl would never do such a thing and I know it."

"That's good, Ms. Renaud," Larousse said gently. "You can be of great help to us."

She looked at Verdun. "You're Karl's friend?"

"Yes," he replied.

"Then you must hate me," she said, the tissue still in her hand.

"I just want to get Karl out of this mess, Ms. Renaud, I really don't–"

"Tell him I'm sorry. Will you do that? For everything, I'm so sorry." She shook her head.

Verdun nodded. "I'll tell him," he said as he looked at Larousse, whose expression showed what every lawyer feels at a turning point in their client's case. It was faint but unmistakable – it was the first sign of victory.

eleven

Verdun was in the process of shaking the rain off his coat when a familiar voice boomed from beyond the reception area.

"There he is. Welcome back – and thanks for bringing this shitty weather with you." Jim Smythe slapped him heartily on the shoulder.

"Hello to you too. How are things?"

"Fine. Thought you'd be sleeping off the jet lag."

"I thought I'd give myself a head start on tomorrow morning," Verdun replied, looking at his watch. He had flown in to Toronto at 7 a.m., and his connecting flight had gotten him back to Ottawa just after nine. He had slept for an hour or so at home before showering and coming in, but he was still feeling a little disoriented by the time changes.

"I was just going down to the corner for a coffee. Have you had lunch?"

"I could use a sandwich."

The two dashed through the rain to the coffee shop just down Elgin, and Smythe secured two armchairs in the corner while Verdun placed their order.

"So how did it go?" Smythe said as Verdun arrived with their sandwiches.

"It went well," Verdun began, describing the pre-trial proceedings, as well as Annie Renaud's surprise revelation afterwards.

"And she'll testify to that effect?" Smythe asked, wiping mayonnaise from the corner of his mouth.

"So she says."

"Well that's good news."

"Yes it is. It still leaves the eyewitness, but Pierre's confident he can deal with him," Verdun added between bites.

"I also made an interesting discovery about the victim while I was there."

Smythe perked up. "Oh yeah, what's that?"

"He was retired from the French diplomatic corps. And guess where his first posting was about twenty years ago?"

"Where?"

"Right here. Except that he killed a pedestrian in a drunk driving accident in Montreal and was whisked out of the country before the cops could ask too many questions."

"Why can't Karl claim immunity anyway?" Smythe asked. "I mean, he was there on a diplomatic posting, wasn't he?"

Verdun shook his head. "I've already looked at that angle, but it's no use. Whatever immunity he enjoyed doesn't apply to criminal acts, and even if it did, his diplomatic posting had come to an end when Malle was killed."

"So he was just your average tourist at the time?"

Verdun nodded. "Technically, yes."

"Still," Smythe said. "If I were Karl, I don't think I'd appreciate the irony of Malle slipping away while he faces the music."

"No, but I met a reporter doing a story on Karl's case on the plane to Nice, and I told McGavin to make the point at Foreign Affairs that the story will compare the way the two governments have treated their respective employees."

"You mean the French protect their own and we throw ours to the wolves?" Jim smiled.

"Something like that. But, I figure it's never too late for a little political pressure."

"So how was France anyway?" Smythe asked after they had finished discussing Roy's case. "Did you manage a little sightseeing?"

"Yeah. It was really beautiful. You should take Margaret – she'd love it. We drove to Monaco and it was–"

"We?" Smythe asked quickly, his interest piqued.

"Oh, just that reporter I was telling you about. She had rented a car for the day–"

"You didn't tell me it was a woman. Come on, spill the beans."

Verdun smiled, then let out an exaggerated sigh. "All right.

But for God's sake, don't tell Margaret. She'll be picking out china patterns. Her name's Isabelle, she's a reporter with *The Citizen*."

Smythe's eyebrows shot up. "Isabelle Jacob?"

"You know her?"

"She's only the talk of the courthouse. Where have you been?" Smythe laughed. "You dog, you. All this time I'm thinking you're toiling away on Karl's case and you're off gallivanting around the French Riviera with an über-babe!"

"How do you know what she looks like?"

"I gave her an interview a couple of weeks ago on my fraud case."

"How come I've never seen her at the courthouse?"

"Don't ask me. But it sounds like you've seen her now – even if you had to go to Nice to do it."

Verdun shook his head. "It wasn't like that. It was a harmless daytrip. We had lunch and a few laughs and that was it really."

"Yeah, I'm sure it was harmless. So are you going to call her now that you're back?"

"What for?"

"You want a map? You're a bachelor and she's an intelligent, beautiful and apparently available woman."

Verdun was smiling again. He couldn't deny that he had thought of little else since that day in Monaco. He really would like to call her up, but he wasn't accustomed to being the pursuer, and he didn't want to rush things. "I might give her a call, I don't know. Besides, I've only been back for a couple of hours. Give me a chance, will you?"

"Make the call, my friend. You don't meet someone like that every day, and besides, it has to be fate."

"What do you mean?"

"You don't think it's strange she ended up sitting next to you on a plane in France. What are the odds?"

Verdun had to admit that their meeting had been a remarkable twist of fate.

"And now that we've got the important stuff out of the way," Smythe said, sipping his coffee. "I can tell you all about what your crazy clients have been up to while you were away."

"Oh God," Verdun sighed, as he awaited the outline of what the week held in store.

Verdun always made a point of complaining to Margaret Smythe about his lonely existence. And even though he knew Smythe saw through this, neither let on. Margaret had been determined to pair him off since they first met, and nobody wanted to spoil her fun. It wasn't as though he didn't wonder from time to time what it would be like to be married – to have a soul mate, as it were. But there was also an undeniable pleasure in being at the centre of one's universe, and in that particular endeavour, Verdun was well versed. It wasn't that he was self-centred – he wasn't. He was a considerate colleague, employer and friend. He was always interested in other people, and in helping them if he could. He was no cad either. He treated the women in his life with the respect of equals, but his default setting was solitude. Up to this point, he had been unwilling to sacrifice his own space to accommodate a partner, even if he was a little lonely now and then.

This Saturday morning started out like all the others. He woke with a chill from a cool fall breeze blowing through his bedroom window. He donned his heavy bathrobe and braced himself as he opened the door to get the morning papers. But instead of an icy blast of air, he found a beautiful fall morning. The sun was breaking out from behind what was left of the clouds and a breeze was rustling the leaves high in the trees. He noted the early birds running along the paths lining both sides of the Rideau Canal and decided he would make a point of doing the same later. It would help to offset the beer and wings he would be having at the pub tonight with a couple of his teammates from his rec league hockey team. After collecting the papers and closing the door behind him, he made his way to the kitchen. He scanned the headlines, then dropped the papers on the table in the breakfast nook, plugged in the kettle and switched on the radio. He listened to the news as he ground coffee and poured cereal. Then, as the water boiled, he measured a careful dose of coffee into the bottom of the press and filled it with water. With his breakfast and the rest of his Saturday before him, he gathered up the local paper without the slightest inkling of how quickly its content would change the course of his day.

Seven hours had elapsed since breakfast and he had gone about his usual routine. Verdun had gone for a run and done a light workout on his home gym. He had picked up his dry cleaning, done some grocery shopping and strolled down to the market and picked up a couple of jazz CDs. With a smoky saxophone filtering softly out of his wireless surround-sound system, Verdun sat in his favourite chair, a cup of tea on the table in front of him and a good book in his hands. But no matter how hard he tried, he couldn't get past the same paragraph. He had felt it all day. He couldn't focus on anything. His perfect Saturday had been held hostage ever since he had seen her picture on page three of his morning paper. He recognized her immediately. Even in a little 1 by 1, black and white square, she was unmistakable. And her picture was just the start. Isabelle's article on Roy had been well written, informative and, most of all, interesting. True to her word, she had used only on-the-record material from her discussions with Verdun and Roy and had managed to distil the complications of the extradition process and the French legal system into a half-page article, beautifully capturing Roy's helplessness in the process. He put his book down and took a sip of tea, glancing at the phone in the process. He had devoted more attention to that little black cordless in the past few hours than in all of its previous lifetime. He desperately wanted to pick it up, and had even taken a few steps toward it, but was confounded each time by an awkwardness he had not experienced since the ninth grade. What the hell was wrong with him? He was an eligible bachelor after all. They had clearly hit it off in France, so what was he waiting for? He grabbed the phone and dialed the number he had looked up a few hours earlier. He waited breathlessly as the ringing was interrupted and he prepared himself to speak. But his anticipation turned to disappointment as the answering machine kicked in. He despised leaving messages, and he debated hanging up. Before he could make up his mind though, the brief message came to an end and the beep sounded. He charged ahead.

"Hi Isabelle," he began confidently. "I read your article in this morning's paper. It was very good by the way. Anyway, I thought of you and wondered whether you'd like to have dinner. Give me a call. Bye."

He hung up the phone and took a deep breath. There, he had done it. He was glad he had left the message. With the ball firmly in her court, he could sit back and wait for her reply. Yes, it was much better this way, he thought as he placed the phone back on the stand. She would get the message and…A feeling of alarm came over him as he realized he hadn't left his name or, for that matter, his number. But surely she would recognize his voice. Should he call back and clarify? No, that would make him look like an amateur. He sat thinking for a moment, then laughed out loud. He was acting like a teenager. He looked at his watch and decided to go get ready – the pub gang would be waiting. By the time he got back, he would probably have a blinking light waiting on his answering machine.

Verdun read through the letter in front of him as his client sat opposite, anxiously awaiting the verdict. "Well," he began, as the young man in his mid-twenties sat up to attention. "As I said, I don't really practice family law." Verdun always began any foray into family law with this disclaimer, partly because it was true, but mostly because he hoped this information would cause the client to seek expert advice elsewhere. But it rarely resulted in anything more than a slightly perceptible shrug in the client's shoulders, followed by an awkward silence indicating that Verdun would not be let off the hook quite so easily. "But from what I can see, you're being ordered to increase your child support payments by $100 a month."

"But I can't afford that!"

"Did you go to the variation hearing?"

"No. I didn't know I had to."

"The hearing's where each side gets to tell their story. I guess the judge took your absence as a sign that you agreed with the version of events that your ex was presenting. Has your income increased?"

"I'm on welfare. What do you think? And whatever she told the judge is bullshit. She's been screwing around with that cop I told you about. Remember?"

Verdun did not. In fact, all he remembered about this unfortunate young man was having represented him on a legal aid certificate about three months prior in connection with an impaired driving charge.

"Why doesn't the cop pay for the child support? Since he's screwing the mother."

Verdun contemplated how to respond to this question without sounding judgmental. Then he remembered the sorry status of his own romantic life and felt even more depressed. It was now Tuesday and he had heard nothing from Isabelle. He had briefly considered calling her again but knew this would come off as too needy. He supposed she was otherwise engaged or, worse, just plain uninterested. Still, he was surprised that she hadn't called back, if only to brush him off. His memory offered him a brief glimpse of her sitting in the passenger seat of the little convertible, the sun gleaming off her flowing brown hair and the crystal blue Mediterranean beyond, before he was abruptly returned to the present by a phlegmatic cough from his client.

"So...What do I do?"

Verdun was spared having to respond by the ringing of his direct line. "Excuse me for just a moment please," he said, reaching eagerly for the receiver. He would welcome a chat with an auditor from Revenue Canada at this point. "Peter Verdun."

"Hello Peter, it's Isabelle."

"Oh." His pulse quickened slightly. "How are you?"

"I just got back in town and checked my messages. I assume that was you – you didn't leave your name."

"Yes." He gave a disarming laugh. "I didn't realize I hadn't left my name."

"I'm sorry, am I interrupting you?"

"Not at all," he lied, turning away from his client's curious gaze.

"Actually, I'm glad you called. I was in Montreal on a story and I got a chance to do some research on Jean-Christophe Malle's victim."

"Really, what did you find?"

"Well, I'd like to take you up on your offer of dinner and then I can tell you all about it."

"Sure, there's a new place on Somerset I hear is very good. Do you like Thai?"

"I love it."

"Are you free tonight, around eight? I can pick you up if you like."

His client looked on as Verdun scribbled something in the margin of the support variation order.

"I'll see you tonight."

He hung up the phone and turned back to his client, who was sitting there with a vacant expression.

"So, what about my case?" he said.

It took every ounce of Verdun's self-control to suppress the grin that wanted to burst over his face. It was another exercise in self-discipline not to tell the man to go pay a family lawyer to deal with his case instead of looking for a pro bono from Verdun. But his sudden elation got the better of him as he looked at the forlorn figure seated across from him.

"Yes," he said, giving a reassuring nod. "Let's see what we can do with your case."

twelve

The address was a tidy little townhouse on the edge of New Edinburgh and must have cost a pretty penny, Verdun thought as he pulled into the driveway. Isabelle met him on the front steps and, after a quick greeting, they drove to the restaurant together, chatting about her article on the way. At the restaurant – a cozy little place that seated thirty or so – they were escorted to their seats and were soon ordering drinks.

"So, how was Montreal?" Verdun asked as the waitress headed to the small bar in the corner with their orders.

"It was ok, I guess. I enjoy going back, but I always feel obliged to stay with my dad. He's had a hard time since his second wife died."

"Oh, I'm sorry to hear that," Verdun said as they settled in. "How long ago?"

"Two years now. Poor Dad." She shook her head. "Anyway, I was there on another story, but I had some time to dig through the archives. It took me a while but I found her. Her name was Angeline Vachon. She was only seven years old – poor thing."

"That's awful. Did you find newspaper articles?"

"Yes, and I managed to track down an accident report through a friend at the Sureté. That's how I found the mother."

"Did you talk to her?"

"Only on the phone. She didn't say much, but she agreed to an interview on Thursday."

"Are you planning to write a follow-up or something?" Verdun was generally curious, but also interested in how the story might affect Karl Roy's case.

"I don't know yet. I generally like to see where the leads take me. It's just the way I do things."

"No stone unturned. That's very good." Verdun smiled as their wine arrived and he dutifully swished a little in his glass, sniffed and tasted it before giving the waiter the nod to pour.

"Are you a connoisseur?" she asked as she took a sip.

"Hardly," he said with a grin. "I saw someone doing that once and thought it looked impressive."

She smiled as he went on. "That is, until my date told me she was a lifelong member of the Opimian Society and exposed my ignorance with a couple of basic questions."

"I'm not going to embarrass you," she laughed. "Wines are a bit of a work in progress for me, but one thing I've learned is that some people just have a knack for choosing the good ones." She raised her glass and smiled. "And you've done very well."

They continued chatting over dinner and it was after ten when the waitress appeared with coffee and a dessert menu.

"I really shouldn't..." Isabelle said, as the waitress listed off the special – a fruit flan. "But I will anyway."

"I'll have the same," Verdun said, as she set down their coffees, and a little silver tray of sugar and cream.

"I can see I'm going to have to walk this off later," she said.

"That's a good idea." He looked out the window. "It's a lovely evening for a walk."

"Yes," she said. "But it will have to be a short one for me. I've got to finish off a piece on student crime before my noon deadline tomorrow and I'm a long way from being done."

Verdun avoided showing his disappointment, nodding instead and taking a sip of the coffee.

"You should come to Montreal with me on Thursday," she said suddenly, adding, "You know how I don't like driving."

He tried to remember his schedule. He was pretty sure he wasn't due in court, and Smythe would cover for his afternoon meeting. "I'd like that. It'll give me a chance to see you in action."

"The interview's set for two, but if you're free, we could leave around mid-morning and you can let me buy you lunch there. That way we'll miss the worst of the traffic."

They finished their dessert and coffee and then strolled down to Wellington and past the Parliament buildings before making their way back to his car. "Thanks for dinner. It was a lot of fun," she said, as he pulled up in front of her house.

"It was my pleasure," he said as their eyes locked for the briefest of moments.

"I'll see you Thursday morning," she said, leaning over and pecking him on the cheek.

"Look forward to it," he said as she got out and disappeared up the steps. When she was safely inside, he pulled away from the curb and made his way back towards Elgin Street. He felt the little smudge of lipstick on his cheek and inhaled the faint scent of perfume that still lingered. He hoped he didn't have anything scheduled for Thursday, because whatever it was, he would be in Montreal.

thirteen

"Here! Turn here," Isabelle said, just as the car was passing a side street. Verdun swerved just in time to make the turn, the force of gravity practically throwing her into his lap. "Sorry," she laughed. "It's been a while since I've been in this part of town."

They had arrived in Montreal just before noon and stopped off for lunch at a downtown deli before making their way east to the address scribbled in Isabelle's day-timer. The drive from Ottawa had offered them a spectacular display of fall colours, and the city itself had basked in the brilliant fall sunshine as they had made their way to St. Catherine Street. Now, the sun was giving way to grey cloud, which exacerbated the pall that hung over this treeless and run-down part of the city. Junk-strewn parking lots and chain-link fences dominated the landscape between the colourless mixture of high-rises and townhouses.

"There it is, on the left. Park over there." She pointed to an empty parking space.

Verdun parked the truck and eyed a trio of tough-looking teenagers leaning on a car across the street, smoking cigarettes.

"Do you want to park somewhere else?"

"No," he lied. "Let's go." They crossed the street and found the number they were looking for above the door of a shabby row house. Verdun knocked on the tattered screen door and they heard muttering from inside. The hinges squeaked and a face appeared behind the screen.

"Ouah?" she said abruptly.

"Mrs. Vachon, my name is Isabelle Jacob. We spoke on the phone on the weekend–"

"Oh, it's you, come in. Your boyfriend too."

"This is Peter Verdun. He's the lawyer for Karl Roy."

"Whatever you say, ma chère," she said with a rough laugh.

Isabelle and Verdun exchanged grins as they followed the old woman inside. The air was rank with cigarette smoke and kitty litter.

"Don't bother to take off your shoes," Vachon shouted over the blare of the television. She turned it down and met them in the kitchen, taking a seat at the little pressed-wood table. She moved the tin of tobacco she had been rolling into cigarettes to the side and waved at the other two chairs. "Have a seat. I don't bite." The rough laugh again.

"We appreciate you meeting with us, Mrs. Vachon. I'm sure this isn't an easy thing for you," Isabelle began.

"It's been so long, but I still think of her every day," Vachon said, looking beyond them at a picture on a sideboard in the next room.

Isabelle turned around to look at the picture of a young girl in a summer dress. "She was beautiful."

"Hmmm." Vachon lit a cigarette. "Too beautiful for this world," she said, slurring her words slightly. "And now the bastard who killed her got his. Tell your boyfriend here I'll do whatever I can to help. This Roy should get a medal–"

"Actually," Isabelle interjected gently. "I was wondering if you could tell us about the accident investigation. How did the police deal with it?"

"That's easy," Vachon said from behind a thick fog of cigarette smoke. "They didn't do a goddamn thing."

"Do you know if Malle was detained at the scene, or questioned?"

"He was at the police station when my brother came to pick me up, I know that much." She got up and pulled a bottle from one of the cupboards. "Drink?"

"No thanks," Verdun said, followed by Isabelle.

Vachon poured a liberal dose into a grimy glass, took a gulp and steadied herself against the counter.

"Are you all right, Mrs. Vachon?" Isabelle got up to offer her a hand.

Vachon waved her off. "He was in the next office with his lawyer. I'd never seen him before but as I walked by, I just stopped and stared." She paused to wipe her eyes. "I stood there staring until he looked up and I knew I was looking into the eyes of the man that killed my baby. I would have gladly slit his throat right there if only..."

"I'm so sorry," Isabelle said, offering her a tissue. She looked at Verdun and wondered if the interview had been a good idea after all. This woman was obviously in a bad way, and by the looks of things had been for some time.

"Is that your son?" Verdun asked, pointing to the picture on the sideboard next to Angeline's and trying to introduce a ray of light into the glum scene.

Vachon nodded and wiped her nose. She walked over to the sideboard and picked up the picture. "So innocent," she said, returning to the table and setting the picture down in front of her. It was a picture of a baby in a little sailor outfit and blue boots, with the hospital bracelet set into the frame below it, the distinctive red logo familiar to Isabelle.

"He's adorable," she remarked.

"He was ten when she was killed – his baby sister," Vachon sighed. "Bruno lost a part of himself that day – something he never got back."

"It must have been very difficult for him to understand."

"Oh, he understood all right. He understood too well that the law doesn't apply to everyone." Vachon took another sip of her drink and lit another cigarette. She seemed to pause to think for a second before her face clouded and she looked at Verdun with a furrowed brow. "Why are you asking me about him anyway?" she said, a sudden defiance in her voice.

Verdun was taken aback. "I...I was just asking about your family, I wasn't–"

"I know what you're doing," Vachon practically spat, turning to Isabelle, who exchanged puzzled looks with Verdun. Vachon downed the rest of her drink and got up from the table. "The past is the past," she said. "And I think I'd like to be alone now."

"I'm sorry if I upset you, Mrs. Vachon. I really–"

"Never mind," Vachon said, gripping Verdun firmly by the arm and pulling him towards the hall. "I'm just an old woman with too many painful memories."

"Well, we appreciate you taking the time to see us," Isabelle barely managed to say before the door creaked shut behind them and they found themselves in a cold shower of rain.

"Come on." Verdun grabbed her by the arm and they bolted across the street to the truck. Once inside, they shook the rain out of their hair and looked at each other. "What the hell was that all about?" Verdun asked.

"I have no idea. She seemed eager to talk when we spoke on the phone."

"I guess I shouldn't have opened my big yap," he said.

"I guess not," she replied solemnly. She waited a few seconds before bursting into a smile. "You look so guilty," she laughed. "It's not your fault. Maybe she's just not a big fan of lawyers."

"I'll bet you didn't mention your own legal background, did you?" he said with a wry grin. They laughed for a moment and Verdun started the engine. "Jeez, it sure turned ugly fast," he said, looking up at a sky that was getting blacker by the minute.

They talked for a while about Vachon's unusual behaviour, and the possible motives behind it, deciding they would get no further answers to their questions sitting there in Verdun's truck. They wasted no time beginning the drive out of town, not wanting to get caught in the late afternoon rush, and within 45 minutes, they were back on the road to Ottawa. But their westward progress was soon halted by a stream of cars blocking both lanes in front of them, their brake lights glowing.

"This can't be normal traffic," Verdun said, craning his neck to see past the gridlock. "There must have been an accident."

"I'm not surprised," Isabelle said, as a fierce downpour pelted the windshield. "I can barely see the car in front of us and we're not even moving."

"Maybe we should have waited for it to pass."

They inched along for about twenty minutes and as they approached an off-ramp, a thick fork of lightning lit up the ky. Verdun looked at his watch. It was three-thirty and they were getting nowhere. He glanced at the sign for the off-ramp.

"Are you thinking what I'm thinking?" Isabelle said, as an

ear-splitting clap of thunder startled them both.

"If you're thinking we should take this exit and find a coffee shop where we can wait this out, then yes, I am."

"Great minds think alike."

Verdun pulled out of the line of traffic and skirted the shoulder until they were at the exit. "This is unreal," he said, trying to make out the turn as the rain turned to hail and pounded the hood of the truck, now rocking noticeably on its axles in the gusting wind.

"Take the left." Isabelle pointed to a sign that indicated a town a few kilometres away. "There's bound to be something there."

Verdun took the turn and crouched over the wheel, driving very slowly down the little country road, making sure he didn't veer into the oncoming lane or into the ditch. After what seemed like far too long, they arrived at the little village of St. Anne de Montfort.

"There's something – over there." Isabelle pointed to her right and Verdun saw the lights of a restaurant or inn, with a number of cars parked outside.

He pulled up and shut off the engine. Reaching into the back seat, he handed Isabelle his only form of shelter from the rain, a windbreaker he had won at a charity golf tournament. "It's the best I can do."

"That's very chivalrous of you," she said, putting it over her head and preparing for the twenty-yard dash to the doorway. The hail had stopped but the rain was still coming down in sheets.

"And a one, and a two, and a thr–"

Isabelle interrupted his countdown by jerking open her door and disappearing into the storm. Laughing, he threw his own door open and followed the sound of her shrieking through the torrent of water. Five seconds later they were standing in the entrance, shaking off the rain. Pulling back a wisp of hair from her face, Isabelle burst out laughing as she took stock of Verdun, soaked to the skin by his short but unprotected sprint. "You poor thing," she said, covering her mouth.

The proprietor of the Auberge du Lac appeared in the doorway with a pair of towels. "Come in, come in out of the rain."

They thanked him and, having dried themselves off, walked into the small lobby of the cozy little inn. The Auberge also featured a dining room and a small bar, both of which were almost full.

"Shall we get a drink while we wait for it to pass?" Verdun said, pointing to the bar.

"Why not?"

They were soon seated at the last available table in the rear corner of the bar, where they could look out at the storm as they sipped their drinks. The jolly owner and his wife, seemingly unaccustomed to such crowds on a weekday afternoon, were doing their best to keep up with the demand for food and drink. As the storm raged and the rain pelted the window, Verdun and Isabelle sensed the camaraderie amongst the sheltering travellers, most of whom were likely not so unhappy to find themselves in a cozy little bar instead of locked in their everyday commute.

"I've never seen anything like it, not at this time of year," the man at the next table remarked, sipping his beer.

"It's something all right," Isabelle said, as a fork of lighting lit up the inside of the pub as if an enormous flash bulb had gone off. When the glare died down, it was replaced by the total darkness of a power failure, followed by a chorus of "oohs," "ahhs," and chuckles.

"Ne vous inquietez pas, messieurs dames!" came the proprietor's voice from behind the bar, followed by the flame of a match. It flickered back and forth across the bar until several candles had been lit, to the spirited applause of the grateful crowd.

"This is too much," Verdun laughed.

"Well, it beats the office, doesn't it?" Isabelle said as the proprietor arrived and lit the little candle at their table.

"Bienvenue," he said. "You were on your way to Ottawa?"

"Yes, we got caught in quite a traffic jam."

"Ah oui," he said with a frown, "an accident - very bad. They closed the highway indefinitely."

"Really?" Verdun asked. "Looks like the back roads for us."

"This is not an evening for travel," the proprietor tut-tutted, looking out at the ever-darkening sky.

"But all is not lost, monsieur, you are in excellent company." He smiled at Isabelle. "And we have a fine dining room across the hall."

Isabelle smiled into her glass. The sales pitch was far from subtle, but the salesman did have charm, she had to give him that.

"Say the word and you can still have my best room for the night. Then tomorrow you can resume your journey relaxed, and with the storm passed."

"Dinner looks like a definite possibility," Verdun said, looking at Isabelle and refraining from any comment on the prospect of sharing a room for the night. Her candlelit smile gave him the sense that she was thinking the same.

"We're certainly not going anywhere for a while," she said.

"Très bien," the proprietor said. "I'll bring you another wine." Before they had a chance to reply, he had gone, leaving them to exchange smiles across the table.

"This is delicious." Isabelle sighed with delight after taking a bite of her cheesecake. The two were in the last phase of a long and sumptuous meal in the Auberge's rustic little dining room. And while the diners all sat in candlelight, it was not of necessity but rather as part of the atmosphere. Though the storm still raged outside, electrical power had been restored to the Auberge and the activity behind its little kitchen door had gone uninterrupted through what was most likely its busiest night of the year. But despite the number of guests, the proprietor had taken great pains not to rush them through their meal. Verdun and Isabelle had been treated to an assortment of appetizers, followed by an entrée of wild game terrine and a cheese plate, all washed down with a couple of bottles of surprisingly good house red wines. It was after eight o'clock by the time the charming proprietor appeared with the dessert menu.

"You have to try this tarte," Verdun said, pushing his dessert plate towards her.

"I can't eat another bite," she said, eyeing the plump blueberries atop the pastry. "Well, maybe one little bite."

"So what did you make of Mrs. Vachon?" Isabelle asked, as they sat over coffee. "Are you as curious about Bruno as I am?"

"There was definitely something about him she wasn't saying," he agreed. "Though I doubt it's of any interest to us. Poor woman."

"Yes, it was kind of depressing, wasn't it?" She shook her head.

"This is fun though," Verdun said, changing tack.

"Yes it is," she said.

"I wonder if they've re-opened the highway," he said, sipping his coffee.

"You're in no condition to drive, counselor," she said. "Besides, I like the road we're on right now."

He smiled back.

"If you'll excuse me, I'm going to freshen up," she said, finishing her coffee and getting up from the table. "Why don't you see about that room?"

Verdun waited patiently for her to disappear around the corner before waving enthusiastically at the proprietor, who was clearing a table on the far side of the dining room. He spotted the sign and came over immediately.

"Oui, monsieur."

"I don't suppose you still have any rooms left for the night?"

"Alas, non, monsieur."

The disappointment on Verdun's face was obvious.

"It's a good thing I saved the best one for you, isn't it?" he said with a wink.

Verdun made his way purposefully up the stairs without a word, with Isabelle following closely behind, her hand in his. Closing the door behind them, they were immediately entwined in an urgent embrace. They kissed passionately, tugging at buttons and zippers and shedding their clothes, as they made their way blindly across the room. Outside, the rain had finally stopped and a dim beam of moonlight was all that lit the bed onto which they softly fell. She rolled onto him and leaned back, pulling her sweater over her head and revealing herself to his gaze and touch. She freed him from his last constraint, pulled at her skirt and leaned forward over him, as the sweet smell of her chestnut hair filled his nostrils and they both sighed with pleasure.

fourteen

Jim Smythe was rubbing his hands together with glee as Verdun walked into his office just after noon on Friday. "Well, well," he began.

"Well what?" Verdun said, trying his best to keep a straight face.

"What! You know damn well what. Tell me all about it."

"I've got to prepare for a meeting. Besides there's nothing to tell–"

"Don't even think about it." Smythe wagged an index finger at him. "You owe me big time. Where would you be without your old friend to appear for you in chambers while you're off cavorting around the countryside?"

"I said thanks on the phone. What more do you want?"

Smythe sat on the corner of Verdun's desk, his arms folded. It was clear he wasn't going anywhere.

"All right, all right." Verdun threw up his arms in mock exasperation. "But I'm not going to kiss and tell."

"Yeah, whatever," Smythe said, moving to the door. "Hold his calls please," he shouted before closing the door behind them.

"Before I say anything, you have to promise not to tell Margaret."

"Are you kidding? She's planning dinner as we speak."

"Well, in that case, let her carry on," Verdun replied, and instead of the rolling of the eyes that Smythe expected, a broad grin appeared on Verdun's face.

"Look at you – all smiles!" Smythe chuckled. "So you drove her out into the middle of nowhere and then used the storm as a pretext, is that it?"

"Something like that, yes." Verdun grinned.

"And you're going to see her again?"

"We're having lunch tomorrow, now that you mention it."

"Well, well. I never thought I'd see the day." Smythe shook his head.

"What can I say? She's great. She's beautiful, smart, funny..."

"So seriously, when do we get to meet her?"

"Soon. We'll do it soon."

"Good, good. How'd the interview go by the way – not that it's crossed your mind since," Smythe asked.

"Oh, it wasn't very productive. Poor woman is a mess. Halfway through, she turned on us and kicked us out."

"Why'd she do that?"

"I have no idea. She seemed a little unstable. Whatever the case, it wasn't much good to Karl."

"Oh, that reminds me." Smythe gestured to Verdun's secretary's desk beyond the office door. "I overheard Julie fielding a call from Pierre Larousse this morning. Sounded like he was anxious to talk to you."

"I'll check with Julie. Anything else I should know about?" he said, looking at his watch.

"No. I talked to Bob Salter this morning and he agreed to adjourn that first appearance until Monday."

"Good, thanks for that. I owe you one."

Smythe got up to leave. "You up to taking the gang out for a drink at five?"

"Sure."

The appearance of Verdun's secretary at the door with a pile of papers would usually have caused him some anxiety. But as he waved her in and began to plan out his afternoon, he realized it didn't matter, and that whatever the day had in store for him, it wasn't likely to erase the smile that lit his face whenever he thought of Isabelle.

At the sound of his phone, Verdun looked up from the letter he was reading. It was almost quitting time and the entire office would soon be heading over to D'Arcy McGee's patio for drinks, but he was eager to touch base with Pierre Larousse before he left. He had called twice and left messages, but it was now well into the night in France.

"Yes?"

"It's Mr. Larousse returning your call."

"Thanks, Julie. I'll see you over there," he said, noting the time.

"We'll save you a seat," she replied as she transferred the call.

"Pierre. Comment ca va?"

"We have a problem, Peter." The flat tone from the usually bubbly Larousse was an immediate indication that something was wrong.

"What is it?"

"I examined the eyewitness this afternoon. It went as we expected, except for one thing."

Verdun waited for the rest.

"The witness recovered a piece of physical evidence at the scene. A piece of jewellery."

Verdun was confused. Roy was not the type to wear jewellery. "What are you talking about? What jewellery?"

"You've heard of Les Canadiens de Montreal of course?"

Verdun was silent for a second as he processed the information. "You mean the hockey team? Well yes, I have, but what does that–"

"The evidence is a small gold pendant in the form of the team's logo. I don't have to tell you this is not good news for our client."

"Are you sure that's what it is? I mean how do the police there know what the Canadiens' logo looks like?"

"Internet," Larousse replied, and Verdun realized how easily it was done.

Verdun was still trying to piece together the puzzle, and some fairly important pieces were still missing. "But where was this evidence before now? I saw no record of any jewellery in the inventory of evidence found at the scene."

"My first question also, Peter," Larousse said. "But they have a very good explanation for this. The witness, you know, is a...clochard."

"A what?"

"Yes. A man with no home, you might say. He found the pendant on the ground near the body and planned to trade it for a bottle, but he ended up a guest of the police the night after the murder and the evidence was confiscated."

"I'm not sure I follow. You mean he was in jail?"

"Yes, as a part of a sweep they do every few weeks starting in the spring. When he was released the next morning, his pendant was gone. He says the duty sergeant took it."

This was making no sense to Verdun. "But how–"

"He didn't mention it in his first statement, but when the detectives interviewed him again about the murder, he told them about the pendant. They questioned the desk sergeant, who gave it up when he realized it might be evidence in a murder investigation."

"But all of this would have been months ago."

"That's true. And it would never have amounted to anything much, except that one of the detectives was curious enough about the logo to find out what it was. And when he discovered it belonged to a Canadian hockey team, well…"

"But they can't use it at trial, surely. What about the delay, or the chain of custody?"

"We're in France, Peter. Our procedures are different and there is a good chance it will go in. And you know what that means."

"You've got to get it excluded, Pierre. No jury is going to believe that kind of connection is mere coincidence."

"I'm going to try, but it will be difficult."

"What about Karl?" Verdun asked. "What does he say?"

"He says he hates this team. He said you would understand."

"He's from Quebec City. Must be an old Nordiques fan."

"What?"

"Nothing. An old sporting rivalry that no French jury is going to understand, much less consider relevant."

"Exactly. So, I will be making a motion next week to exclude the evidence, but I'm not very confident."

"Is there anything I can do, Pierre? I feel helpless over here."

"You could try the political route again, but I think it may be too late for that."

"I'll talk to McGavin and see if he has any ideas. Call if you think of anything else I can do."

"I will. Goodnight, Peter."

Verdun put the receiver down and rubbed his temples. Suddenly, the rendezvous at the pub had lost its significance. Since leaving Nice, Verdun had felt growing confidence that Roy's position was improving and that it was only a matter of time before he would be released and returned home. This new development was a considerable turn for the worse in that it caused him to consider seriously his client's version of events – something he hadn't done since the very beginning. As he tried to think of an explanation for the presence of the pendant, Verdun had to admit that nothing plausible came to mind. For a moment, he allowed himself to consider the possibility that Roy might not have told him the truth, but he quickly dismissed those doubts. If he knew anything at all, it was that Karl Roy was innocent.

Verdun left a message on McGavin's voice mail with his home and cellular numbers, then shuffled a few of the papers on his desk before turning off his computer and locking up. On the short walk to Sparks Street, he tried not to think of Roy, but it was impossible. In the five-minute stroll down Elgin, he had convinced himself that, however coincidental, the discovery of the pendant was immaterial. He chased the logical conclusion to the far recesses of his mind and decided instead to redouble his efforts to prove Roy's innocence.

fifteen

"How about over there?" Verdun said, pointing to a wide expanse of lush, green grass, at the far end of which stood a large willow. Isabelle nodded and they both left the bike path and made their way across the grass, still green though most of the leaves had now turned. In the brilliant fall sunshine, the trails in the Hog's Back area were at their most spectacular. Verdun brought his bike to a stop and carefully removed the picnic basket from the carrier behind his seat as Isabelle gently laid her bike on its side.

"It's so beautiful," she said as Verdun spread out a blanket and offered her a seat.

"After you," he said, putting the basket down and opening it slowly, keeping its contents out of her view.

"That's quite a basket. What have you got in there?"

"A little aperitif for starters," he said, passing her a wine glass. He pulled out a bottle of Niagara ice wine, uncorked it and poured them both a glass.

"Cheers," she said, touching his glass with hers. "This was a wonderful idea."

They sat on the blanket looking out over the glass-still waters of the nearby canal and talked and laughed for a while before Verdun returned to the picnic basket that he had purchased and carefully provisioned the night before, treating her to an array of salad, smoked salmon, pâté, cheeses, and finally, a small selection of pâtisseries he had bought across the River in Gatineau before picking her up. As they enjoyed the last of their wine in the sun's warm glow, they moved for the first time beyond talk of their respective work, into the realm of their personal lives, trading little snippets of information. After they had each divulged something intimate, they returned to work, and eventually to Karl Roy. Verdun had already told her of Larousse's call the day before, and of his struggle to reconcile it with Roy's version of events. It was clear that the news had affected her as well.

"Just playing devil's advocate," she began. "How else would you explain the presence of a Canadian hockey team's logo at a crime scene in France? I mean, unless there was another Canadian we could point to, that leaves the jury with Karl."

"True, but there are other possibilities," he replied, without much conviction.

"Like?"

"The French police aren't stupid," he said. "And they're not above planting evidence either, especially when their only eyewitness is a drunkard. What better way to bolster his less than stellar credibility?"

"But if you accuse them of planting evidence without some proof, don't you run the risk of looking desperate? With conspiracy theories as your only defence to what the jury will see as the obvious explanation?" Isabelle noticed the barely perceptible slump in his shoulders and decided she'd gone further than she had intended in making her point. "Sorry," she said sheepishly.

"You're a little too good at being devil's advocate," he said before trying a different tack. "Let's say it wasn't planted. Karl can't have been the only Canadian in Nice at the time." He stopped, taking note of her silence. "You're right. It just doesn't look good, whatever way you slice it."

"Hey." She touched his arm. "I didn't mean to bring you down. Hopefully Pierre will get it excluded and it won't even be an issue."

"Yeah, let's hope so. How about your follow-up piece on Malle's victim, how's that going?"

"You mean now that the mother has decided to clam up? I'm not sure if I'm going to pursue it. I'm going to see if I can find the brother, and if that doesn't work I may have to abandon it."

"So how do you go about tracking someone down anyway?"

"Provincial registry. The records are all electronic now. You just fill in a form and pay a fee. Piece of cake."

"What, no cloak and dagger meetings with informants in back alleys?"

"Not yet. I won't get the results on Bruno Vachon until Monday. Once I get a full name and date of birth, I have people in the business...," she said coyly.

"Sounds very mysterious." He smiled, leaning towards her.

"A good reporter never reveals her sources. You know that."

"Not even for me?" He leaned closer, so that their cheeks brushed.

"Well, maybe for you," she said, putting her arms around his neck and kissing him as they sat back on the blanket.

Verdun sat outside the little coffee shop off Bank Street and sipped his brew. There was very little traffic, even for a Sunday morning, and though the morning air was brisk, it was worth it to take in the fall colours on the tree-lined side street. He envied Malcolm McGavin, who lived in the area – probably in one of the stately old Victorians with hundred-year-old trees in the yard. He had called Verdun at home the night before to arrange the impromptu meeting, saying he wanted to discuss Roy's case. As he waited, Verdun's thoughts turned to Isabelle and a smile creased his lips. After their picnic, they had returned their rented bikes and gone to his place for coffee, where they had spent a glorious evening together, capped by a moonlit stroll along the canal path. He hated having to get up this morning and disturb her, but they would see each other again tonight for a movie – and more coffee afterwards, he hoped.

"Glorious morning, isn't it?"

Verdun was roused from his pleasant daydream by McGavin's voice from behind him.

"Good morning, Malcolm. Yes, it is."

McGavin placed his mug on the table and sat across from Verdun.

"Thanks for meeting me. I hope I didn't get you up early, but there weren't a lot of options today. My grandson has a swimming lesson in an hour that I promised to watch, and I'm leaving town this afternoon for a week or so."

"Not at all," Verdun lied.

"Have you heard from Karl?" McGavin inquired.

"No, I haven't spoken to him since I was in Nice," Verdun replied, wondering if the meeting had any connection to Larousse's call on Friday. "Have you?"

"Not directly, but I did hear from a former colleague at the mission in Nice. There's been a new development."

"I think I know what you're about to say. I got a call from Pierre Larousse."

"About new evidence linking Karl to the murder?"

"Bad news travels fast, I guess."

"What is it?" McGavin leaned over the table.

"A pendant with the Montreal Canadiens' logo was found at the crime scene, if you can believe that."

"You've got to be kidding."

"I'm afraid not."

Verdun explained the version of events Larousse had described as McGavin sat, shaking his head. "Of all the bad luck," he said finally.

"He's certainly due for a break," Verdun agreed.

McGavin swirled his coffee around, as if pondering his next question. "Do you find the Crown's handling of Karl's case unusual, Peter?"

"You mean the last-minute evidence? I wouldn't say it's standard, but it's not the first time something like that's happened. The French system has its flaws, just like ours."

"I meant our Justice Department, not the French prosecutor."

"I'm not sure I know what you mean."

"It's just that from my perspective, things seem to be playing out quite differently from what I would have expected. I've seen the Justice Department, not to mention Foreign Affairs, rush to defend much less deserving behaviour in the past, and I just find it difficult to reconcile the way Karl's been treated."

"Well, it is a murder case–"

"Yes, I know all that." McGavin waved at him. "But it almost seems as though Justice wants him to be convicted."

"Have you raised this with your colleagues in government?"

"Yes, and my confrères at Justice are being unusually tight-lipped, which makes me even more convinced there's a hidden agenda behind their approach. Now, with this new evidence…It just seems all too convenient."

"You're not suggesting Justice Canada had anything to do with the discovery of the new evidence are you?"

"No, of course not," McGavin said, as if asking for confirmation that this was too ridiculous to consider. "But I am troubled by the apparent lack of support for his case."

"I think they have to make a judgment call about whether to protect an innocent citizen or hand over one they're not so sure about," Verdun said, finishing his coffee. "In this case, there's no doubt they made the wrong call, but I have to believe they are honouring their treaty obligations, not conspiring against one of their own for some other reason."

"You're right, I'm sure," McGavin said. "I just have the strangest feeling… Maybe I'm getting old."

"I have to admit, I'm a little unsettled myself about this new evidence."

"Oh, really?" McGavin raised an eyebrow. "You're not questioning Karl's innocence, are you?"

"No, no. I'm just wondering how to limit the damage if it does go in."

McGavin nodded. "Well, I hope you and Pierre can come up with something soon, for Karl's sake."

"Hello?" Verdun called as he closed the door behind him and laid the bag of croissants on the hall table. Hearing no reply, he continued on to the bedroom, but found his rumpled bed empty. On his way to the living room, he heard a faint voice and as he arrived, he noticed the patio door to the balcony was open. Sitting on a patio chair with her cellular phone at her ear was

Isabelle. She was dressed in his flannel bathrobe, with her shapely legs tucked up under her and her long dark hair tied back in a ponytail.

"Bonjour." She smiled as he leaned down and kissed her and handed her a coffee. "Oui rappelle-moi plus tard," she said, ending her conversation and closing the phone.

"Sorry, I didn't mean to interrupt," he said, taking the seat next to her.

"It's ok, just a contact in Montreal, confirming a meeting later this week."

"You're going back to Montreal?"

"Yes. Part business, part pleasure. It's my father's sixty-fifth birthday on the weekend."

"Really?"

"Yes, and his horrible new girlfriend has arranged a stuffy party."

"I take it you two don't get along."

"That's an understatement. She's a real bitch. I don't know what my father sees in her." She sighed. "But, he seems happy, and I'm prepared to tolerate her for his sake."

"The dutiful daughter."

"Now you're mocking me." She leaned over and kissed him, the neck of her robe coming undone enough to display a lovely combination of neck, collarbone and cleavage. "Just for that, I should make you come with me. You can see first-hand just how dutiful I really am."

"When is it?"

"I'm going over on Wednesday, but the party's on Saturday if you'd like to meet me there."

"I'd love to."

"It's a date," she said, leaning back in her chair and sipping her coffee. "How was your meeting?"

"Malcolm had heard about the new evidence and was looking for confirmation. He seems to think there's something rotten either at Justice or Foreign Affairs."

"What do you mean?"

"Unusual resistance to helping Karl. Former sources drying up, that sort of thing."

"Sounds interesting."

"I think it's a little paranoid frankly. I don't see what the government would have to gain from conspiring against Karl."

"Hmm, you never know."

"I forgot I was talking to a reporter," he said with a wink. "Oh, I picked up some croissants from the bakery around the corner," he added, getting up. He went inside to get them and as he picked up the bag, he turned to find her standing in front of him, her robe opened down the middle.

"I was thinking we could work up an appetite for breakfast," she said, sliding her arms around his waist and pulling him close.

"What a good idea," he said, as the bag of croissants dropped to the floor.

"Saturday night – eight o'clock," Jim Smythe said, striding into Verdun's office. He had just returned from a sentencing in youth court and was removing his tabs and undoing the top button of his court shirt.

"What's on Saturday night?"

"You're bringing your new lady over for dinner – no ifs, ands or buts. Margaret won't wait any longer. What with all these extra hormones she's carrying around, she can be pretty unreasonable."

"Sorry, pal, she'll have to wait just a little longer. I'm taking her to a party in Montreal on Saturday."

"Are you now?"

"Her father's sixty-fifth birthday bash."

"Meeting the family now, are you?" Smythe smiled broadly. "Boy, you really are making progress."

Verdun smiled.

"All right then, the following Saturday, and don't even think of weaseling out of it."

"I'll have to see if she's in town–"

"Yes, yes, I know." Smythe waved a hand. "But that's plenty of notice. Don't forget how hard Margaret's toiled for you all these years. Where would you have been without all those impromptu encounters with the fairer sex?"

"Probably a lot better off for the most part," he muttered. "Did I tell you Heather left a message on my machine the other day? It's been months–"

"Heather?" Smythe rubbed his chin.

"You know, from Margaret's fitness class."

"Oh yes, now I remember – the stalker. Ok, that wasn't such a good match, but that's all water under the bridge now, isn't it?"

Verdun scowled as his phone rang.

"Coffee later?" Smythe whispered. "And don't forget – next Saturday," Smythe said from the doorway, pointing a finger in Verdun's direction before disappearing.

Verdun picked up the phone.

"Peter, it's Pierre."

"Hello, Pierre," he said, immediately wary of Larousse's tone. "What's up?"

"Bad news, my friend. The evidence of the pendant will go in."

"Ah." Verdun clicked his tongue in frustration.

"Karl's trial will begin in two weeks – not the best of timing."

"What do you mean?" Verdun asked.

"Have you read about the WTO ruling on wine names?"

Larousse paused for the reply as Verdun racked his brain. He vaguely remembered hearing something about a trade dispute between Canada and France over Ontario wines recently, but hadn't given it much thought. "A little, yes. Well, not really."

"It's a very unpopular decision to reduce tariffs on Canadian wines sold in France. I don't have to tell you how important wine is to France."

"No, I guess you don't. So now Karl's going to suffer the fallout from a trade war. This is too much."

"Our client is in need of a reversal of fortune."

"Is a postponement possible?"

"At this stage, no. Besides, I'll succeed only in angering the judge by asking."

"You're probably right." Verdun rubbed his eyebrows.

"Karl is here with me now. He would like to talk to you if you have a moment."

"Of course." Verdun waited as Larousse handed over the phone to his client.

"Peter?"

"Yes, Karl, how are you?"

"I've been better. I need you to contact my family for me. My parents have been helping out with my legal fees, but they've hired a private investigator to look into Malle, and I'm afraid they're being taken advantage of. This is all bad enough. I don't want them squandering their life savings as well. Would you talk to them?"

"Of course. I've got your father's number here. I'll call him today and arrange to see him."

"Thanks, Peter, I appreciate it."

"Don't worry about it," he said, searching for comforting words to offer. Finding none, he rang off with a promise to call back once he had spoken with Roy's parents.

Verdun went out to the reception area and returned with the morning papers. He was soon focused on a story on the front page of *The Globe*. It summarized the WTO ruling on wines, describing the French reaction as "outrage." He threw the paper down on his desk in disgust.

sixteen

Verdun took two champagne flutes from the tray and handed one to Isabelle.

"Thank you," she said, taking the glass and tapping it lightly against his before taking a delicate sip.

"Good health," Verdun said, looking at his surroundings. The ballroom was packed with affluent-looking people decked out in the finest of evening wear. It had been a while since Verdun had worn his tux, and by the way the vest was pinching, it might be time for a trip to the tailor, or the gym. He had rescued it from the far recesses of his closet upon hearing that the party was to be held at the Ritz Carlton on Sherbrooke Street.

"My God, I haven't seen most of these people in years," Isabelle said. "I hardly recognize most of them."

"Your father has a lot of friends," Verdun said.

"Oh," she said, leaning in close and lowering her voice. "You see that man over there with the blonde."

"Yes," Verdun replied, noticing at once the disparity in age between the dapper, but nonetheless sixty-something, man and the young blonde at his arm.

"That's Guy Cardin," she whispered.

"Who's that?"

"Accused of murdering his socialite wife – must be fifteen years ago now. Dad got him off, but I'm sure he did it, though Dad always refused to talk about it."

"He's looking pretty happy."

"With that young tart?" Isabelle said with obvious disdain. "Must be his flavour of the month. Ah, there's Dad. Ready?" She took him by the hand and set off across the ballroom floor.

"Darling, I'm so glad you came." Georges Jacob smiled and

kissed his daughter on both cheeks. He was a very distinguished-looking man who looked at least ten years younger than his actual age. Tall and trim, the elder Jacob shared the same hair colour as his daughter, though his was streaked with grey.

"This is Peter Verdun," she said, as Verdun shook his hand.

"Glad you could come, Peter. Isabelle's told me all about you and that interesting extradition case you've both been working on. I'd love to hear all about it," he said, pausing as a blonde woman in her forties arrived at his arm. "Later on perhaps."

"Isabelle, so lovely to see you," the woman said, giving her an elaborate embrace designed to avoid smudging any make-up.

"Hello, Josianne."

"And who is this charming young man?" she said as Verdun extended his hand and introduced himself. "Of course. You're the lawyer from Ottawa. Now, there's no talking shop here." She wagged her finger at Verdun. "You lawyers are all the same. If I left Paul alone for five minutes, he'd find the only other lawyer in the room and be discussing some supreme court case and ignoring all of his guests." She laughed while Verdun noticed Isabelle squirm just a little. "I keep telling him to retire, but he insists on going to work, day in, day out," she continued.

"That's because he loves his work," Isabelle interjected. "Everyone should be so lucky."

"But why not take more time to relax and enjoy life? That's all I'm saying."

"Isabelle, I want to say hello to Marie," said Isabelle's father. "You remember my old secretary?"

"She's here?"

"I bumped into her downtown the other day and invited her. Do you remember her?"

"Of course I do. She was like a second nanny to me."

"She's over there," Jacob said, pointing to the nearby corner.

"I see Judge Deschamps has arrived," his girlfriend said. "I guess I'll see he's properly greeted if you insist on spending your time with an old secretary."

Isabelle watched her walk off in a theatrical huff before turning to her father. "Dad, why on earth–"

Her father cut her off with a wave of his hand. "Don't start, my belle, not tonight. Come along, Peter," he said as they made their way through the crowd, the elder Jacob making the first of many introductions.

"You looked beautiful tonight," Verdun whispered in her ear as she lay across his chest, her long brown hair splayed over his stomach.

Isabelle looked up and kissed him gently on the chest. "You didn't look so bad yourself," she replied. "You made quite an impression on Madame Angelil, I noticed."

"The hospital trustee?"

"You know very well who. I could tell you were enjoying her teasing. I thought she was going to grab you by the ears and shove you down her dress."

"It was a little low-cut, now that you mention it," he admitted, reaching down into the pants that lay balled up at the side of the bed. "And look, she gave me her number," he said, waving a business card.

"She gave you her number, did she?" Isabelle looked coy.

"Yes, she did," he said, trying to gauge her response.

"And to think I was standing twenty feet away – the nerve. Let me see that."

He passed her the card as she sat up on the bed.

"She's quite a wildcat, you know. Goes through husbands like cars. She likes to update the model every few years. None of them can keep up with her voracious appetite."

"Is that so?"

"She's a bit of a swinger too, if the rumours are true."

"Really? She didn't seem the type."

"Are you joking?" she laughed. "So, did she ask for a test drive?"

"Not in so many words, no."

"Good, because I want you to call her up and ask her a favour."

"Seriously?" Verdun was taken aback.

"Men – always thinking with their minds in the gutter." She slapped him playfully on the thigh. "Look at this." She pointed to the business card. "It's the same logo as the one on the baby bracelet we saw at Josée Vachon's house."

"The baby picture of her son Bruno?" he said. "Yes, I think you're right. But so what?"

"So, she's on the hospital board. She can help you find his hospital records."

"You're still looking for him?"

"I want to finish that follow-up piece on Karl's case, and it's bugging me that I can't find him."

"I thought you were using your sources."

"Didn't work out. My search turned up no birth certificate for a Bruno Vachon of the right age bracket."

"But if there's no birth certificate, why would there be hospital records?"

"He was born there, right? There would have to be something, under Josée's name if not his."

"I suppose."

"You're not curious about him?" She stroked his chest.

"You mean because Mrs. Vachon got so defensive when I mentioned him?"

"You have to admit, there was something she wasn't saying. And he is the only other person I know of who would have a motive for killing Malle."

"But that was so long ago. Besides, there are plenty of jealous husbands on the other side of the Atlantic who are likelier suspects than Bruno Vachon."

She nodded. "I suppose you're right. But I have my background piece on the victim to finish, and I don't like loose ends."

"So what do you want me to do?"

"Call Mrs. Angelil tomorrow and say you're looking for the records in connection with a case of yours. That's basically true anyway. Offer to take her to lunch, whatever. Give her a little tease – but that's all!" she said, wagging her finger at him. "She's been around a little too much for my liking."

"So basically, you want me to prostitute myself for your story. And ask for nothing in return..." He sighed dramatically.

"What did you have in mind?" she asked, leaning over him.

Verdun stood outside the restaurant and looked for a cab, anxiously eyeing his watch. He pulled out his cell phone and dialed a number as a cab pulled up. "Isabelle, I'm across town and running late. Can I meet you at the train?"

"I was starting to get worried about you," she said, a little mischief in her voice. "Did your charm work?"

"We'll have to wait and see," he said, getting into the cab.

"I'll bring your bag with me," she said. "I'd better get going. You can tell me all about it on the way back."

Twenty minutes later, he was waiting for her as she came into the train station.

"Hello, lover boy." She kissed him on the cheek.

"You weren't kidding, were you?" he said. "She was all over me. It's a good thing we were in a well-lit public place or she would have eaten me alive."

"She must have been upset that you didn't play along."

"Oh, I played – just not the same game she had in mind. We parted on friendly terms, I think."

"So she'll do it?"

"She promised to look into it and call me with the information. Who knows if she will or not?"

"Well done," she said as they headed to the platform and boarded the train for Ottawa.

"And by the way," he added, "I told her you were my fiancée. Even that was barely enough to spare me." He located their seats. "Here we are," he said, stowing their bags.

"Now," she said as they settled into their seats. "I want to hear all about it. What she wore, what she said. Spare nothing."

"You're shameless," he said as a voice announced their impending departure over the speaker.

seventeen

Verdun checked the street number again in his day-timer and made sure he had the right house. Although he had already spoken to them about canceling the French detective's contract, Roy's parents had been on their way to Quebec City to visit an ailing relative, and this was the first chance Verdun had had to actually meet with them since his conversation with their son.

Their modest but tidy little house was on a quiet street within sight of the walking trails of Gatineau Park. The first snow was just a few days off, but even now, in early November, the abundant trees were adorned with a wide array of different coloured leaves. Those that had already fallen crunched under his feet in the cold morning air as he walked along the sidewalk and through the little iron gate. The front door opened as he climbed the two steps to the front porch, and the figure of Roy's father appeared behind the screen.

"Bonjour, Monsieur Verdun. Thank you for coming," he said with a smile and opened the screen door to let him in. Through the screen, his sparse crown of snow-white hair and the woolen cardigan gave the impression of kindly old man. But as Verdun came face to face with him and felt the firm squeeze of his handshake, he realized that first impression was wrong and that Jacques Roy was a man of robust health. He also conveyed a friendly strength of character that Verdun had to admire.

"Please come in. Ah, here's Adèle, my wife."

"Hello," Verdun said, as Roy's mother appeared from around the corner.

"Don't worry about your shoes," she said, waving as he stooped to untie them.

"I don't mind, really–"

"No, no," she insisted, pulling a face that called for obedience on Verdun's part.

"Come in and join us for coffee," Mr. Roy said, leading him into the kitchen, where they sat at a lovely pine table that looked, despite the well-worn surface, that it was made to the standards of another time.

"So how's Karl?" Verdun began, as Mrs. Roy filled a china mug with rich-smelling coffee.

"We spoke to him from Quebec last night," Jacques Roy said, keeping a brave face. "He says he's well, but I think this latest twist has changed him."

"What do you mean?"

"He sounded tired. Very tired," Mrs. Roy said, looking down at her coffee.

"He's all right, Adèle, he's strong."

"I know he's strong, Jacques, but sapristi…" She shook her head.

"Pierre Larousse is a very experienced criminal lawyer," Verdun said, putting his hands around his mug. "I'm sure he'll do an excellent job."

"He'd better, for what he's charging."

"A criminal defence is very expensive, Mr. Roy."

"I know, I know. And I didn't mean anything by it. It's just that…" He trailed off, looking down at his hands. He seemed not to know what to do with them.

"It's been very hard for us, Mr. Verdun," Mrs. Roy said, trying a weak smile. "Karl's savings are gone, and between Maitre Larousse and that crook of a detective, so are most of ours."

"Adèle," Jacques Roy admonished her. "He's not here to listen to our complaints."

"It's all right," Verdun said. "How much did you pay this detective?"

"We paid him ten thousand up front, and then he would call and tell us he just needed another thousand or two to make real progress," she said, oblivious to her husband's looks.

"Dollars?"

"Euros."

Verdun sighed. "Did he uncover anything?"

"Nothing worth a damn," Jacques Roy grumbled. "This Malle had so many girlfriends it was hard to keep track. He kept saying he had found one with a violent boyfriend or husband, but it never came to anything. We should have known he was just out to take advantage.

"Does Pierre know how much this detective was charging?"

"No. He warned us there was no guarantee he'd uncover anything useful. Had he known about the fees, he would have put a stop to it, I'm sure. But we were desperate."

"Do you have a name? Maybe we can try and get some of your money back."

Jacques Roy fished a worn business card from his wallet. "There. That's him. But there's no way we'll get it back."

Verdun knew as much, and didn't want to get their hopes up. He looked at the card and wrote down the name. "I'll make some calls, but you may be right, Monsieur Roy."

"I don't care about the money anyway," he said with a frown. "If I have to sell everything I own, so be it. I want my son back home."

"What are his chances?" Mrs. Roy asked, the fear evident in her voice.

"Of acquittal? It's difficult to say, Mrs. Roy." He sipped his coffee, trying to think of what to say. He had tried to prepare for this question, and as he sat at their table, in the expectant silence, he wanted desperately to soften the blow. But that would be unfair. "Not much better than 50-50, I'm afraid," was all he could manage.

"Because of this damned hockey pendant?" Jacques Roy asked.

"It certainly doesn't help."

Jacques Roy let out a grim chuckle. "Karl hated le Canadien. He was a Nordiques' fan right up until the end," he said, referring to the NHL hockey team's move from Quebec City to Denver in the late eighties.

"And if he is convicted?" Adèle Roy could barely keep her voice from trembling.

"We're a long way from that, Mrs. Roy," he said.

"Would they let him serve his sentence here?" Jacques Roy said, taking his wife's hand as she began to sob quietly. "I can't think of him in a foreign jail–" He broke off abruptly, his own voice wavering.

"It's possible. But again, let's not get ahead of ourselves. Karl is innocent until proven guilty, and I've seen worse-looking cases turned into acquittals."

"You're right," Roy's father said, regaining his composure. "We can't give up hope – not yet." He rubbed his wife's arm.

The wind had picked up when Verdun said goodbye and returned to the street. As he approached his vehicle, he zipped up the front of his coat and shivered. He started his truck and looked out across the park. The bright morning sky had turned a dull grey and cast a pall over the trees. As he watched them sway in the wind, he thought of Roy's parents and felt a hollowness in the pit of his stomach. He thought of them huddled together, trying desperately to stifle the dread that accompanied their every waking hour. Verdun was overcome by a desire to help. Until that moment, with his role in Roy's legal defence at an end, he felt his involvement in the case was over as well. But as he pulled away from the curb, he was determined to find some other way to help them.

eighteen

"Here we are," Verdun said, shifting the truck into park and switching off the ignition.

"It's very nice," Isabelle said, surveying the front of Jim and Margaret Smythe's red brick home. Even with many of their leaves now missing, the huge trees that lined the streets still dominated the scenery of this Westboro neighbourhood, only a few minutes from downtown. Jim and Margaret had moved here the previous year, and though it was an older house whose repairs and upgrades ate up a lot of Jim Smythe's weekends, it made a beautiful home that had already increased in value by ten percent if not more.

"So are you ready for the third degree?" Verdun asked.

"I'm sure it won't be as bad as you keep saying," Isabelle replied as he took her by the hand and led her up the front path.

"You don't know Margaret," he chuckled as Jim Smythe came to the door, dressed in a bright red cardigan.

"They're here, honey," he called over his shoulder as he opened the door.

"Here you are," Verdun said, handing him a bag with two burgundies he had spent a lot of time debating over at the LCBO.

"And this is for the mother-to-be," Isabelle said, handing Smythe a bottle of blueberry wine. "It's non-alcoholic," she added.

"How thoughtful," came Margaret's voice as she pushed past her husband to get a look at the new girlfriend. "Come in, come in. Jim would have you stand on the front porch all night," she tutted. "It's freezing out there."

After their coats had been hung up, they made their way into the living room. "It's a lovely home," Isabelle said, looking around and taking note of the beautiful old-fashioned hardwood floors, the high ceilings and the intricately carved mantel over the living room hearth.

"Would you like the dime tour?" Margaret said quickly. "Why don't you boys take care of the drinks?" she said, waving at them dismissively as she gently but firmly directed Isabelle back out to the front hall. "Come on, I'll show you the upstairs first."

Verdun winked at Isabelle before she disappeared around the corner and up the stairs. "I suppose she'll be all right, will she?"

"Best to let Margaret have her way," Smythe said, patting him on the back. "Let's go have a beer."

"You've painted in here – again?"

"You haven't been here in a while, have you?" Smythe said, passing him a bottle from the fridge. "I did this over the summer actually – colour number three."

"Sure you got it right this time?" Verdun asked. Margaret's habit of changing the colour schemes every few months was a running joke.

"Cheers," Smythe said, knocking his bottle off Verdun's before taking the first sip. "I'm off the hook now anyway – can't be exposing the fetus to paint fumes, you know."

"Good answer. This baby thing has its advantages."

"Oh, before I forget. Are you interested in Senators tickets tomorrow night? Bob Wright offered me a pair, but you know how Margaret is about the Corel Centre. I can't get her to go all the way out there to save my life. And now with her motion sickness – forget it." He looked upstairs. "Is Isabelle a hockey fan?"

"I'm not sure, to be honest. But isn't tomorrow the Leafs game? You're not telling me you're going to miss that?" Jim Smythe was a die-hard Ottawa fan who never missed an instalment in the bitter rivalry between the hometown Senators and the team's arch-enemy from Toronto.

"For you to impress your lady friend, I'm prepared to give them up, yes," Smythe said soberly.

Verdun looked at him for a moment while he thought. "Nice try. You've got better seats, haven't you?"

"What do you take me for?" Smythe said in mock reproach.

"Someone with tickets to a box."

"Oh, all right, you got me," he laughed. "I'm going with Sam," he said, referring to Margaret's brother, an executive with an insurance company that had a corporate box.

"So now I'm only worthy of your leftovers. I'm insulted." Verdun laughed. "But sure, I'll take them off your hands."

"Good," he said, quickly retrieving the corkscrew as the sound of footsteps announced the return of the women to the main floor.

"Oh, here they are, hiding out and drinking beer, and forgetting their manners," Margaret said as she entered the kitchen, followed by Isabelle.

"I couldn't find the corkscrew," Smythe offered weakly.

"It's so lovely," Isabelle said. "Margaret was telling me everything you've done since you bought it. You must be quite the handyman," she said to Smythe, who beamed proudly as he uncorked the blueberry wine and poured her a glass.

"Oh, I don't know," he said.

"I didn't know he had it in him," Margaret said, giving him a hug and a peck on the cheek. "But he really does have hidden talents."

They moved into the living room with their drinks and chatted while Margaret scurried back and forth to the kitchen to monitor the roast.

"So what's the latest with that interesting extradition case?" Margaret asked, sitting on the edge of the sofa, ready to return to the kitchen at the first smell of burning. "The one that brought you together," she added with a smile.

Verdun couldn't help a chuckle. Margaret obviously approved of Isabelle, and even though she'd had no role in the matchmaking, it was clear that she was in her glee.

"We were just discussing it on the way over actually," Verdun said, putting his hand in Isabelle's.

"Any word from the woman you told me about?" Smythe asked.

"What woman?" Margaret perked up, her interest – or perhaps it was concern – aroused.

"Didn't I tell you? Peter's moonlighting as a gigolo."

"What?" Margaret frowned. She looked at Isabelle to gauge her reaction and was surprised to see her laughing.

"Relax, dear. She put him up to it," Smythe said, waving at Isabelle and explaining the luncheon of the previous week.

"It was just lunch, Margaret, really," Verdun said with a wink. "And no, she hasn't called, so apparently I'm losing my touch with the fairer sex."

"Shouldn't we let Isabelle be the judge of that?" Margaret said.

"Yes, we should." Isabelle played her role. "And Peter's just being modest. If you'd seen the way that woman was eyeing him at the party. If only I could have read her mind!"

Verdun laughed. "Well, even if she decides not to help us out, Isabelle's called in a favour from a colleague in Montreal. He's in the investigation business."

"You should talk to Vic Seguin if you're looking for a P.I.," Smythe said, getting up.

Verdun looked puzzled. "Who's Vic Seguin?"

"You know, my fraud case," Smythe replied. "He was so happy with his acquittal that he practically begged me to give him work he could do for free."

"Well, depending on far we get, I might ask you to give him a call," Verdun said, sipping his beer.

"Do you smell anything?" Margaret said, suddenly standing up from her perch on the edge of the sofa.

"You were just in there." Smythe shook his head. "It's not burning."

"Well, it's got to be ready by now. Why don't we let these two enjoy a quiet moment together while we look after dinner?"

"Uh, sure," Smythe replied, reluctantly getting up.

"I have the strangest feeling," Isabelle whispered in Verdun's ear, as she leaned closer to him on the couch. "Like we're in high school and our friends are trying to set us up." She giggled.

"I warned you," he whispered back, laughing.

"I didn't say it was a bad feeling."

"Well, we shouldn't waste the opportunity then, should

we?" He leaned into her and gave her a kiss that, together, they turned into a long, lingering embrace.

"It's gone all quiet out there," Margaret called from the kitchen. "Is everything all right?"

"We're just fine, Margaret," Verdun called back. "Just enjoying those lovely smells from the kitchen."

"They're such a nice couple," Isabelle said, sipping her wine.

"Yes," Verdun said. "They complement each other very well."

"I'm glad you brought me here," she said, stroking his arm.

"So's Margaret. Can you tell?"

"She certainly seems happy for you."

"She can tell that I'm happy, and she's smart enough to know why," he said.

"Hmm, never underestimate that female intuition."

"I guess not."

"I'm glad I met you, Peter," she said, kissing him again. "You make me very happy."

nineteen

Verdun sat at his desk, reading the morning mail and sipping his coffee. He paused to look for a file and noticed for the first time that big, fat flakes of snow had begun to fall. It was the first snowfall of the year and he hoped it would continue all day. He loved winter, at least the first half of it. By late January or so, even skating along the Rideau Canal on crisp, bright winter days had lost its luster and ranked a distant second to a tropical beach. But not yet, and especially not this year. This year was going to be different. He was already planning a ski trip with Isabelle, and that was just the beginning. There would be skating and sleigh rides, hot toddies and long nights by the fire. He was even considering taking her to Nova Scotia over Christmas to meet his parents. In fact, he was having trouble thinking of anything but her lately, and he had to admit that it was a good feeling.

His mental image of Isabelle in his arms in front of a roaring fire was shattered by the shrill tone of his telephone that brought him abruptly back to the reality of Monday morning at the office. It was his direct line, and his phone displayed a number he didn't recognize. "Peter Verdun."

"Hello, Peter," said a sultry and familiar voice. "It's Chantal Angelil."

"Chantal, how are you?" Even over the phone her voice smouldered with sensuality.

"I'm so sorry I didn't get back to you earlier. You must have thought I was teasing you," she said suggestively.

"Oh, not at all," he replied.

"I had such an enjoyable lunch last week. Next time you're in Montreal you must let me return the favour," she purred.

Yes, of course," Verdun said, after a moment's hesitation. He didn't want to encourage her any more, but he didn't want to be rude either.

"Perhaps you'll let me show you some of Montreal first. We can work up an appetite..."

"Uh, yes."

"How's the lovely Isabelle? Have you grown tired of her yet?"

"She's very well," he said, his discomfort growing. It must have been obvious in his voice.

"I'm joking, darling. You make a wonderful couple."

"Thank you."

"About the name you asked me to find, I'm afraid I've let you down."

"Well, at least you tried."

"I can probably tell you why you couldn't find him under his mother's name though."

"Why's that?"

"I found the records for Josée Vachon, and her records indicate that she had a boy named Bruno, but the space for the father's name is blank. Things weren't quite as liberal back then as they are now. In those days, unless the mother was married, the hospital didn't recognize the father's name. People had enough trouble getting the government to record births of unmarried parents, let alone a Catholic hospital."

"So Josée Vachon wasn't married then?" Verdun said. He was sure Vachon had told him otherwise, or had it been Isabelle?

"Of course there's always the other possibility..."

"What do you mean?"

"Don't play the innocent, Peter. You're a man of the world."

"You mean she was married, but the husband wasn't Bruno's father?"

"Perhaps it was an innocent dinner, followed by dancing and then a marathon of every erotic pleasure two people can share... Of course there are precautions now that didn't exist then," she added quickly.

"And you say there's no record of the father's name," he said, ignoring the come-on and focusing on the facts.

"I'm afraid not," she sighed.

"I see. Well, you've still shed some light on why we have no record of Bruno Vachon, and we're very grateful."

"We?"

"I mean me. I'm grateful."

"So when do you plan on returning to Montreal?"

"I'm not sure," he said vaguely. "I'm really busy around this time of year."

"Well, you must promise to call me when you're in town. And of course, if there's anything else I can do, you have only to ask."

"There is one thing. But you've done so much already–"

"Tell me what it is, I'm yours for the taking."

Verdun tried to ignore the urge to hang up and swallowed his pride. "I was just wondering whether there would be a list of children – boys actually – born at the hospital in that year."

"I suppose there would be, yes."

"Could I trouble you for it? Any leads I could get to narrow the search at the birth registry would be very helpful."

Angelil had gone silent, perhaps awaiting something more from him. Verdun swallowed before adding, "I wouldn't forget it."

"Well, I'm sure it won't be too much trouble. Let me look for you. But now you must really promise to let me take you out and show you a good time."

"Yes, of course."

"I'll call you back in a day or two."

"Thank you so much."

"Bienvenue. Bisous cherie."

Verdun hung up the phone and let out a sigh. That woman was something else. But she had given him something to go on, however small. He dialed Isabelle's number right away, both to tell her the good news and to purge the guilty feeling the call had left, like a lipstick stain on his collar. He chuckled to himself. There was no way he was going anywhere near Montreal for the foreseeable future.

"Thank you, Your Honour," Verdun said brightly, bowing his head ever so slightly in deference to the judge, in part in his capacity as an officer of the court, but mostly because of the very light fine and the suspended sentence his client had just received. A very muttered "thank you" was the best the disgruntled prosecutor could manage. She glared at Verdun as the clerk called the room to order in preparation for the judge's departure.

"Don't look at me like that," Verdun said, after the judge had left. "I told you you weren't being reasonable insisting on jail time."

"I'll have to consider an appeal on this sentence," she said, shaking her head. They both knew she would do no such thing. As an experienced Crown attorney who disliked losing as much as anyone else who made their living sparring in the Elgin Street courtrooms, she had learned the importance of choosing one's battles carefully.

"Great job, counselor. Thanks." The young man seated next to Verdun had been prepared for a much stiffer fine, perhaps even accompanied by some period of incarceration, and his relief was genuine. He was only twenty-two, and although he would still have a criminal record, it could have been much worse.

"You're welcome, John," Verdun said, shaking his hand and starting to pack up his briefcase. "You were lucky. Stay out of trouble from here on in, all right?"

"Sure," he said. The fact was, John Brett didn't need luck. His parents had money instead – and lots of it – to get him out of all sorts of trouble. Verdun's legal fees were a pittance compared to the repair bill on the brand new Porsche young John had snuck out of his dad's Rockcliffe garage and wrapped around a pole in a drunken escapade. Who knew, maybe the kid really had learned a valuable lesson? And no one had been seriously hurt.

"Thank you so much, Mr. Verdun," Mrs. Brett said, taking her son by the arm. She had been very attractive in her day, and though her lightly tanned skin would betray her age someday, her life of pampered leisure had delayed that event so far. "I'll have Henry settle up with you as soon as he's back from Singapore," she whispered, as if talking of such things in public was a sin.

"Yes, of course."

Verdun made his way out of the courtroom and down to the Elgin Street entrance. As he was leaving the building, he heard a familiar voice calling his name from the sidewalk, and he smiled as he caught sight of Isabelle's delicate features. "What a nice surprise. I thought you were in Toronto until tomorrow," he said.

She was dressed in a knee-length suede coat, with a brightly coloured woolen scarf wrapped around her neck. The chill in the air had put a rosy blush on her cheeks and a sparkle in her brown eyes. He put his arms around her, and as they kissed, he noticed how wonderful she smelled.

"I dropped by your office to surprise you. I thought we'd get a drink, but Jim told me you were still in court." She stood back and appraised him. His peacoat was undone and he was still wearing his waistcoat and tabs, having bundled his robe under his arm.

"I could never resist a man in tabs."

"Very funny." He jabbed at her arm playfully.

"So are you finished fighting the good fight for today?"

"Barring something ugly waiting for me back at the office, yes."

"Oh, Jim wanted me to tell you he spoke to the investigator and he's going to join us for a drink. Here, let me carry that." She draped his legal gown over her arm and took his free hand in hers as they headed south towards the office.

"I missed you," he said, kissing her on the cheek.

"Well, I'm glad I wasn't the only one."

"What do you say I cook you dinner later?" he said as they crossed Lisgar Street.

"That sounds great. I'll bring dessert."

"Yes, you will."

"So how's Margaret feeling?" Isabelle asked as she and Smythe settled around a table in the corner of the crowded basement pub while Verdun looked after their drinks.

"She's doing well. A little queasy from time to time but over it for the most part, I think."

"You must be so excited."

"We are. I've never seen Margaret so happy. Although I think you're part of the reason for that," he said.

"Ah, yes," Isabelle laughed. "Peter told me he's sort of become Margaret's pet project. Well, I'm happy to oblige. I don't know why he hasn't been snapped up."

"Are you two talking about me?" Verdun said as he gently deposited a red wine and a pair of draught beers in the centre of the table.

"I was just saying what a great catch you are, and wondering why you haven't been snapped up already, that's all."

"And it was going so well…" Smythe shook his head in mock despair. "Now you have to come clean, old boy."

"Very funny," Verdun said, sitting down. "The truth is I've been waiting for someone worthy of all of Margaret's efforts."

"To Margaret then," Isabelle said, raising her glass. "And her very good taste."

They all drank and shared a laugh.

"There's Vic now," Smythe said, getting up to wave him over. Vic Seguin was tall and dark, with the rugged features of a man who had endured his share of time outside. He greeted them with a disarming smile as he unbuttoned his overcoat, but the smile did nothing to dispel the sense that he was man possessed of a certain degree of power – the kind of authority over people that helped him in getting what he wanted most of the time. He had been a cop in Montreal for ten years, which was long enough to learn a few things, and to decide the pension plan wasn't worth sticking around for. After a brief stint doing private security, a friend had asked him to help out with his investigation firm and after a few years of catching cheating husbands and wives, he'd gone out on his own. For the most part, his work was finding long-lost relatives for probate firms, but he enjoyed the occasional diversion.

"So I hear you need some help tracking someone down," he said, taking a seat and looking first at Verdun, then Isabelle. Verdun explained what little they knew about Josée Vachon's son, from the approximate year of his birth at St. Augustin.

"And you're sure about the hospital?" Seguin asked as Smythe returned with his drink.

"That much we're sure of," Isabelle said with a nod.

"He grew up in Montreal and spent some time in the military," Verdun added.

"And I wouldn't be surprised if he spent some time in jail," Isabelle said. "I got the impression from the mother that he'd had some troubled times – but that's just a guess."

"Well," Seguin said after they had finished. "It won't be easy without a last name, but the hospital's a good place to start."

"What are the odds of finding him?" Smythe asked.

"Like finding a needle in a haystack," Seguin replied. "But I'm good at what I do and I owe you one, so I'll give it my best shot. I've got to go to Montreal next week anyway so I'll be able to get started then. Who knows? In a week or two I may have something for you."

"What sort of fee are we looking at?" Verdun asked.

"Like I said, I'm going to be in town on another job anyway so there's no overhead. Let's see how it goes. I'll touch base before I get into any major disbursements."

Verdun nodded.

"And you say this guy's a potential witness?"

"It's a possibility, but a remote one," Verdun replied.

"Anything else you need to tell me?" Seguin asked, sipping his drink and looking up at Verdun. As a side door opened and a bright beam of light lit his face, Verdun noticed for the first time the discoloration of a scar high on his right cheekbone.

"What do you mean?"

"I just like to know if I'm looking for someone who doesn't want to be found, that's all. I don't like surprises."

"There's no reason to think he knows I'm interested in finding him," Verdun assured him. "In fact, Isabelle's more interested in him for her article."

Seguin drained his glass and let the ice slide back from his teeth to the bottom of the glass before putting it down. "All right then. I'll be in touch."

"Thanks," Verdun said.

"Don't thank me yet," he said as he got up to leave. "You never know what I'll find."

twenty

Verdun made his way out through the doorway into the brilliant morning sunshine. The sentencing hearing had been much shorter than he had anticipated, and the judge had called a brief adjournment after submissions in order to come to an immediate decision rather than reserve for another date. Verdun hadn't bothered to put on his coat, and the chill of winter filled his nostrils and braced his skin as he stepped out into the stone courtyard at the rear of the courthouse. He took a deep breath and strolled up some stairs towards a water fountain that had been winterized months before. The air was much warmer in the direct sunlight, so that sitting on a park bench with only his court clothes and legal gown was quite tolerable. He watched the people walking by and wondered what was going through their minds. Whatever their troubles, they probably weren't facing five years in a federal pen. Verdun's client was a troubled teen who had dropped out of school and spent his youth with the wrong crowd. It hadn't taken him long to graduate from petty theft and vandalism to break and entering, compiling quite a juvenile record along the way. But all that changed when he was arrested and charged with armed robbery at the age of nineteen. Verdun believed he hadn't intended to use it, but the kid was caught on the corner store's video camera brandishing a large hunting knife. He had tried to emphasize his client's tender age as much as possible in his sentencing submission and had pleaded for some form of youth diversion in lieu of incarceration, but he knew that, as a legal adult, the boy would be going to jail, and not some juvenile day camp either – this would be the real thing. To look at him in the courtroom, you would think he should be shooting hoops or playing Nintendo – not sitting in a jail cell. Verdun was still trying to reconcile the image of the young man he had come to know with the violent thug depicted in the damning video. Whatever happened when the judge recalled the court to order, Verdun had the sinking feeling that this kid was already lost, another depressing statistic.

Verdun took a deep breath and watched the steam as he exhaled into the cold. He got up and stamped his feet, turning his mind to the much more pleasant image of a sleeping Isabelle lying in his bed as he was leaving this morning, her chestnut hair contrasted against the crisp white linen. He felt like talking to her, suddenly needing the warmth of her voice, if he couldn't have her physical closeness. He reached under his court robe for his cell phone and as he did, its shrill ring tone went off. He didn't recognize the number but it was from the Montreal area. "Hello?"

"Peter." It was a gruff voice he couldn't place.

"Yes, who's this?"

"Vic Seguin. You got a minute?"

"Oh, hi Vic. Sure, what's up?" he said, surprised to be hearing from Seguin already. It was only Wednesday and he hadn't expected much for at least a week or so.

"I think I found your man."

"You're kidding."

"Well, I found his name anyway. It's Bruno Jacques, 36 years old. I stumbled onto him when I cross-referenced the hospital records with army and prison records, using the first name. Your girlfriend was right about him doing time. He's done more than his fair share."

"That's amazing. Do you know where he is now?"

"That's the hard part. He's had a couple of addresses in Montreal but nothing recent. The last place I know he was for sure is Kingston Pen. After that, the trail goes dead."

"Well, I can get the records from Department of Corrections and track him down that way," Verdun said.

"I thought you probably could."

"Still, I can't believe you found him this fast."

"Piece of cake," Seguin replied. "Listen, if you want to take it from here I'll consider myself square with your partner."

"You must have some expenses or something."

"Naw, I'm good. Listen, I've got to run. If you need any help following up, let me know. I'll be back in Ottawa next week."

"Thanks. I think it's me who owes you one now."

"I've got no plans of needing a criminal lawyer, but you never know." Seguin gave a raspy chuckle. "Good luck."

Verdun pulled out a pen and scribbled the name and age on the palm of his hand. He was truly amazed at how easily Seguin had found him. He was about to call his secretary for the number of a contact at Corrections when he saw the clerk looking around by the entrance doors. Spotting Verdun beside the fountain, she waved him in, indicating it was time for his young client to face the music. The excitement of Bruno Jacques' discovery faded, replaced by a grim sense of foreboding as he returned to the courthouse.

twenty-one

Verdun's heart rate jumped as he felt the ominous feeling of his vehicle sliding. He instinctively took his foot off the gas, fighting the urge to brake, and in that instant, he felt the tires regain their grip and return the vehicle to a straight path. He hated black ice, especially when it lurked beneath a layer of dry snow. He was anxious to get to Kingston, but not enough to risk arriving in an ambulance. Verdun had spent two frustrating days since Vic Seguin's call, and now, nearing noon on Friday, he saw the first of the series of exits off Highway 401 for Kingston. He had ignored the weather forecast as he left the clear skies of Ottawa behind him around mid morning, but with the snow increasing in intensity and the winds whipping up, he was glad he would soon be leaving the highway. Four-wheel drive or not, he had reduced his speed to 70 km, and he would be taking it easy until he saw the sign for his exit emerge from a white cloud of driving snow.

Verdun had wasted no time in calling his contact at Corrections in Ottawa and had been provided with a sketchy history of Bruno Jacques' lengthy prison record. Spanning a fifteen-year period – his adult life, in fact – it had taken him through a half-dozen prisons in Quebec, including the maximum-security Port-Cartier, Archambault and Donnacona institutions, before moving on to Ontario in the latter part of his career, most recently, Millhaven and Kingston. But for a man with such a history, his file was relatively thin, to the point that Verdun's contact suggested a visit to Kingston to see if there wasn't more in a file on site. A few phone calls later, he had ended up talking to someone in the prison's administration who confirmed there would in fact be a file in their records. As they arranged a time for

Verdun's visit and the formalities he would have to go through to get access to the files, they discovered that they had been classmates in university, and Verdun had been quick to offer him lunch.

He followed the signs to the prison and, after what seemed like an interminable drive through the white fog, arrived at the administration building. As he parked and saw the length of the walk to the doors, he realized how unprepared for a winter storm he was. He sighed and pulled the collar of his leather jacket up around his ears as a poor substitute for a toque or parka hood and made a dash for the doors, almost losing his footing as soon as his dress shoes hit the icy pavement. He caught himself and cursed, making his way gingerly to the partially cleared path, finally getting some traction on the salted asphalt.

He came through the doors with a blast of cold air and a mist of snow, and once inside the reception area, he shook his jacket and blew into his hands.

"It's taken quite a turn out there, eh?" the receptionist said with a smile.

"I've got to start listening to the weather forecast," he replied.

She nodded. "Can I help you find someone?"

"I'm here to see Bob Gregory."

"I'll let him know you're here. You can hang your coat up over there and help yourself to coffee if you like." She pointed to a coat rack in the corner, next to a couple of plastic chairs. The coffee machine was sitting on an adjacent table.

"Thank you." He took off his coat and hung it up, but decided against the stewed-smelling coffee, taking a seat instead as the receptionist announced his arrival. A few minutes later, he saw the familiar, if slightly rounder, features of Bob Gregory approaching the reception area. Although they had each pursued different degrees in university and hadn't kept in touch, Verdun remembered Bob well from frequent outings to the campus bar. He'd always been a lot of fun.

"Peter, how are you? My God, it's been too long."

"Hello, Bob. You're looking well."

"You mean well-fed," he joked, slapping him on the shoulder. "So you're a big-shot lawyer now, hey? How's that going?"

"Minus the big-shot part?" Verdun grinned. "It's a living, what can I say. How about you? Criminology? I never would have guessed."

"You mean you thought I'd end up on the other side of the bars, right?" Another laugh. "Come on," he said, taking Verdun by the arm. "I pulled the file and found you some working space. Don't worry, it's not the place we use for the conjugal visits."

Verdun laughed. Bob had certainly kept his sense of humour over the years. He had a feeling lunch would be very entertaining.

They walked down a hall of offices and Verdun was introduced to a series of people in the offices.

"That's me," Bob said, as they passed an open door.

"The corner office. So you're the grand poombah – I should have known."

"Flattery will get you everywhere, my friend. And here's your spot." He led Verdun into a small conference room just around the corner from Gregory's office. There was a banker's box on the table. "Make yourself at home. I'd offer you a coffee, but the stuff they brew out there tastes like shit, and I wasn't about to freeze my nuts off to go get you a decent cup."

Verdun smiled. "That's fine," he said, looking at his watch. "What time do you want to go to lunch?"

"I've got a meeting in five that'll take me to about one-thirty."

"Lunch after that then? That'll give me time to get started with the file."

"Sure. Make yourself at home, and if you need anything, just ask one of these layabouts," he said loudly as a colleague came out of an office a few doors down and gave a mock salute.

Verdun settled in a chair and opened a box. It was about half full, containing a dozen or so different-coloured files stacked one on top of the other. He picked out the first, flipped it open to the top page and started reading.

"How's it going?" Verdun looked up from his file and saw Bob Gregory standing in the doorway.

"Good. Very interesting reading." He looked at his watch. "How about some lunch?"

"Sure, but you're gonna want to look outside before we think about anywhere but the cafeteria," Gregory said.

"It's that bad?"

"Come on," he said, leading the way down the hall to the reception area. Once there, they both peered out through the front windows at a full-blown snowstorm. Verdun couldn't even see his SUV, and the cars that were closer were covered in a foot of the white stuff.

"Wow!"

"See what I mean?"

"All of a sudden cafeteria food doesn't sound so bad," Verdun said. "Though when I said I'd buy you lunch, that's not exactly what I had in mind."

"Don't sweat it. The food's not bad. Follow me."

Gregory led him along another hallway, then down a flight of stairs into a large cafeteria. Most of the lunch crowd had gone and they had their choice of tables when they had picked out their food.

"So how do you like Kingston?" Verdun said, biting into his sandwich.

"The town or the Pen?"

"Both, I guess."

"I like the job for the most part. And it's not a bad place to live – when it's not buried in snow. I've got a nice house and the lifestyle's hard to beat. How about you?"

"Well, you know what Ottawa's like. It'll never change. But I started a firm with a partner a couple of years ago and it's going pretty well."

"Married?" Gregory asked, sipping his soup.

"No," he said, thinking of Isabelle and thinking it somewhat of a betrayal not to mention her importance to him. "How about you?"

"Nossir," he said with a broad grin. "And no plans to be. I've always lacked the necessary maturity," Gregory laughed. "It's not as though I've ever tried to hide the fact. But you…"

"Well, I'm seeing someone actually."

"Ah, I knew it."

"What's that supposed to mean?" Verdun said, feigning offence.

"Strait-laced lawyer like you? Come on."

Verdun laughed and took another bite of his sandwich.

"So, you find what you were looking for in those files?" Gregory asked.

"I don't know. I'm only halfway through but it seems like Bruno Jacques spent time in just about every prison in Quebec before coming here. Is that unusual?"

"Not necessarily. Depends on the length of the sentence, populations, any number of things. What was he in for?"

"You name it," Verdun replied, pushing his sandwich plate to the side and turning to his salad. "Theft, assault, drugs, weapons charges. That's what I've seen so far."

"Classic repeat offender. Jack of all trades and master of none."

"Didn't stop him being paroled over and over."

"It usually doesn't. We can't afford to keep them all inside so they get released at the earliest possible opportunity. It's a question of money – or lack of it." Gregory shook his head.

"Jacques had his share of run-ins with other inmates too. Got a few months added on to his sentence a couple of times."

"This guy in a gang?" Gregory asked, wiping the corner of his mouth with a napkin.

"I don't know. Why do you ask?"

"Sounds like he fits the profile, that's all. And if you're trying to track him down, that's the first place to look. These guys are pretty tight, and they don't waste any time going back to their roots when they get out."

"I never thought of that. I didn't see anything in his file though."

"It wouldn't necessarily show up in the official files, but that doesn't mean we don't know exactly who's running with which gang. I'll check this afternoon."

"That would be great, thanks."

Gregory looked over Verdun's shoulder at the window on the far wall. "Are you planning on driving back to Ottawa tonight?"

Verdun nodded.

"You might want to reconsider." Gregory gestured to the window.

"It doesn't look good, does it?" Verdun didn't relish the thought of the return trip. The 401 was dangerous enough on a clear day. But in a blizzard, after nightfall, it was asking for trouble.

"You're welcome to crash at my place if you want. We could hit a club and have a few beers for old times' sake."

"I might just take you up on that, but I'll get a room downtown. I don't want to cramp your style."

"Sure, whatever. There's a new bar just opened this month I've been meaning to check out – supposed to be very popular with the ladies." He winked.

Verdun smiled. He had no intention of ending up in a hotel room with a stranger, and if it wasn't for the storm, he'd prefer to get back home to Isabelle. But as long as he was stuck here, he knew a night out with Bob Gregory would be good for a laugh.

They finished their lunch and headed back upstairs. "Let's have a look at our friend's professional affiliations," Gregory said, leading the way into his office and taking a seat in front of his computer. He began tapping at the keyboard and clicking on the mouse as the computer loaded a database. "It's Jacques, right? Bruno Jacques?"

Verdun nodded as Gregory entered the name and hit enter. "Well, whaddaya know? Your pal's a biker. Lifetime member of the Rollers."

"Who are the Rollers?" Verdun asked, taking out his pen and jotting down the name.

"Montreal-based bikers. They used to have a virtual monopoly over the drug trade but they've lost some of their turf to rivals. They're still major players though. They're also into gambling and prostitution and all the rest. A pretty violent bunch."

"And what is that, a biker database or something?"

"It provides names of inmates with known links to organized crime, whether it's a biker gang or not." Gregory paused and clicked the mouse a few times before furrowing his brow. "That's odd," he said.

"What?"

"There's no picture."

"I was going to ask you about that. I haven't seen one in the file either."

"There's got to be," Gregory said with the certainty of experience. "There's always a separate ID file. But we usually have a picture on here too." He tapped the monitor with a finger. Just then his phone rang, and taking note of the number displayed on his phone, he looked at Verdun.

"It's the boss-man."

"Go ahead and take it," Verdun said, getting up. "I'll be next door." He returned to his conference room.

A few minutes later Gregory was at the door. "I've gotta go to a meeting on the third floor. I'll be a couple of hours. You ok here?"

"Sure, go ahead."

"With this weather the place'll be clearing out early. I'll come back and get you when the meeting's done and we'll make for happy hour. How's that?"

"Sounds good."

"By the way, make all the copies you want. It's just down the hall here." Gregory pointed to the right.

"Thanks, Bob. See you later."

Verdun was vaguely aware of a sound in the distance, just enough to interrupt his peace. It became more insistent and shrill, and in the few more seconds it took for his foggy brain to process the sound, he became suddenly aware of his foreign surroundings. He groaned as he became aware for the first time of a pain in his head, and groped in the direction of the sound until his hand reached the cell phone on the bedside table.

"Hello?"

"Hello, stranger, did I wake you?"

Verdun recognized Isabelle's voice immediately. "Where are you?" he said, looking at his watch.

"I'm in Ottawa. Where are you? You sound like shit."

"It's a long story. Jeez, it's almost ten o'clock." He shook his head and visions of the night before entered his mind. Beer and wings, followed by a very loud bar and a lot more beer. He vaguely remembered a tray of shooters and he felt suddenly ill, remembering the bitterness and pungency of the liquor. "I called you last night but didn't get through. I figured you'd wait out the storm in Toronto before flying back."

"Yeah, I had no choice," she sighed. "They cancelled everything around from six o'clock last night until early this morning. What a mess. So how was Kingston?"

"I'm still here. I wasn't about to hit the highway last night. I met up with an old friend from my undergrad days."

"Aha, so that's why you're still in bed at this hour, and sounding so hoarse. What did you get up to?"

"Good clean fun...I think," Verdun said with a laugh. The truth was, most of the night was a blur, though he seemed to recall that when they parted ways at closing time, Gregory had a rather attractive blond on his arm. Her friend had made her play, but thankfully, Verdun had enough of his wits about him to politely refuse. He looked around the hotel room, as if to confirm his recollection of events. He was relieved to find only his own clothes scattered on the floor.

"Fun?"

"Yeah, it was. I haven't been on a bender like that since... Well, I don't even know."

"And what about our friend Bruno?"

"Bob showed me the whole file, and then some. It turns out Bruno's a biker."

"Really?"

"Yeah. Bob ran his name through some database and he's linked to a Montreal biker gang called the Rollers. That part wasn't in the file."

"Well, that's interesting. Good to have friends in the right places."

"The file didn't have a picture either."

"That's strange," Isabelle remarked.

"Yeah. Bob double-checked and apparently the identification file is missing. He's going to see if he can find it and get back to me. In the meantime, we may want to call up Vic Seguin again and see what he can find out about the Rollers."

"I've got a better idea," Isabelle said, as she chewed on something at her end. "A friend of mine in Montreal writes on bikers. He'd be a good place to start."

"Sounds good." Verdun rubbed his tired eyes. "What are you eating?"

"Pain au chocolat. Fresh from the bakery. I bought some for you, but I guess you're going to have to wait a while now."

"Hmm." Verdun felt his stomach gurgle and realized he had better eat something, and soon. "Can I buy you dinner tonight?"

"Sorry, I've got plans," she replied, and Verdun felt his heart sink a little as she paused a moment before continuing. "I'm cooking for you tonight, over here. I picked up a set of cookware in Toronto that I'm dying to try out."

"Sure, I'll be the guinea pig."

"Good. What time are you coming back?"

"Oh, I don't know," he sighed. "Time to get a shower and grab some breakfast and I'm out of here." He got up and drew the curtain on a winter wonderland. "I don't know what the road's going to be like."

"You be careful. I want you here in one piece. Why don't you come over around five? We can have some wine and maybe I'll let you help out in the kitchen."

"I've been known to swing a pot or pan around."

"Good. See you then. Drive safely."

"I will." He smiled. "It's nice to hear your voice. I missed you."

"I missed you too."

Verdun flipped the phone shut and sat back on the bed. His headache returned instantly and he groaned out loud. He was too old for carousing, he decided. He wondered how Bob could do this on a regular basis. The aching subsided as he visualized Isabelle, standing in her kitchen with her bright eyes and beautiful smile. He wanted her so much he could almost taste her lips. He got up and made his way very slowly to the shower.

It was after one by the time Verdun pulled into his driveway. The roads had been well cleared, but there had been an accident in the eastbound lanes of the 401 that had delayed the already slow drive even more. As he had planned to return home the night before, he was still in the same clothes, and all he could smell was cigarette smoke and stale beer. He would need something to eat, followed by a long visit to the gym to sweat out the remaining ill effects. He might even go for a late afternoon nap, time permitting.

The previous day's storm had left a clear blue sky in its wake, with a resulting drop in temperature, and the snow crunched under his shoes as he waded through it up his front steps. He grumbled at the prospect of having to remove it before someone broke their neck and put the key in the lock. Once inside, he noticed the cool immediately. He swore under his breath, recalling the furnace repairman's assurance that he had fixed the temperature sensor. He dropped his briefcase and kicked off his shoes, heading straight for the thermostat. Having turned it up, he tried the cold-water tap in the kitchen and was relieved to see a steady stream of water flowing into the sink. He went back down the hall to the powder room and tried the tap in there as well before heading upstairs to his bedroom. He noticed the pile of clothes he had left on the floor and added laundry to the mental list of things to do. He stopped to open the curtains to let in the light before going to the ensuite and turning on the tap. It too emitted a smooth flow of water, and as he turned it off, his relief at having avoided frozen pipes gave way to shock as he noticed something on the mirror in front of him. His shock turned to horror as the halogen bulbs over the medicine cabinet lit the mirror in front of him and he made out the text written in bold, black letters: YOU'RE LOOKING AT A DEAD MAN IF YOU DON'T MIND YOUR OWN FUCKING BUSINESS. NO COPS – THEY CAN'T HELP YOU ANYWAY.

Verdun took a step back, physically shaken by what he saw in front of him. The house seemed suddenly large and dangerous. He stepped cautiously back into the bedroom and grabbed the old nine-iron he kept inside his closet, turning on the light and checking it out before proceeding any further. He slowly made his way through the house, turning on lights and checking behind doors and in closets before sitting at the kitchen table. He laid the club across the table and noticed for the first time that his hands were shaking. As a thought occurred to him, he got up and checked the patio door. It was locked and when he opened it and examined the outside of the door and the jam, there was nothing to indicate it had been forced. He did the same with the front door, with the same result, before checking all of the ground floor windows. No sign of forced entry of any kind. Nobody else had a key, other than his parents, and he wondered how the messenger had gotten in. But more than anything else, he was struggling to make some sense of the message.

Taking the golf club with him, Verdun returned to the ensuite and re-read the message. Mind his own business about what? It could only be about Bruno Jacques, but how could he know of Verdun's interest in him? And what's more, why did he care? There were too many questions. Verdun thought about calling the police but decided against it. He found himself wiping the message off the mirror with a tissue, though common sense told him to leave it there. Standing back and looking at the smudged mirror, all he could think of was getting out of there as soon as possible. He threw a change of clothes into his gym bag and headed back downstairs. He looked at the telephone and debated making a call. To Smythe, or Isabelle? The police entered his mind again but left just as quickly. He would shower and change at the gym and go somewhere to think.

twenty-two

"Peter, I wasn't expecting you until..." Isabelle paused, seeing an unfamiliar expression on his face. "What's wrong?"

"Can I come in?"

"Of course."

He had been wandering around since leaving the gym, unsure of what to do next, or who to tell. "Something's happened," he said, as she shut the front door.

"What is it? You're scaring me."

"Someone broke into my house last night."

"Oh, my God." She put her hand over her mouth. "Did you call the police?"

"No. They didn't take anything, but they left me a message."

"What do you mean, a message?"

"Written on my bathroom mirror – telling me to mind my own business, and not to tell the police."

"I don't understand," she said.

"It must have something to do with my visit to Kingston."

"You mean Bruno Vachon?"

"Or Bruno Jacques, or whatever his real name is. But it doesn't make any sense. I was only at the prison yesterday. How could anyone have found out so fast?"

"Could it be one of your clients?"

"I thought of that, but it doesn't make any sense." He shook his head and noticed Isabelle was dressed in jeans and a sweatshirt, her hair tied back in a ponytail. He wasn't accustomed to seeing her this way. She looked more beautiful to him than ever. "I'm just glad to see a friendly face," he said.

She put her arms around him and he held her close. She kissed him. "Here we are, standing in the porch. Take off your coat and come in."

Verdun unbuttoned his coat and followed her into the living room, where a Mozart concerto was playing from somewhere unseen. There was a mug of something next to an open book on the coffee table. "I'm sorry to unload all this on you. I didn't know who else to tell."

"Don't be silly. Come," she said, sitting on the loveseat and patting the cushion next to her. "Tell me everything."

Verdun proceeded to fill in the details, describing the message, as well as what he had found in Kingston. When he was done, Isabelle sat back and considered the situation. "Here's what we'll do. I told you about my friend in Montreal."

"The one who writes on bikers?"

"Yes. We're going to talk to him first. He's very discreet, and he'll know what to do."

"Let me talk to him," Verdun said. "I don't want to drag you into this."

"I'm already in this, in case you hadn't noticed, "she said. "I'm the one who wanted to find Bruno, remember?"

"Yeah, but–"

"But nothing. I'll call him right now," she said, getting up.

Verdun grabbed her arm. "Don't, please. I don't want you involved. Let me call, and not from here."

She looked at him and sensed the urgency in his eyes. "I'll call from a payphone if you like."

"You're going to call him now? It's Saturday."

"We never rest in the journalism business," she said. "Besides, he's not really a friend, he's family. He'll do anything for his favourite cousin. Come on."

Before he had time to think about it any more, Verdun found himself donning his coat and following her out to his truck. He drove downtown and found a payphone off Elgin Street.

Isabelle made the call with Verdun standing at her shoulder. "It's the machine. Shit." She fumbled in her pocket and fished out a scrap of paper. "I'll try his cell." She dialed the second number and after a few seconds her frustration revealed that she was listening to another recorded message. Then her eyes brightened and a smile came across her face. She hung up the phone and looked at Verdun. "We're in luck."

"What is it?" he asked.

"That was his service. He's traveling but he'll be in Ottawa tomorrow. He always stays at the Lord Elgin. We'll leave a message at the front desk for him."

As they got back in the truck, the late afternoon sun was fading and a very light dusting of snow was coming down, the flakes sparkling in the last remnants of daylight. "Don't worry," Isabelle said, sensing Verdun's unspoken anxiety. She rubbed his arm as he drove them home. "René will know what to do."

"Thanks." He grasped her hand and held it.

"Let's talk about something else," she said. "How was your boys' night out?"

Verdun laughed. "You'll have to meet Bob. He's quite a character," Verdun began, and before he knew it, they were back at Isabelle's and he had forgotten the whole, awful ordeal.

"Let's have a drink," she said, closing the front door behind them. "Go sit in front of the fire and warm yourself up."

He did as he was told and she joined him a few minutes later with a couple of wine glasses. As they sat on the floor, she kissed him gently.

"I'm glad you were here today," he said.

"Wait until you taste dinner, you'll be really glad."

Verdun smiled and as he leaned back against the loveseat, she lay across his lap. They sat, looking into the glow of the fire, soft music in the background, and it occurred to him that there was nothing else more important, nowhere else he felt he should be, or would rather be, than right here, right now. All his cares and worries melted away into insignificance, and it was then that he realized. He was in love.

Verdun followed as Isabelle led the way across the floor of the café. "Bonjour René, ca va?" she said, approaching a table occupied by a dark-haired man who looked up from his newspaper.

"Cousine," he replied and got up to accept a kiss from Isabelle on each cheek.

"This is Peter Verdun," she said, taking Verdun by the arm.

"René Bourassa. Please, have a seat," he said in perfect English, gesturing to the two empty seats at the table. "Isabelle told me what happened. It's very...unsettling."

"Yes," Verdun nodded, as they took their seats and a waiter appeared offering coffee.

Bourassa accepted for them all. Though he was dressed simply in a black roll-neck and jeans, and even sported a day's worth of stubble, it was obvious from his tone and manner that Bourassa was used to giving orders, and having them followed. From what Isabelle had told him, her cousin had been groomed to take over her uncle's business, but had decided to follow his own path, changing his academic course from business to medicine. But after a brief stint in medical school, he had dropped out and pursued journalism instead. He had spent several years as a crime writer before writing the first of several books on organized crime in Canada and the U.S., specifically on motorcycle gangs. He had since branched out and become a consultant with Interpol in Paris, but his career choices, fraught as they were with risks, combined with his obvious independent streak were probably why Isabelle liked him so much. It was clear as she exchanged family-related gossip with Bourassa that Isabelle looked up to him.

"So, Peter," he began, ready to get down to business. "Tell me what the message said."

Verdun repeated it verbatim, adding with some embarrassment that he had erased it.

"Ah," Bourassa said, waving his hand dismissively as if it was of no consequence. "And you say it was on a mirror. Where exactly?"

"My bathroom mirror. It was a marker of some kind. I could smell it when I wiped it off."

Bourassa nodded. "And nothing was taken?"

"No. And no sign of forced entry anywhere. I checked all of the doors and windows."

"No," Bourassa said, nodding again.

"In fact, except for the message, I'd never have known anyone had been in there."

"And you don't think it was a client?"

"No. I've run through every client I can think of, past and present, and this doesn't fit with any of them. I can only imagine this being related to Bruno."

"He's a member of the Rollers. Do you know them?" Isabelle interjected.

"Yes, but it's been a while since I've followed the Montreal scene. I don't know the individuals anymore."

"What I can't understand is the timing," Isabelle said. "I mean, Peter gets access to Bruno's file after noon and they're breaking in that evening? It doesn't make sense."

"Hmm." Bourassa stroked his chin. "You shouldn't underestimate how well-connected these people are. They have elaborate networks for gathering information. But they tend to be a little more dramatic."

"What do you mean?" Verdun asked.

"Bikers operate by using fear to their advantage. Intimidation, pure and simple – that's their stock in trade. If they'd gone into your place, they'd have torn it up, smashed a few things, just to make sure you got the message."

"Well if it wasn't Bruno or his heavies, who then?" Isabelle asked.

"You must have made arrangements with someone over the phone before going to the prison, no?"

"Yes, but he's an old university buddy. What would he have to do with–"

"It wouldn't necessarily have anything to do with him. But as you know, a request for a file can set off any number of alarms. Whether it's someone in records, an electronic tag, whatever."

"I'm not sure I understand," Verdun said, looking puzzled.

"It may not be Bruno or his gang that's giving you the warning," Bourassa said, sipping his coffee as this advice sank in.

"You mean someone in Corrections?" Isabelle shared Verdun's look of doubt.

"Like I said, bikers use intimidation very well. It's one of the reasons it's so hard for police to gather evidence from witnesses, and why they so often have to rely on informants."

"You mean you think the police broke into Peter's place and left that message?" Isabelle said, lowering her voice, as a waiter arrived to freshen their coffee. He poured the rich-smelling brew from a silver decanter, taking the subtle wave of Bourassa's index finger as his cue to give them another moment or two before asking for their order.

"It wouldn't be the first time they protected an informant, and it would certainly explain the timing," Bourassa said, turning to Verdun. "Besides, why would the Rollers care about you looking into Bruno's records? You'll forgive me for putting it this way, but as a criminal lawyer you're more on their side of the fence than the other, aren't you?"

Verdun sat back and considered Bourassa's reasoning. It had an undeniable ring of logic. "And they do this regularly?"

"Of course not," Bourassa replied, shaking his head. "But from what you've told me about this Bruno's record, he's been in and out of enough of the right prisons to make him a very valuable source indeed. And when it comes to the rare sources like that – if indeed he is one – they'll stop at nothing to protect him."

Bourassa stirred cream into his coffee in the silence that followed. Verdun looked deep in thought.

"So what are we supposed to do now?" Isabelle asked.

"You mean what am *I* supposed to?" Verdun said, looking up at her. "I should never have dragged you into this, Isabelle."

"You're right, of course," Bourassa said soberly. "But you have a lot to learn about my favourite cousin, whose beauty is matched only by her stubbornness. If you hadn't told her, she would have found out one way or another." He was grinning now.

"I'm a big girl, Peter," she said, putting her hand on his. "Besides, this is Canada. Even if the police did go so far as breaking into your house to scare you off, that's still a far cry from actually harming you, much less me."

Bourassa nodded. "She's right, but I would think very seriously before I dug any deeper into this man. The police are one thing, but if the Rollers were to become aware of your interest, that's quite another matter."

"But you said they wouldn't care one way or the other."

"Another tactic the police sometimes use is disinformation." Bourassa paused to sip his coffee, enjoying the way Verdun and Isabelle waited for the rest. "Let's say some false information about the nature of your inquiries made it to the right person, perhaps even via Bruno, that changes the Rollers' opinion of you."

Verdun nodded.

"And attention from a gang like the Rollers *is* something to worry about, I assure you," Bourassa added.

"So you think I should back off?"

"I'm telling you the possibilities if you don't, that's all. Whether you proceed will depend on how badly you want the information," he concluded, as the waiter returned.

"Would you care to order?"

Verdun watched as Isabelle placed her order. Whether it was because he was in love with her or not, he had felt a growing urge to protect her from the dangers of this world. He knew that, despite her conviction and strength, whatever the importance of finding Bruno might be, it paled in comparison to his need to keep her safe.

twenty-three

Verdun stepped out onto Elgin Street from his office, bracing himself for the cold evening air. And though a winter wind nipped at his ears, the darkness he had expected to see was brightened by an array of coloured lights all the way down Elgin to the War Memorial. Though only mid-November, the awesome six-week display of Christmas lights in the downtown area had begun for another year. As he walked north, he took them all in, first the white lights lining the street, then the multi-coloured ones in front of the courthouse and beyond. The War Memorial was brightly lit, as was the Chateau Laurier and the East Block of the Parliament buildings, which he could just see as he crossed Elgin on his way towards the canal. It had been cold for the past few days, but skating on the frozen waterway was still several weeks off. As he turned up the path along Queen Elizabeth Drive and the lights of downtown faded behind him, so did their accompanying cheer. With the darkness, came thoughts of the troubling call he had received from Pierre Larousse late in the day. With all of his preliminary motions exhausted, Karl Roy's day of judgment was fast approaching.

While Verdun had spent the last two weeks struggling with his decision to stop his inquiries into Bruno Jacques, he had tried to keep the quickly approaching trial at the back of his mind while he considered other options, of which there were, of course, none. Isabelle had gone to Nice to cover the start of the trial for her paper and had been giving him regular updates on the prosecution's progress. To say that things did not look good for Roy would be an understatement at this point. And while most of Verdun's own bad humour was due to his client's misfortune – and Verdun's inability to help – he also knew it was inextricably linked to Isabelle's absence. She had been gone for only six days, but it seemed a lifetime.

As small, dry flakes of cold snow began to fall, collecting like confetti on his coat, Verdun took advantage of a short break in the traffic to scamper across to Delaware Street and up his front steps. He rid himself of coat, boots and briefcase before heading to the kitchen, where he poured himself a whiskey. Ignoring his mail, he switched on a floor lamp and sank into his favourite armchair. He sipped his drink, recalling Larousse's description of the prosecution's case so far, and the unspoken request for something – anything – that Larousse might use to slow the growing momentum. Verdun had noticed the change in Larousse's voice immediately, devoid of the usual confidence.

Verdun sighed as he noticed the flashing light of his answering machine on the corner table, and though his first impulse was to ignore it in favour of his drink, he couldn't resist checking it in case it was Isabelle. He pressed the button and returned to his chair. The first message was indeed from Isabelle, saying she would be delayed in Paris by another day on the way back, meaning he wouldn't see her until Sunday. As if this wasn't bad enough, the second message was from Roy's father, asking in muted tones for a return call as soon as possible.

As the machine emitted a long beep to indicate the end of messages, Verdun rubbed his eyes and leaned back in his chair. Too depressed to call Mr. Roy in his current state, he picked up the remote and switched on the television. Jumping from channel to channel, he decided on a sportscast giving hockey scores. After a breakdown of the Senators' win in an afternoon game, the focus shifted to accusations of links between organized crime and several members of the Montreal Canadiens, including their top scorer. Verdun shook his head. Weren't they content just to play the game they loved and collect their fat salaries?

He switched off the television in disgust and looked for his day-timer and Isabelle's number in Nice. He knew her voice was the only thing that could cheer him up.

"So how was Karl?" Verdun asked, as he lay back on the soft pillows at the head of Isabelle's bed, where they had soon ended up after meeting at the airport. She lay face down next to him, an arm draped over his naked torso.

"Stressed," she replied, pulling herself up onto her elbows. "I worry about what a guilty verdict will do to him."

"So do I," Verdun sighed.

"It's good to be home," she said, smiling.

He stroked her long brown hair, running the back of his finger over her cheek. "I think I'm in love with you," he said after a moment.

She cocked her head to the side. Then she smiled. "You *think*, do you?"

He smiled at her.

"I love you too," she said, pulling herself up to plant a soft kiss on his lips.

"Where's the olive oil?" Verdun asked, rummaging through a cupboard in Isabelle's kitchen. She sat at a table on the other side of the breakfast bar, reading the morning paper over a cup of coffee.

"Ah, here it is. You're going to love this omelette – my specialty."

"I'm sure I will," she said, looking over and laughing as she watched him cross the kitchen floor in a t-shirt and boxers, a carton of eggs in one hand and a frying pan in the other.

"Most important meal of the day," he said, cracking the eggs into a bowl.

"Did you hear about this thing in Montreal with the hockey players?" she said, still reading the paper.

"The gambling thing, and the ties to organized crime? Yeah, I saw something about that on TV."

"A gambling ring run by bikers."

"I didn't know it was bikers." Verdun looked up from the stove.

"That's what it says."

He returned to his cooking, pouring the egg mixture into the pan. Isabelle sipped her coffee.

"You thinking what I'm thinking?" he said after a noticeable silence.

"The hockey pendant found at the scene?"

He stopped poking at the eggs with a spatula, hesitating before speaking. "You don't think it's an incredible coincidence that a hockey pendant would be found at a crime scene in the South of France?"

Isabelle nodded. "It's pretty odd, I must admit. But what of it?"

Verdun didn't respond, and appeared to be deep in thought.

"You think it's possible Bruno's connected to Malle's murder somehow?"

"Put it this way, from what I know of Bruno Jacques, I wouldn't want to be the guy who killed his baby sister."

Isabelle shook her head. "I can't see it. Bruno strikes me as a common thug. Not someone with the wherewithal to track someone down on another continent more than twenty years after the fact, much less hop a plane to the French Riviera to perform a neat little execution for his baby sister Annie."

Verdun stopped poking the eggs and looked at her. "What did you call her?"

"Annie." Isabelle looked puzzled.

"Why'd you call her that? Her name's Angeline."

"That was his pet name for her."

Verdun stood there, the spatula in his hands as the eggs burned on the stove. "How do you know?"

"It's in my research somewhere. The eggs!" She pointed to the plume of smoke behind him.

He pushed the pan off the burner. "What research?"

"I don't know. I read it somewhere. What's gotten into you? What's the matter?"

"Think, Isabelle. Where did you read it?"

"You're creeping me out, Peter. Jesus. It was...the obituary. I copied her obituary, that's it."

"Is it here? Show me."

"What are you talking about?"

"The obituary. Show me the obituary!"

"All right, all right. It's in my file, come see for yourself if you don't believe me." She led him to her study and a manila envelope by her computer. She rifled through its contents and retrieved a photocopied page. "Here."

Verdun took the page and read the encircled text, mourning the death of Angeline Vachon. "...Annie leaves her big brother to mourn her..." He stood back, realizing that the spatula was still in his hand. "Do you know what this means?"

"I wish you would tell me."

"The eyewitness in Nice," he began breathlessly.

"The homeless guy?"

He nodded. "He heard the killer say one thing after he cut Malle's throat. I just assumed he was talking about Karl's fiancée, Annie Renaud."

"What, Peter? What did he say, for God's sake?"

"That's for Annie."

twenty-four

As he waited at the airport for Isabelle's return flight from Toronto, Verdun's thoughts drifted to Karl Roy's trial. As soon as he and Isabelle had made the connection between "Annie" Vachon and the comment overheard by the eyewitness, Verdun knew he had to concentrate on tracking down Bruno once and for all. And though it made him a little uneasy, he also knew there was no way to keep Isabelle out of it. She was as keen as Verdun to find out if there was more than a coincidental connection. They had gone immediately to her cousin with their discovery, who directed them to Jean Martin, a writer in Montreal who specialized in true crime – organized crime specifically. He was especially knowledgeable about the current Montreal biker scene. That had been three days ago, and while they were waiting for a reply from Martin, Verdun had debated whether to risk involving the police, if for no other reason than to expedite the process. The fact was, they were running out of time. Verdun was in regular contact with Pierre Larousse, and Roy's trial was leading to a rapid conclusion – and a conviction – unless something drastic happened in the interim.

"So what's new? Isabelle said, startling Verdun from his reverie.

Her return flight had arrived a few minutes early, and with no checked baggage to collect, they paused only long enough for a pleasant kiss before leaving the terminal.

"We'll talk in the car," he said.

Verdun pulled away from the parking booth and made for the exit road leading to the airport parkway. "Well," he began, stepping on the accelerator in an attempt to make the most of their jump on the crowd of deplaning passengers. "As a matter of fact, I spoke to Jean Martin a couple of hours ago. He called to give me an update on Bruno."

"And?"

"He found him all right."

"Really?" Isabelle couldn't contain her excitement. This was the first time anyone had actually confirmed the existence of the mysterious Bruno Vachon, a.k.a. Bruno Jacques, in the flesh.

"He's a member of the Rollers, and seems to be pretty high up, though Martin's not really sure about his place in the organization."

"How did he find him?"

"I'm not sure. Through his sources, I guess. He said he got the impression Bruno likes to keep a low profile, which usually means he's in operations."

"You mean he's not a knee-breaker."

"Yeah, that's right. He's more of a strategist who looks at new markets, and alliances with other gangs."

"Sounds like a VP of corporate development," Isabelle said, looking out the window as the traffic thickened around them. It was four-thirty and most of the traffic was heading the other way as they made their way north past Carleton University. The grey sky was turning dark and little flakes of snow were falling, melting as they hit the windshield and making the dark asphalt shine with reflected light.

"I guess he is, in a manner of speaking," Verdun said, as he flicked on the wipers. "Anyway, Martin said he would be in Washington for a few days to cover a big biker rally."

"The 'drive to DC.' I read about that in this morning's paper," Isabelle said.

"Can't get anything past you," Verdun said as she smiled. "Martin said he'd be heading back to Montreal on Wednesday and picking up where he left off, putting a file together with pictures and whatever information he can get. He suggested we meet him there on the weekend. You free?"

"For a weekend with you in Montreal? It's a date." She put her hand on his.

As the Airport Parkway turned into Bronson Avenue, the flurries turned to snow and Verdun changed lanes to avoid a long line of traffic. "I was going to make you a nice dinner," he said, checking the adjacent lane in his side mirror. "Did you want to go home first?"

"No. I just want a long shower. You might like to join me."

"That's pretty hard to refuse." Verdun grinned as he took a right turn and came to a stop in a line of traffic headed east. He leaned over and kissed her, breathing in the sweet smell of her hair, until the car behind them beeped impatiently. "All right, all right," he sighed, returning to the steering wheel.

"Why don't we order in?" Isabelle said as the snow really began to fall. "It looks like a good night to spend under the covers."

Verdun looked up from a draft motion he was reading to the clock on his office wall. It was three o'clock on Wednesday and he still had not heard back from Jean Martin to firm up the upcoming weekend meeting. As he began to look for his number, Verdun's direct line rang and Isabelle's cellular number appeared on his phone. "Hello there," he said, as Jim Smythe entered his office, saw Verdun on the phone and indicated with a hand signal that he would return shortly.

"You sound in good spirits," she said.

"I am now," he replied.

"A penny for your thoughts," Isabelle asked.

"Well, there's last night…"

"Don't you men ever think of anything else?"

"Actually, I was just thinking of calling Pierre Larousse about this weekend," Verdun said. "You haven't heard from him, have you?"

"No, nothing. Why don't you give him a call? You can tell me all about it tonight over dinner."

"Who's cooking?" he asked.

"Nobody. I'm taking you out for a night on the town. Dinner at Sans Pareil followed by the NAC orchestra. I got us great seats."

"You're too much."

"The tickets are freebies from work. You can thank me later for dinner."

"Is that the little place in Hull?"

"The one and only."

"I don't know what to say. I can't wait."

"Good. I'll be home around six. Dinner's at seven. Gotta run – don't forget to call Pierre."

"See you tonight," he said as they hung up. "Home," as she had put it, was her place, where they had been effectively co-habiting since the break-in at Verdun's. He had moved the bulk of his clothes and personal things in over the course of the past couple of weeks and he felt comfortable there, as she appeared to be as well.

"When are you going marry her and get Margaret off my back?" Smythe was leaning in the doorway.

Verdun laughed.

"Look at yourself, man, I've never seen you like this." Smythe pointed at him.

"What are you talking about?" Verdun asked.

"You're grinning like a Cheshire cat half the day, in your own dream world the rest."

"Don't be such an old woman, Jim," Verdun scoffed, with a dismissive gesture.

"You laugh, but it's true, and you know it."

Verdun had little choice other than to acknowledge what was apparently obvious. "I have to admit, the thought had crossed my mind–"

"I suppose it has. She's really a keeper."

"I just don't want to scare her off. I mean, what if she's not thinking of anything serious?"

"For God's sake, strap on some balls," Smythe said, taking a seat in a client chair.

"If Margaret could hear you–"

"She'd agree completely." Smythe rubbed his top lip with an index finger. "But you might be onto something."

"What?"

"Well, you know how good Margaret is at obtaining information."

"Better than most of the interrogators we see on the stand

across the street," Verdun said.

"Exactly. Who better to ask if you need a little help figuring out Isabelle's intentions? Margaret was saying last night it's time we had you over for dinner again."

"Come on, Jim, we're not in high school."

"Well, get on with it then."

"You know, you really are starting to sound like Margaret."

"Anyway, I'm sure you'll do the right thing," Smythe said. "And I was serious about dinner."

"We're in Montreal this weekend."

"There you go – romantic city–"

"To meet with Jean Martin."

"Oh, right. What's new with Karl?"

"The judge took ill and it was adjourned until next week. After that, there's probably no more than a couple of days left."

"Well, I hope Martin can help you out."

"Me too," Verdun said.

"I could use your help next week if you're available," Smythe asked, getting up to leave. "I've got that sexual assault I was telling you about – the teacher."

"Yes, you wanted to try and exclude the similar-fact evidence."

"You said you had some research."

"A fat file of it. Sure, I'll be around. We'll be back on Sunday."

"Good. Well, I'm off to the holding cells. You think about what I said."

"Yes, Mom."

"And use my jeweller. I can get you a deal, thanks to his son's drug problem."

"You're quite a resource, Jim."

Verdun found the card with Jean Martin's numbers and dialed the first one.

"Allo?" a gruff voice answered.

"Jean Martin?"

"Oui."

"C'est Peter Verdun."

"Peter, hello," Martin switched to heavily accented English, which was at least better than Verdun's French. "I've been meaning to call, but..."

Verdun sensed hesitation in his voice. "Is this a bad time?"

"It's my cell. Give me five minutes and I'll call you back on a hard line."

"Sure." Verdun hung up and returned to his draft motion, curious about what Martin had to say. Ten minutes passed before the phone rang again, indicating a Montreal number. He snatched it up. "Jean?"

"Yes. Sorry about that."

"No problem. I was just calling to see if we're on for the weekend."

"We should definitely meet, but not here. C'est un vrai dûr, your Bruno."

"What do you mean?"

"I've been doing this for years, but this is the toughest nut I've had to crack. Not many people know more than his name, and the few that do are not keen to talk."

"Really?"

"And I think I'm being followed. That's why I think it would be a lot safer if we met outside Montreal."

"Where?"

"Gatineau. Boulevard St. Joseph."

Verdun wrote down the number.

"I'll be there Friday night," Martin continued. "I've got a meeting lined up here tomorrow night with a source I trust."

"Is there anything you can tell me now?" Verdun couldn't contain his curiosity.

"Better we wait until Friday."

"All right. See you then." Verdun hung up and sat back in his chair, feeling a mixture of excitement and frustration. It seemed clear that Martin was onto something, but just as clear that he would have to wait until Friday to find out what.

twenty-five

"So how did he sound on the phone?" Isabelle asked as Verdun changed lanes on Wellington and turned onto the Portage Bridge.

"Rattled, I guess. He said so little it was difficult to tell."

They had both been anxiously awaiting the evening's meeting, especially since Jean Martin's call from the road late on Friday afternoon to confirm its time and location. Verdun undid his tie as he drove, loosening his collar in the process. He had been held up at work and hadn't had time to change before picking Isabelle up at her house. They sat in silence as they crossed the Ottawa River and were greeted by the massive grey complex of government buildings looming out of the darkness on the Quebec side.

"All he really said was, 'a 21 heures,'" Verdun added, turning left, then right up Montcalm. "You sure it's at this end of St. Joseph?"

"He said 21 heures?" Isabelle asked, ignoring Verdun's question.

"Yes, what's the matter? I thought all you francos were on military time."

"But that's nine o'clock, not eight."

Verdun continued in silence. "You're right. What was I thinking?" He shook his head, looking at the dashboard clock, which read 7:57 pm. "Should we wait until nine?"

"We might as well see if he's there, now that we're here."

"Yeah, I guess." Verdun stopped at a red light. "I don't know why I thought it was eight o'clock."

"Espèce d'anglo," Isabelle laughed, as the lights changed and they headed up towards St. Joseph Boulevard. "There it is." Isabelle pointed to a modest two-storey with a light on over the front porch. Verdun parked the truck and they got out into the cold night air. The street was a mixture of residential and commercial and with only a few of the houses lit up and none of the businesses, it was quite dark. As they approached the house, bounded by a vacant-looking house on one side and a plumbing store on the other, Verdun noticed the front end of a van parked in the alley between the house and the store, likely the plumber's. An older model Trans Am was parked in front.

Verdun and Isabelle climbed the front steps and he knocked on the screen door. They waited a few seconds and then he tried again, this time hearing a thud from within.

"Here he comes," Verdun said, though a few seconds later there was still no one at the door.

"That's odd," Isabelle said.

Verdun opened the screen and noticed that the door was ajar. "It's open," he said.

"Maybe we should wait, Peter."

He rapped on the door with his knuckles and it creaked open. "Allo?" he called out, pushing it open a little farther. "Jean?"

"This is giving me the creeps," Isabelle said, shivering from the cold.

"I'll just have a quick look. Why don't you wait here?" he said, turning to her.

She looked up and down the darkened street and made up her mind she would rather not. "Let's go," she said, waving him in.

Verdun led the way into the front hall, calling Martin's name again. The house was dark, except for a thin ray of light coming from a doorway towards the rear of the main floor, which he guessed was the kitchen. He walked slowly across the creaking hardwood of the front room, noticing it was bare of furniture except for a table and chairs by the side window. Arriving at the doorway, Isabelle behind him, he called out Martin's name once more before pushing the door open.

What he saw stopped him dead in his tracks, causing Isabelle to stumble into him. Lying on his back in the middle of the kitchen floor was Jean Martin, his legs akimbo and his hands –

covered in blood – clutched over his chest. A deep red stain had soaked into the fabric of his white shirt.

Isabelle cried out when she saw him, jolting Verdun back to reality. Martin heard it too. Still alive, he craned his head towards them and tried to speak, but only a faint gurgle came out. As Verdun moved towards him, he heard the sound of an engine starting, then revving up as it went into gear, followed by a short squeal of tires as the vehicle hit the asphalt in front of the house. Verdun raced back out to the side window and pulled back the curtain just in time to see the van he had noticed in the alley disappearing into the night. He cursed and returned to the kitchen, where Isabelle was still standing, helpless and frozen, over Martin's motionless form.

"Call 911," he said, taking her by the shoulder and directing her to the phone on the wall. She seemed to be released from her shock by the motion, and she picked up the receiver.

Verdun kneeled next to Martin, leaning over him. "Jean, can you hear me? We're going to get you an ambulance."

Martin opened his eyes and looked towards Verdun, though he might have been looking right through him. "Cold," was all he said. The back door had been left open and the kitchen was freezing. Verdun whipped off his jacket and laid it over Martin.

"Br…" Martin said, and Verdun began to remove the blazer he was wearing. "No," Martin said, gasping for breath. "Br…uno."

"Bruno did this?" Verdun asked quickly, leaning closer to hear better. Martin was wheezing and gurgling with every breath. "Blink once for yes, Jean," he said, hearing Isabelle giving directions to the dispatcher in the background.

Martin blinked twice.

"Who was it, Jean? One of Bruno's people?"

Martin blinked twice again.

"Bruno's…" Martin paused, fighting for the strength to get the last words out. "…protect…"

"Bruno's protected? By who?"

Martin closed his eyes, as if to summon some internal strength, then opened them again, looking not at Verdun's face, but moving deliberately to his chest. Verdun followed the path of the dying man's eyes, noticing that a bloody finger had uncurled to point in the same direction. Martin returned his gaze to Verdun's face and managed a final whisper before his expression faded and his eyes glazed over into a death stare.

"What did he say?" Isabelle asked, now at Verdun's shoulder.

"Déjà," he said, turning towards her and looking into her dark brown eyes, watching them well with tears. He stood with her and held her in his arms in the middle of the freezing kitchen, the sound of her sobbing broken only by a growing wail of police sirens.

twenty-six

Verdun and Isabelle sat in a small office at the police station to which they had accompanied Detective Marc-André Théberge of the Sureté du Quebec from the house on St. Joseph. Verdun looked at his watch, noting it was almost midnight. Isabelle was quiet under his arm, stirring only to wipe her nose with a tissue from the box Théberge had left with her when he stepped out for a moment a couple of hours before. With the door shut and the blinds down, the little office was quiet, but Verdun could sense the frantic pace of a lot of people outside the room. He looked around the office, squinting from the bright fluorescent lights above, but every time he closed his eyes, the gruesome scene of Jean Martin's final moments played itself out in vivid detail. It all seemed so surreal, and though Verdun's logical side was working on an explanation, another part of him was still having trouble believing that he and Isabelle were here, and had seen that terrible sight just a few short hours ago. Verdun had defended several clients on murder or manslaughter charges and was no stranger to the darker side of human nature. But the impact of descriptions by witnesses, police reports and forensic photographs – no matter how vivid or grisly – paled in comparison to the first-hand experience. The expression of terror on Isabelle's face was burned into his memory as well, and disturbed him almost as much as Martin's death mask.

"Are you ok?" he whispered to Isabelle, as if his regular voice would unsettle her in her fragile state. She sniffed and nodded her head slightly.

"I'm so sorry, Isabelle. I'm so sorry."

"It's not your fault," she said softly as he rubbed her arm. "When are they going to let us go home?" she asked.

"I don't know," he sighed. "They'll want a formal statement before we go anywhere."

Verdun had already provided Théberge with a lot of information at the scene, including why Martin had been hired and a sketchy description of the van, an old model Chevy, dark in colour. Unfortunately he had no licence plate to offer or physical description of the killer, or killers. But Théberge was most likely talking to the anti-gang division of the Sureté, putting out feelers on which members of the Rollers were in the area. He couldn't help thinking Théberge had spent part of the time confirming his and Isabelle's personal information and occupations, not that they were very likely suspects since they had called in the crime. Just then the door opened, and Théberge entered the office, followed by a younger man in uniform.

"Sorry to be so long," Théberge said in his heavy accent. It had taken him about five seconds of conversation with Verdun in French to determine they would be better off in English.

"Any luck finding the van?" Verdun asked.

"No, but it's very early, Mr. Verdun."

"Of course."

"I was at the coroner's office," Théberge said, motioning to the younger officer. "This is Lemoyne, he's going to take your statements. If you'd please come to the interview room, we can get started so you can go home. I know this has not been a pleasant evening for you."

Verdun got up slowly, motioning for Théberge to join him by the door. "I'd like to suggest giving a statement on behalf of both of us. It's been a long night."

Théberge looked at Isabelle's forlorn figure on the chair and nodded. "We may ask her to come back at a later date, but that's fine for now," he said. He had probably already ruled them out as suspects and, in any event, he was well aware that his chances of keeping a lawyer and a crime reporter against their wishes were slim indeed if they decided they wanted to walk out the door.

Verdun returned to Isabelle and offered her his hand, and they both followed Théberge out of the detective's office. He led them down the hall to a stark room with a large rectangular table in the centre, surrounded by several chairs. "Please sit. Can I get you some more coffee?"

"No thanks," Verdun said. Isabelle shook her head.

"Do you mind if we record the statement?" Théberge asked, pointing to the recording device at the end of the table, in front of Lemoyne.

"No," Verdun said. Théberge nodded to his colleague, who popped a tape in the recorder and placed a microphone in front of both Théberge and Verdun.

"Ready?" Théberge asked.

Verdun nodded.

Théberge began by asking him how well they knew Jean Martin and why they were meeting. Verdun expanded on the information about Bruno Jacques that he had given at the scene – information that had been of obvious interest to Théberge – and explained that the meeting was to discuss Martin's findings.

"And had the victim provided you with any information about Bruno Jacques before this evening?"

"Not really. He said he thought he was a pretty senior member of the Rollers, but he was supposed to meet with a source last night in Montreal to confirm it."

"Did he give you the name of the source?"

"No."

Théberge asked Verdun to describe their arrival at the house on St. Joseph, a process that Verdun found difficult, but with Théberge's gentle prodding, managed to complete. Then he discussed the van and Martin's final words.

"Déjà – already. Do you know what he meant by that?"

Verdun shook his head. "I've been racking my brain about it, and it doesn't make any sense."

Théberge asked some more questions about Martin's state when they found him, before moving on to the physical evidence at the scene – whether the doors at the front and back were open or closed, whether there was any indication of more than one assailant, footsteps or anything. When Verdun had answered his questions, Théberge paused and pulled a pocket-sized notepad out of his jacket pocket. Verdun glanced at his watch. He had been giving a statement for almost thirty minutes and he was growing tired.

"Just a few more questions, Mr. Verdun. I won't keep you much longer."

Verdun nodded and looked at Isabelle, who managed a feeble smile.

"Do you know if Mr. Martin used drugs?"

"I have no idea," Verdun said, surprised at the question.

"Did you see any physical evidence of narcotics either in the premises or on the victim?"

"No." Verdun frowned. "Why?"

"Just a lead we're following, that's all." Théberge flipped his notepad over and nodded at the young officer at the far end of the table, who switched off the tape. "Those are all the questions I have for Mr. Verdun, thank you."

"What's all this about drugs? Did you find something on him?"

Théberge looked at him, considering whether to respond. "I'm really not free to discuss–"

"Oh come on. I've cooperated fully. I think it's only fair that you let me know whether the guy I discovered dying was killed in a drug deal."

"Some drugs were found on him. But between you and me, I don't think it's a factor."

"What kind of drugs?"

"We're waiting on confirmation from the lab," Théberge replied, getting up. Verdun had the feeling he was lying.

"What news on the biker connection? Surely that's got to be the main thrust of your investigation."

"Like I said, it's early to say anything for sure. But your information has been very useful."

"I'd like to be informed if you question Bruno Jacques. As I've said, he may have valuable insight into a case that's currently before the courts."

"I'll see what I can do. Thank you again, Mr. Verdun. I'll have you driven to your car if you like."

Verdun nodded and shook Théberge's extended hand as Isabelle excused herself to the washroom.

"It's Peter," he said, fishing out a business card from his jacket pocket. Théberge accepted it and gave him one of his own.

"I'll be in touch," Verdun added, as Lemoyne led him out to the lobby.

twenty-seven

"Peter! Peter, wake up!"

Verdun bolted upright in bed, opened his eyes to find Isabelle shaking his arm, a panicked look in her eyes. "What?" he said, disoriented and realizing his forehead was dripping sweat.

"You were having a nightmare," she said, trying to calm him down.

"Jesus." He lay back down and wiped his brow. "You're right. I could see him, he was calling out to me. It was..." He shook his head.

"It's all right now," she said, kissing him gently.

"What time is it?"

"Almost seven."

"Were you up?"

She nodded. They had finally arrived home around one-thirty and collapsed together in Isabelle's bed. As his mind cleared, the details of the previous evening came into focus again. He looked at her. "How are you doing?"

"Better than you, I guess."

He smiled and touched her cheek, the salty tracks of her tears still visible. "Poor Jean."

"Do you think they'll find Bruno?"

"I'm sure they will. They have to." He kissed her and pulled the covers up as she nestled on his chest. They both lay there in silence, the first light of day creeping through the bedroom window.

"Hello, it's Peter Verdun calling. Just wondering if there's been any progress since we spoke yesterday. Please give me a call when you get a chance. Thanks." He hung up the phone and retrieved the Sunday paper as Isabelle came out of the bathroom wrapped in a towel, her long hair combed back over her shoulders.

"Detective Théberge?" she asked.

"Not there. I left a message."

"It's still early."

He nodded.

"Maybe we should go do something fun today. I mean, to take our minds off it," she said, rubbing mousse into her hair with her fingertips. "Yesterday was so depressing, moping around here."

"You're right," he replied. They had spent the entire day at home, not knowing what to do with themselves, trying to deal with Martin's death in their own little worlds, unable to talk about it for more than a few moments at a time. The only other person they'd told was Jim Smythe, who had come over late in the afternoon with Margaret to offer them whatever comfort they could.

"The police have got both of our cell numbers. I'm sure they'll call when there's any news. What did you have in mind?"

"I don't know," she said, picking up her hairdryer. "Do you ski?"

"Haven't lately, but I'm reasonably capable. I suppose you're the queen of the moguls."

She laughed. "Mont Tremblant's too far for today. What about Mont Cascades? You'll be all right there."

"Very funny. Sure, let's go." He looked at his watch. "If we leave soon, we can get the better part of a half day in."

Verdun felt the rush of cool air on his face as he careened down the slopes in hot pursuit of the svelte figure in the tight red ski suit just ahead. After the first few tentative runs, Verdun had found his old form, but it didn't hold a candle to hers. She was a natural. He watched the neat sprays of powder she left in her wake as she carved her way through the steepest parts of the slope with expert ease. Arriving at the bottom, she turned to greet him and waved towards the chalet. "Drink?"

"Sure." His legs were tired already, and he knew he was going to pay the price tomorrow as it was. They popped off their skis and walked over to the chalet. Finding a table in front of a large window overlooking the slopes, they pulled off their hats and gloves and she took a seat. A waitress came by to take their order, and as she left, Verdun found himself staring at Isabelle as she looked out the window. The cold had left a rosy glow on her cheeks.

She turned back to him and caught him looking. "What?"

"How do you manage to look so good in a snow suit?" he said, smiling.

"Pretty hot stuff yourself," she said, looking at his cobbled-together ensemble. His old ski suit was so full of tears it couldn't be worn, and now, he looked like an overstuffed mattress.

"It's ok," she whispered, leaning close. "I know what's under all that goose down – the real you, that is."

He smiled as the waitress returned. "This was a great idea," he said, as they drank and sat back.

She nodded, and they sat in silence for a moment, before she put her glass down and looked at him. "Are you still thinking about him?"

"Yes, but I'm trying not to. You?"

"Same."

"I'm surprised Detective Théberge hasn't called."

"Do you think he'll let you know if they find Bruno?"

"He'd better. And I'll be going over to Gatineau first thing tomorrow if I haven't heard back. Karl's trial is almost over. We don't have the luxury of waiting around for the Sureté."

"I'm sure he'll call."

"Yeah," Verdun said, without much conviction. They sat, looking out at the late afternoon sky as the sun began to dip behind the hill.

"Oh," he said, "remind me to drop by my place on the way back. I need to pick up my blue suit."

"Sure," she said. "I thought you'd brought them all over already."

"No," he said, sipping his drink. "But I seem to have brought most everything else. Your closet's getting crowded."

"A friendly takeover." She smiled.

"Let's call it a merger."

"I like that."

He looked at her, her features framed by the setting sun behind her. That smile. "I've been thinking about that lately, now that you mention it."

"Really?"

"Well, I've basically been freeloading off you since...you know."

"True." She nodded slowly.

"And I thought maybe instead of paying you rent, I could offer you something else instead."

"Sounds interesting,"

"Do you like the Maritimes at Christmas?" he said. She said nothing but he thought he detected a little glimmer in her eyes. "I was planning on going home for the holidays," he continued. "And I wondered if you would come with me. I've been looking into renting a place just outside Halifax for a couple of weeks. It would give me time to show you around. You know, show you where I grew up. Meet my old friends...my parents. That sort of thing." He found himself nervous all of a sudden. Though he remained cool on the outside, his heart pounded inside his turtleneck.

Agonizing seconds passed as she sipped her wine and put down the glass. She leaned over the table and beckoned him near. "I would love to," she said.

twenty-eight

Verdun's morning was not shaping up well at all. He was due in court in less than fifteen minutes, and he had discovered, upon arriving at the office and turning on his computer, that he had forgotten all about a deadline for filing a defence in one of the few civil litigation matters he was handling. He had refused Jim Smythe's offer to take over his files for a few days, deciding immersion in work was better medicine than a lot of free time to think about Jean Martin. But his mental state had taken a turn for the worse as he listened to the morning newscast's clinical description of the case. Frozen in front of the mirror, his face half covered in shaving cream, Verdun had hung on every word of the twenty second report, waiting for some word or detail that would reconcile it with the desperate scene he had experienced firsthand as the life of another human being had been extinguished before his very eyes. The morning anchor was well into the hockey scores before Verdun realized that Martin's story was over, the listeners left to draw their own conclusions from stock phrases such as "foul play suspected" and "drug-related." He stood there motionless, unable to acknowledge the unspoken but unavoidable conclusion of the story – that it was just another drug deal gone bad.

Shaken but determined not to falter, Verdun had made it in to work, with the intention of easing into the week. Now, he would have to spend what was left of his day after court scrambling to get a defence filed on a case he hadn't touched in weeks.

Where were his meeting notes? he asked himself as he rifled through the unruly mass of paper on his desk. He picked up the phone in frustration. "Julie, I'm due in court in fifteen minutes and I can't find my meeting notes on the Pickett file. Any idea where I might have put them?"

His secretary was at the door a few minutes later with a file folder in her hand. "Are you looking for this?"

Verdun looked up from his frantic search, reached for the folder, and, flipping it open, breathed a sigh of relief at the sight of a yellow sheet of handwritten notes. "Thank God," he said.

"Why not thank me instead?" she said. "There's a detective Théberge on hold for you. Do you want me to take a message?" She looked at the clock on his wall.

"No. No, I'll take it."

"All right," she said, turning to go.

"Julie," he said. "Thanks. I don't know what I'd do without you."

She smiled. "I'll transfer the call in."

Verdun answered on the first ring. "Detective Théberge?"

"Mr. Verdun, I'm sorry I didn't get back to you sooner, but I was waiting on the results of some tests."

"I heard the news this morning and I have to say, I was shocked. Anyone would think that Jean Martin was a career criminal, not a respected crime writer."

"Well, we don't write the news, Mr. Verdun."

Verdun sighed in frustration. "What about Bruno Jacques? There was no mention of him. Have you had any luck finding him?"

"Actually, he's not a suspect. But we are pursuing several leads as we speak."

"What do you mean, he's not a suspect? After everything I told you, you don't think it's a little coincidental that Jean Martin ended up dead after making enquiries about Bruno Jacques?"

"Look, Mr. Verdun, I know you have your own views on this matter, but the evidence we have does not lead to the same conclusions."

There was silence as Verdun collected his thoughts. He was baffled by Théberge's comments, and he noticed a certain distance that wasn't there before. "Look, Detective, I have to be in court in a few minutes but I'd really like to discuss this with you. Can we meet later today?"

"I'm afraid that's not possible, Mr. Verdun. You can understand that I have my job to do as well."

Again, Verdun noted the coolness in his voice. He was becoming very annoyed. "Is there anything you're not telling me, Detective?"

"I'm conducting a murder investigation. Of course there are things I'm not telling you. But I've been more than cooperative–"

"Were you told by someone to lay off Bruno Jacques?"

"I know you were shocked by Friday's events, so I'll forgive your letting your imagination get the better of you, Mr. Verdun," Théberge said pleasantly. "Perhaps if you had known Mr. Martin better, you'd understand," he added.

"What the hell does that mean?"

"He owed a lot of money to a lot of people, some of them not very nice."

"You mean people like Bruno Jacques?"

"No...I can't go into detail but I can assure you that the Sureté will stop at nothing to find Mr. Martin's killer. Just let us do our job. Now I really do have to go. Good day to you."

Verdun put down the receiver and stared at it for a moment, trying to make sense of Théberge's words, and his tone. He needed to call Isabelle, but he didn't have time. He grabbed his briefcase and ran for the door. He would have to sprint down Elgin to make it on time.

Verdun's motion had been mercifully quick, and he found himself back on Elgin Street within thirty minutes. He dialed Isabelle's number and he walked back to the office, impatiently listening to her dial tone.

"Hello?"

"Isabelle, thank God you're there."

"I was in a staff meeting. What is it?"

"Théberge called this morning. They're not considering Bruno as a suspect. Can you believe that?"

"But...Why not?"

"He gave me a load of crap about other evidence pointing him in other directions, but I could tell he was lying."

Isabelle was quiet for a moment. "You thinking what I'm thinking?" she said finally.

"Something funny's going on. I don't know if it's his superiors directing his investigation, or…"

"Or what?"

"I don't know," Verdun replied as a new thought occurred to him. Perhaps Théberge had been the victim of the same type of intimidation as had Verdun. A beep suddenly interrupted the call. "Hang on, I've got another call. Can you hold?"

"Yes, but hurry. I've got to get back."

"Hello?"

"Peter, it's Julie. Pierre Larousse just called to say that Karl was convicted this morning. Sentencing is in two weeks. He wants you to call right away."

"Oh, Christ. All right. I'm almost there." He pressed a button and returned to Isabelle. "That was the office. Karl's been found guilty," he sighed.

"Oh no."

"Listen, this day is really going to shit. I've got a deadline this afternoon for a defence I haven't even started, and I've got to look after it. I don't even know when I'm going to have time to call Larousse. Are you going to be around this evening?"

"Yeah, my follow-up on the Health Minister's business connections in Montreal is on hold, so I won't be going anywhere. See you for dinner?"

"That's a date," he said as he crossed Lisgar and arrived at the door to his office, pausing before going inside.

Isabelle sat in her little blue BMW, scanning the parking lot as a group of men and women in uniform crossed towards the coffee shop located just across the street from the police station. After her meeting was over, she had wasted no time getting into her car and crossing the Chaudiere bridge into Gatineau. It had been clear from his voice on the phone this morning that Verdun was under a lot of stress, and with her main story on hold, she had a little more time than usual. She had considered the routine approach but decided that she most likely would not get past the reception area. Théberge would be no more eager to see her than Verdun and was sure to be conveniently unavailable to respond to her inquiries. She scanned the crowd entering the shop and returned to the text of an article she was re-working. After a few minutes she looked up to see a man in his forties crossing the lot. Tall and dark with a tidy moustache – there was no mistaking Théberge. She waited for him to enter the coffee shop before getting out of her car, locking the door and hurrying across the lot. She joined the queue behind her target and stayed close but out of his sight as he chatted with some of his colleagues who were seated at a nearby table.

Just before Théberge reached the head of the line, Isabelle leaned forward as if to scrutinize the pastries behind the glass, pretending to notice him for the first time as she straightened up. "Detective Théberge?"

"Ms. Jacob," he said. "What are you doing here?"

"I was doing an interview for a story I'm working on," she said, switching to French.

"And the person just happens to live near here, is that it?" Théberge commented, without much humour.

"Yes, actually. How about you?"

He looked at her with a raised eyebrow and proceeded to order his coffee.

"All right, I'll cut the crap," she said. "Let me buy you that coffee."

"I'm very busy, Ms. Jacob."

"Isabelle."

"I have an investigation to get back to."

"You don't think we're going to just leave it alone, do you?"

"We?" He turned to look at her.

"I spoke to Peter this morning. He told me about the unusual turn in the investigation. Look, all I want is five minutes and I'll happily leave you to your business. That doesn't sound so bad, does it?" She leaned to the server and ordered a coffee, nodding to Théberge and adding, "His too," before passing her a ten-dollar bill.

"Five minutes," he grumbled.

She followed him to a table in the corner, where they both sat and sipped their coffee. "So, Peter tells me you're not considering Bruno Jacques as a suspect. Surely you can see why we're both puzzled."

Théberge shook his head. "It's not as simple as you think. You said your cousin referred you to Martin. Did he know him well?"

"Not really," Isabelle replied. "He worked with him for a short period a long time ago. My cousin gave us his name by reputation more than personal knowledge. Why?"

"He had some very bad habits."

"Such as?"

"Off the record?" Théberge leaned in ever so slightly.

"All right."

"A nasty drug habit for starters. Heroin."

"Is that so?"

"He had other expensive tastes as well. Things that are usually beyond the means of your average crime writer. High-end strippers and a lot of gambling."

"You seem to be painting a very negative picture of Mr. Martin. What happened to respect for the dead?"

"You think I'm making this up? Check it out for yourself. You'll find he owed money all over the place."

"My money's on one of the creditors living in Montreal, driving a Harley and going by the name Bruno."

Théberge leaned back and sighed. "You see, you're not even prepared to listen to the facts. You think you've got it all figured out, don't you?"

"All right, suppose it's all true. Martin's the poster boy for living on the edge. Doesn't that make it even more likely that someone like Jacques would be involved in his death?"

"Not when he was about to bring down the Rollers' arch-rival," Théberge said.

Isabelle looked puzzled, trying to recall the name of the biker gang that was trying to infiltrate the Montreal scene with the backing of affiliates in the U.S.

"The Dogs?"

Théberge nodded. "He was working on an exposé on the Dogs, but it seems they found out about it before he had finished.

They've been relying on their relative anonymity to get a toehold in their war with the Rollers. I'd say that gives them a pretty strong motive and all but exculpates anyone from the Rollers altogether."

"Who told you all of this?"

"Reliable sources," he said emphatically. "You have yours, and so do we."

"Come on," she laughed. "Do you know how crazy that story sounds from this side of the table?"

"I don't really give a shit how it sounds to you."

"But you're saying you're relying on it to abandon the investigation of Bruno J–"

"There never was an investigation of Bruno Jacques because there was never any credible evidence against him," Théberge interrupted, putting the lid back on. "Your five minutes are up."

"And you're wrong if you think we're just going to drop this."

Théberge leaned in close, his mouth enveloped in a visible snarl. "I don't give a fuck what you and your boyfriend think. Make it your life's work if you want. And if you try and print any of this, I'll deny it, and I'll have your job while I'm at it." Just as quickly, he had reverted to a smile, bidding her goodbye and leaving the table.

Isabelle was a seasoned journalist and had developed a very thick skin over the years. All the same, she was shocked by the sudden intensity of Théberge's vitriolic warning. But she quickly recovered her composure and returned to her car. Starting it and feeling the power of the engine, she felt her spirit renewed. She looked in the little mirror under the sun visor and checked her hair. Pausing for a moment to take stock of her reflection, she felt a sudden anger at the way Théberge had tried to intimidate her. She took a deep breath and flipped the visor back up. If that bastard thought he had scared her off, he had another thing coming. Her adrenaline still pumping, she stomped on the gas pedal and raced out of the parking lot, squealing her tires as she regained Maisonneuve headed back over the river.

Verdun walked out the front door of the little house on the edge of the Des Fees parkway, down the path and through the front gate, closing it behind him. He looked up to see Adèle Roy, still standing in the doorway, waving him goodbye. He returned the wave and headed for his car, his shoulders heavy with the weight of emotional exhaustion.

Verdun had called Pierre Larousse mid-afternoon, while his secretary worked on a draft of the defence, to discover that Roy's father had requested that Verdun look in on his wife and break the news that her son had been found guilty of murder in a foreign land. For financial reasons, Verdun discovered, only one of Roy's parents had been able to attend the trial. Larousse had described the effect of the verdict on Roy's father as "devastating," and it was with a great deal of dread that Verdun made the trip over to Gatineau late in the day, after finishing the bulk of the defence document and entrusting its filing to one of the associates.

Mrs. Roy greeted him with her usual hospitality, likely sensing from the start that something was wrong. He decided to break the news as gently, but as quickly, as possible, so as not to string her along. She deserved nothing less than the truth, after all. She wept upon hearing the news, but gathered herself enough to offer him coffee, which he gratefully accepted. He spent the better part of two hours talking with her about Roy's life – his work, his girlfriends, his hopes and dreams before all of his current "troubles," as she called them. She asked him about the upcoming sentencing, as well as appeal and any other options that might better the unfortunate fate to which Roy now seemed destined. He answered as best he could, explaining what he knew of the options, but trying not to attach too much weight to the likelihood of the success. Finally, he was humbled by her gratitude for all he had done, which to Verdun, now seemed terribly insignificant.

At Verdun's suggestion, Mrs. Roy had asked a friend to come over, and after she arrived and he ensured that Mrs. Roy was in good hands, Verdun had withdrawn. As he now walked to his truck, he felt the events of the past few days catching up with him. He seemed to be jumping from one crisis to the next, and it was taking its toll. As he got in his truck and shut the door, he sighed and ran his fingers through his hair. He closed his eyes and images raced through his mind: Roy's astonished face as he heard the verdict that would most likely place him in a foreign jail for the next twenty years or more, Jean Martin's morbid, pallid face, those staring eyes pleading with him to grasp the meaning of some unspoken message. He opened his eyes and started the truck, needing a refuge from all of this negativity – solace that could only be found in one place. He pulled out his cell phone and turned it on, noting he had several messages. As he descended into Hull, he looked at the green glow of the phone's display and recognized her number. She had called while he was with Mrs. Roy. He desperately needed to be with her now, to forget about all of this for a while. He checked the time and tried her at home.

"Hello?"

"It's me," he said.

"Where were you? I've been trying to reach you all afternoon."

"I'm just leaving Karl's mother's place. She was pretty upset."

"Oh God. That must have been awful for her. And for you."

"Yeah, it was. How was your day?"

"I had a chat with Théberge this afternoon," she said.

"You did?"

"I had a little more time today than you did, so I took a trip over to see him."

"What did he say?"

"All in good time. We've both had a long day. I've got a nice white chilling in the fridge. We'll have a relaxing drink and I'll tell you all about it when you get here. Drive safely."

"I'll be there in ten."

In spite of everything that had happened that day, Verdun couldn't help smiling. It was amazing, the invigorating effect she had on him. As he crossed the Portage Bridge and caught sight of the Supreme Court in the fading grey light, and the Parliament buildings beyond, he turned on the radio and found himself humming along to a song. There was no drug that could match this. He would be asking Jim Smythe about his jeweller as soon as he got the chance.

twenty-nine

Verdun stepped out of the cab into a whirlwind of thick wet flakes that obscured anything that was more than five feet from his nose. He squinted at the wind and slammed the cab door shut, hurrying to the nearby entrance to the East Memorial Building, past a few hardy smokers huddled against the swirling wind. Once inside, he stamped his feet on the thick carpet covering the marble floor and moved to the guard's desk, brushing the wet flakes from his jacket. "Hell of a morning out there," he said.

"It's that," the grey-haired commissionaire said.

"I've got a meeting with John Grimes – name's Peter Verdun."

"Verdun, hey?" The commissionaire scanned a list, ticked off Verdun's name and handed him a temporary visitor's pass.

"Elevator's that way, sir." He pointed down the hall. "You're going to the fifth floor."

"Thank you," Verdun said, removing his overcoat and placing the sticker on the lapel of his suit jacket. He picked up his briefcase and walked off towards the elevators, his rubber overshoes squeaking as they hit the marble floor. The old building opposite the Supreme Court served as Justice Canada's headquarters and comprised offices off a series of long hallways leading to an inner atrium at the base of which was the law library.

Verdun disembarked on the fifth floor to find himself in an airy reception area encircling a large cherry wood coffee table, and with a counter at the back. He presented himself to the woman behind the counter, who asked him to be seated while she called to announce his arrival. After hanging up his coat and removing his overshoes, Verdun sat down and scanned the selection of newspapers and legal magazines on the table, some of which he recognized from the pile of non-urgent mail that always littered the side table in his office. He picked up a copy of a departmental magazine that he hadn't seen before and flipped through the articles covering recent developments or government initiatives in a wide range of legal fields, from environmental regulations to major lawsuits against the Crown, to proposed changes to the Criminal Code. Most familiar with the last category, he focused on the few pages dedicated to criminal law initiatives. As he reached the last page of that segment, he was drawn to an article topped by a picture of a silver-haired man at a podium. The headline read: "Fearless Former Prosecutor Appointed ADM." Verdun scanned the article, which described the highlights of the man's career, from his days as a young prosecutor, through his appointment to lead a Justice anti-crime task force, to his leading role in a couple of high-profile biker cases in Quebec. Verdun felt an undeniable respect for Robert "Bob" Desjardins as he read about the multiple death threats the latter had endured, especially for a government salary. As he looked at the picture again, Verdun saw an intensity in the man's eyes that matched his description as fearless, but that inspired confidence as well as authority. Surely, with such a man as an adversary, the Bruno Jacques of the world would have few places to hide. He was looking at the bottom of the article for details of Desjardins' appointment when he heard his name from across the room.

"Peter, sorry to keep you waiting. I'm surprised you managed to find the building in this weather!"

Verdun shook his hand. John Grimes was an affable sort, always ready to cut the inevitable tension of litigation with a well-timed joke. Verdun didn't deal much with the civil arm of federal Justice, but he knew Grimes from the early days, when the latter had been a partner at Verdun's articling firm, before he made the move to Justice.

"Good to see you, John," Verdun said as Grimes led him down the hall to his office, a small but nicely decorated area with a large window looking onto what would have been a lovely view of the Supreme Court and the Ottawa River beyond, if not for the blizzard outside. Verdun inspected a picture on top of a bookcase as he laid his briefcase on a chair.

"My grandson. He's two," Grimes said.

Verdun noted several other group pictures in the background, remembering Grimes had a large family, though he wasn't sure if he had four or five children. "You're a grandfather. Congratulations."

"Two more on the way at last count." Grimes was obviously proud. "Before Ben arrived, I thought being a grandpa would make me feel old, but the little tyke reminds me of chasing my own kids around when I was a younger man." He laughed as they both sat. "You married?"

"No," Verdun said. "Though I've been thinking a lot about it lately," he was surprised to hear himself say.

"Good for you. It's a wonderful thing, to have a family," Grimes said. "But you didn't come here for advice on family matters, did you?"

The pleasant mental image of Isabelle holding their toddler's hand as he made his first steps across a lush green lawn disappeared abruptly as Verdun returned to the present with a little sigh. "No, John, I didn't," he said, pulling a file folder out of his briefcase and preparing to make his pitch for discovery of Crown documents.

Verdun's meeting with John Grimes had been relatively successful, resulting in an undertaking to give him access to most, if not all, of the documents he had been looking for. And he had accepted Grimes' invitation to join him for lunch in the Justice cafeteria, the weather being too miserable to warrant venturing out onto Sparks Street. As they chatted over coffee, Verdun thought of the magazine article he had seen in the reception area. "While I was waiting earlier, I was reading about a guy named Bob Desjardins – a recently appointed assistant deputy minister," he began. "He was described as a fearless former prosecutor," Verdun added, recalling the headline.

Grimes nodded as he swallowed the last of his coffee. "Yeah, that was a while ago that he was made ADM. Spent most of his career in Quebec fighting the bikers."

"That's right."

"He must have a lot of balls, I'll give him that." Grimes shook his head. "But to be honest, I don't know him personally. Different portfolio and Justice is pretty big."

"So where would he fit?" Verdun asked.

"His portfolio? God knows. I haven't been here long enough to figure out all the acronyms myself. He'd be somewhere in federal prosecutions, I would imagine. The corporate side is on the fourth, I think." Grimes looked up to the many office windows above them facing the interior atrium at the base of which they were seated. "Why? You defending a biker?"

"No. Just curious. Bikers aren't a client base I'm going after right now."

"Glad to hear it. They're a nasty bunch."

As Verdun finished his coffee, Grimes looked at his watch and smiled. "Well, it was good to see you again." He extended his hand as they stood. Verdun shook Grimes' hand and thanked him for the undertaking to disclose. "Go up these steps and hang a left. That'll bring you back out to Wellington," Grimes said, bidding him farewell as he went the opposite way.

As Verdun passed a bank of elevators and a set of doors slid open, he decided to jump on. Riding it up to the fourth floor, he got off and found himself in another reception area similar to that on the fifth but featuring a locked door and an electronic keypad next to a glassed-in reception counter. There was no one seated on the other side of the window and he considered pressing the intercom for assistance, but feeling somewhat deterred by the increased security, he decided instead to take one of the business cards by the window and retreat to the elevator. He had the distinct feeling he wouldn't be getting in to see anyone today regardless.

Verdun had waited twenty minutes for a cab as the intensity of the storm picked up and a real accumulation hampered the flow of downtown traffic. Now safe in the warmth of the office, he felt the recent lack of sleep catch up with him, and though he didn't relish the prospect of going anywhere, he needed a caffeine boost desperately. He went to his door and looked around. He knew

Julie was visiting her mother in Toronto, but even so, it seemed deathly quiet for mid-afternoon.

"Where is everyone?" he asked the receptionist.

"Mr. Smythe is in court all afternoon with Todd. And Betty had to pick up her son from school," she said, referring to Smythe's secretary. "They closed it because of the storm."

"They're closing the schools?"

"Most of them," she said. "It's supposed to get worse as the afternoon goes on."

Verdun considered the receptionist's commute to Barrhaven and looked at the empty client chairs. He didn't have any appointments for the afternoon and it wasn't much of a day for walk-in traffic. "Why don't you get out of here while you still can? Traffic's going to be a nightmare later on, and there's not much going on here anyway. You can forward the calls to the answering service. Anything urgent will go to our direct lines anyway."

"Thanks, Mr. Verdun." Smiling, she hurriedly punched a code into the phone and gathered her coat and bag.

"Drive safely," he called after her, returning to his office and leaving the door open to ensure he would hear anyone coming up the stairs.

Verdun was catching up on the pile of non-urgent mail, which never completely went away no matter how often he went through it, when the phone rang.

"Peter, how are you doing?"

He sensed that Isabelle's voice lacked its usual warmth. "Better than yesterday. How about you?"

"I've got to go to Montreal tomorrow," she said. "And I'm really not in the mood for a road trip. Any chance you could get away?"

He sighed. "I wish I could, but I've got a trial starting Thursday –"

"The assault? Is that this week?"

"Yeah. I could ask Jim to take it. I'm sure he wouldn't mind."

"It's ok," she said. "I'll take my dad out to dinner or a show."

"How long are you going for?"

"I'll be back by the weekend. Anything new on Karl's sentencing?"

"No, but I may have stumbled onto someone who could help us," Verdun said.

"Who?"

"Bob Desjardins. He's a senior bureaucrat – assistant deputy minister of something – with a lot of experience going after bikers."

"How'd you find out about him?"

"I was over at Justice for a meeting and his name came up by fluke. He's got a reputation for being a bit of a gunslinger – and somewhat fearless. Sort of like the anti-biker poster boy. Headed up task forces and prosecuted high-profile bikers in Quebec."

"Sounds like someone we should definitely talk to," Isabelle agreed.

"I'm going to try and arrange a meeting this week if possible."

"What are you going to say it's about?"

Verdun hadn't really thought about that, but he sensed Isabelle was thinking further down the road than him.

"I don't know. What do you suggest?"

"You want to keep it general enough that he doesn't think he needs a week of briefings before he meets with you, but interesting enough to make it worth his while."

"Sounds a little more political than my usual approach."

"Listen, whatever his background he's a politician now. Say it's an anti-gang initiative certain members of the defence bar are considering proposing. Something you'd like the benefit of his considerable experience on. He might think it has some political benefit for him."

"That sounds good."

"I've gotta run. See you tonight."

As Verdun hung up the phone, he heard voices and footsteps out in the reception area. He came out to investigate and found Jim Smythe brushing snow off his coat, apparently oblivious to the thick layer that had settled on top of his brown hair. "Well, if it isn't Santa Claus!"

"Ho frikken ho," Smythe muttered, noticing Verdun's amused glance and sensing the presence of the white halo. He leaned forward to brush it off and cursed again. "Boy, it's bad out there."

"I sent the staff home. I've got a light afternoon and figured we're not going to be getting many visitors."

"Good idea," Smythe said, hanging up his coat and shivering. "Jeez, it's freezing in here. Any idea how to work the coffee machine?" Like Verdun and most of the staff, he usually bought his coffee at one of the many shops along Elgin and rarely, if ever, drank the office brew.

"I was just going to ask you to run out and get us some," Verdun joked. "Yeah, we can probably figure it out if we put our heads together."

Smythe found the filters in a drawer, while Verdun retrieved a large can from the fridge, and before long, they were pouring steaming coffee into mugs.

"Tastes better when you make it yourself, right?" Verdun said, noticing Smythe's grimace after taking a tentative first sip.

"At least it's better than going out there again," Smythe said.

Verdun laughed.

"What?" Smythe asked.

"You looked like a yeti when you came in. Is it really that bad?"

"Oh sure, laugh it up." They both chuckled and sat drinking their coffee for a while. "So how are you doing?" Smythe asked quietly.

"I'm all right," Verdun said.

"Don't underestimate the impact of something like that. Maybe you should take some time. I'm sure you could get an adjournment for the trial under the circumstances. I can handle it for you if not."

Verdun shook his head. "I think I'm better off working. I really do. But thanks for the offer, I appreciate it."

Smythe nodded before taking a sip of his coffee.

"I should know better, I guess, but I just thought it would all be resolved by now," Verdun said. "Bruno Jacques should be behind bars right now, but instead, the police have ignored him and all but abandoned the investigation."

"Do you know if what they're saying about Jean Martin is true?" Smythe asked.

"I don't know." Verdun shook his head. "Neither does Isabelle, to be honest. Even her cousin hadn't been in touch for a long time, so who knows?"

"And how's Isabelle taking it all?"

"She's doing what I'm doing. Trying to keep busy. She's off to Montreal this week on a story."

"Why don't you go with her?" Smythe suggested. "I told you I can handle your trial."

"Actually I may have stumbled onto someone who can help with the Gatineau cops."

"Oh yeah?" Smythe drained his cup.

"Ever hear of Bob Desjardins?"

Smythe shook his head.

"I was over at John Grimes' office this morning. He's with the feds now."

"Yeah, I remember John."

"Anyway, I was reading an article in the reception area about a former prosecutor recently promoted within Justice. His background was in biker prosecutions. A real gutsy guy by all accounts."

"Now that you mention it," Smythe said, raising an index finger. "I do remember hearing something about him. He handled one of the mega trials in Montreal."

"Right. Anyway, I was thinking of trying to pick his brain about what to do with the Martin investigation. Who knows? Maybe he could even pull some strings."

"Sounds like it's worth a shot."

"I was going to call and try and set something up this week."

"Good luck," Smythe chuckled.

"I know, I had that conversation with Isabelle, but she gave me some ideas. She knows her stuff."

"She's a keeper all right," Smythe agreed.

Verdun laughed. "By the way, you said you knew a good jeweller…"

Smythe looked surprised. "You serious?"

"I'm asking, aren't I?"

thirty

Isabelle waved at the waiter as he passed by with a coffee pot and pointed to her cup with a smile. The young man, dressed the part of the cash-strapped student in scruffy jeans and a wrinkled t-shirt, was only too happy to oblige a beautiful female patron and was soon filling her cup with fresh coffee.

"Can I get you anything else?" he asked, ignoring the impatient waves of a group of male students in the corner.

"Just the bill, thanks," Isabelle said, as he turned to leave, a little deflated. The grungy café had been a regular stop during her days at McGill, but she hadn't been inside in a couple of years. She was glad to see that their tradition of cheap food and good, hot java hadn't changed. She took a sip of coffee and returned to her notepad, finishing off her notes of the morning's meeting with one of the members of the McGill Board of Regents. Her topic was the funding crunch facing universities in the Ottawa area, but her editor had thought it useful to get the views of their Quebec counterparts. For her part, Isabelle couldn't help wondering whether the real reason was to get her away from Ottawa for a while, for some "perspective," as her editor had put it. This had been in response to her repeated requests to do an intensive report on Jean Martin's case requests that had been adamantly refused from the outset. Instead of using Isabelle's unfortunate first-hand experience as an asset, the paper's management had felt it unwise to have her assigned to the case, because of a lack of objectivity. It was all too clear to her that her replacement lacked her enthusiasm for the case and had done little more than report the material that had been spoon-fed to him by the Gatineau police.

Despite her lack of interest in the university story, and whatever her employer's motives, Isabelle was thankful for the trip. To be here in her old university haunts was quite therapeutic. She looked outside at the brilliant sunshine and the thin layer of snow on the ground and decided it was a perfect day for a stroll through campus. She had another meeting scheduled for the following morning but a light afternoon of research ahead. She only wished Verdun were here to join her. She had come to rely on him a lot lately, to the point that she felt something missing when they were apart. She was looking forward to the trip east for the holidays, and imagined them sitting in thick sweaters, sipping brandy in front of the fire.

"Here you go," the waiter said, slapping a receipt on the corner of the table and breaking her reverie.

"Oh, thanks." She reached for her purse and began gathering her things. As she put her phone into her bag, she considered calling Verdun but remembered his trial. Better to wait until this evening. She left enough for her bill and a generous tip and headed out into the crisp air, flipping her scarf over her shoulder and heading up Sherbrooke towards McGill campus. As she walked, she wondered whether Verdun had gotten his meeting with Desjardins, and it occurred to her that, with her afternoon free and with access to a good library, she might be able to help out from here. She took the cold air deep into her lungs and smiled. She loved winter.

Isabelle stifled a yawn and refocused her eyes on the small screen of the microfiche reader. She scribbled some notes before moving the scanner over page after page of newspaper articles, looking for the next in a series of articles she had discovered in *The Montreal Gazette* dating back a dozen or so years. As she relaxed her grip on the button, she was jolted by a buzzing sensation on her hip. She grabbed her phone and recognized Verdun's cell number on the display. "Hello?" she said quietly, looking at the students scattered around the tables and chairs in the basement of the library.

"Isabelle? Why are you whispering?"

"Hang on," she said, getting up and going into a nearby study room and closing the door. "There," she said, returning to her normal voice. "I'm in the library."

"What library?"

"McGill library."

"Oh. How's it going?"

"Fine. How's your trial?"

"It's all right. I'm chipping away, but who knows?"

"Did you have any luck with Desjardins?" she asked.

"Not yet," he said. "But there's a good chance the trial will wrap up tomorrow, so I could still meet him on Friday if I can arrange a meeting. So your story's keeping you in the library overtime?"

"No, the story's a bit of a bore. But that's not why I'm here. What time is it anyway?"

"Seven."

"My God, I've been here for hours. No wonder I'm so hungry. I decided to get a little background on Desjardins and came across some pretty interesting reading."

"You're a real little gumshoe, aren't you?"

She laughed. "Seriously though, this Desjardins has a very interesting past."

"How so?" Verdun's interest was piqued.

"There's a series of investigative articles on an informant who ran amok in the early nineties. He was a really bad dude, accused of just about everything, including several murders before he ended up dead himself. After his death, someone started looking into his files and discovered that, despite a ton of evidence against him, he was not only never charged with anything, but actually paid handsomely with government dollars – presumably for information."

"What's this got to do with Desjardins?"

"He was said to be in charge of a secret informant program – if you can call it that – run in conjunction with the RCMP, though neither he nor anyone from the Mounties would comment on it."

"Was there an investigation or anything?"

"There was pressure for one, and a lot of articles in the weeks following this informant's death, but it seems to have died off. After that, there was just this one writer who continued to file his articles."

"Who's the writer?"

"Jean LeCompte. I found an obituary from five years ago. Looks like him. I've got a call into my cousin to see if he's heard of him."

"Well, Desjardins certainly seems to have left anything shady well behind him. Maybe this LeCompte was just a conspiracy theorist."

"Maybe. But he wrote in a lot of detail about the mole program, from how it recruited young thugs, then threw money at them and gave them immunity for virtually anything in exchange for information on organized crime. It was all very secret – not to mention illegal – and Desjardins' name appears in a lot of the articles as a key person, along with an RCMP officer named Jeff Cory."

"What about Cory?"

"He's retired. I put a call in to a friend in Ottawa who's looking for his coordinates."

"Boy, you're really thorough, aren't you? I hope you're not going to do a background on me."

"I'm checking with my sources as we speak," she laughed.

"When are you coming back?" he asked. "It's bizarre to be at your place without you."

"Friday. And I like it that you're there. I just wish I could be too."

"Oh, while I think of it, I got a call from the travel agent and the place is booked for Christmas."

"The farmhouse? That's wonderful. I'm really looking forward to it."

"You're going to love it. Big stone hearth and plenty of firewood to keep us warm. We can even chop down a Christmas tree on the grounds and drag it back ourselves."

She laughed at the mental image. "That I have to see."

"What? You don't think I can live off the land?" he joked.

"I'm sure you're capable of anything you set your mind to, Peter."

"That's better. Oh," he said as a loud beep sounded in the background. "That's the oven. I'd better go before I burn the place down."

"What's on the menu?"

"Frozen lasagna. Hurry home."

"I love you," she said. "I have a mental picture of us in front of that big stone hearth to keep me warm until the weekend."

Isabelle hung up and returned to the microfiche reader, switching it off. She had gotten enough information for one day. She collected her things and left the library. Outside, it was dark and as she made her way back to Sherbrooke along the path through the main gates, a light snow began to fall. It was only a short walk to her hotel, where she would freshen up before finding somewhere to eat. So Desjardins had given Verdun the slip so far. She would have a couple of phone calls to make first thing in the morning.

thirty-one

Verdun's heart skipped a beat at the sound of the car's horn blaring behind him. He jumped from the street into the pedestrian area as the driver shouted obscenities and sped off down York Street. His mind had been wandering as he walked to his lunch rendezvous with Malcolm McGavin. He spent the majority of the fifteen-minute walk thinking of Karl Roy, and despairing at the fact that all that was left of his defence were submissions to try and reduce the sentence. As he reached the Empire Grill, Verdun looked up at the sky, which had grown darker during the last part of his walk. The wind had picked up too, and he felt a slight tingling in his cheeks as he entered the warmth of the restaurant. He spotted McGavin already at a table and waved his way past the addled server.

"Peter, thanks for coming."

"My pleasure. How are you?" he said, removing his coat and draping it over the back of his chair before sitting.

"Oh, you know. Counting the days to retirement."

"Really, you don't look like a retiree."

"Less than a year to go. I'll have been with the department for thirty years by the end of next summer."

"Wow, that's quite a stretch. Congratulations."

"Thanks."

"What's next then?" Verdun asked, trying to imagine McGavin gardening full-time. It didn't quite fit.

"I'll probably do some consulting. I should really stick it out for another five years and get a full pension, but I'm too old-fashioned for the department nowadays." He shook his head and sighed. "Things are changing more and more, not necessarily for the best."

Verdun wondered if there was something more that McGavin wasn't saying.

"Take Karl, for example. It's an absolute disgrace the way he was abandoned. You think that would have happened twenty years ago? Not on your life."

Verdun nodded as the waiter appeared to take their drinks order.

"But that's enough griping from me," McGavin said as the waiter left. "Tell me what I can put in this affidavit that might be of help."

"Right. Well, as I told you on the phone, Pierre plans to make several submissions at sentencing and we thought, as a senior official, you would be a good person to speak to his integrity."

"Of course," McGavin said.

"I also wanted your opinion about asking someone in the French government to do the same. I know you spent a lot of time in France and must have extensive contacts, but I can imagine not everyone would be enthusiastic, given…"

"Given Karl's been convicted of killing one of their own," McGavin finished his thought. "Karl impressed his counterparts in the French diplomatic corps, I can tell you that. As for protecting their own, your instincts are right, but we shouldn't forget Malle was no poster boy for the French government. He had a rather forgettable reputation from their perspective. I'll make some calls and see what I can do."

"That would be great."

"Yes, I can think of a couple of people that might be willing," McGavin said as their drinks arrived, and they each ordered one of the specials.

"So what ever happened to that reporter from *The Citizen*? She was looking into some link to the young girl Malle had killed in that accident years ago."

Verdun sighed and gave a brief summary of the events leading up to Jean Martin's death.

"Oh my God!" McGavin exclaimed. "I read about it in the paper, but the police seemed to be chalking it up to the drug trade."

"Yeah," Verdun said. "I think that was their intent."

"But this is preposterous. Surely there is something that can be done to pressure them into at least questioning this Jacques fellow."

Verdun shook his head. "We've tried, believe me. In fact, I'm trying to arrange a meeting with an ADM at Justice to see if he can help."

"Who?"

"Robert Desjardins. He used to prosecute bikers in Montr–"

"Bob Desjardins?" McGavin repeated, his face registering shock.

"Yes. What's wrong?"

"Well, I'm surprised you're asking him to help."

"Why?"

"Because he was one of the main reasons Justice never went to bat for Karl on his extradition," McGavin continued as Verdun looked on, perplexed. "You remember I said there was a group in Justice that seemed adamantly opposed to helping Karl and I couldn't explain why? Well I'm told that Desjardins was the main ringleader."

"What would he have to do with extraditions?"

"Nothing, technically, but he is on very close terms with the minister. I guess he had his fingers on the pulse of Karl's file."

"Maybe there were political reasons not to oppose the extradition. That doesn't necessarily mean he won't help Karl out at sentencing, does it?" Verdun asked.

"No, but there would be a certain irony if he did help now."

Their meals arrived and the conversation returned to the specifics of Roy's affidavit, before concluding with casual chit-chat. Before he knew it, Verdun was looking at his watch and calling for the cheque. "This time I'm paying. I insist," he said, flagging down the waiter.

They parted company, with McGavin promising to send him something by the end of the week. All the way back in the cab, Verdun considered Desjardins' role behind the scenes of Roy's extradition, finally deciding that the motive must have been political. As he got out of the cab in front of his office, he ran into Jim Smythe, headed for afternoon court.

"Hey, I made that call for you," Smythe said.

"The jeweller?"

"He said to drop by tonight after six. Can you make it?"

"Yeah, I think so," Verdun said.

"The address is on your desk."

"Thanks, Jim. I owe you one."

Isabelle sat on the bed in her hotel room, her wet hair wrapped in a towel and a map of the city spread out in front of her. She pointed the remote at the television at the foot of her bed and turned the volume down so that the morning news was reduced to background noise.

"Valcartier, Valcartier, where are you?" she asked herself, tracing her finger through the fine print of the index. "There you are – B5." She located the sector on the map, in the east end, and planned a route from the hotel. She looked at her watch and decided it was long enough after the rush hour peak to brave Descarie Boulevard. She quickly blow-dried her hair, put on a bare minimum of make-up and dressed. Going out the door, she grabbed her phone and tossed it in her purse.

Isabelle tried to remember if she had accepted the additional insurance on her rental car as she squeezed into a quickly disappearing gap in the three lanes merging into an on-ramp. Advancing at a painfully slow pace, she spotted an opening and found herself directly opposite a young man in a dented old Toyota with racing stickers on the windshield. He had obviously seen the same space and, for a split second, the two stared at each other. Isabelle gave him a big smile, enough to make him hesitate for the instant it took her to step on the gas and jump into the opening. As it closed behind her, the other driver was left in the snarl of traffic, cursing in defeat.

With some open road ahead, Isabelle's mood lightened as she joined the morning race across the city. This was far from the breakfast meeting she had planned in a trendy café near the hotel, but when the financial officer from the university called to postpone their meeting until late afternoon, she had decided to make the most of her time instead of cursing her bad luck at having her trip home delayed. Her first call was to Robert Desjardins' office, but it had been too early to do anything but leave her number on voice mail. As she was considering how to get her hooks into him for an interview, her phone rang – this time with good news from Ottawa, that the ex-Mountie she was looking for had retired to Montreal.

Before long, Isabelle was descending an off-ramp into a rather spartan part of the east-end that seemed familiar, though she wasn't sure why. She soon found the address and parked outside a bungalow in a nicer area than what she had driven through, across the street from a little park. She walked up the front steps and, seeing no doorbell, rapped on the screen door.

After a few seconds, a woman in her fifties or early sixties opened the door, leaving the screen shut, if not locked. "Yes?" she said. Her tone was neither inviting nor unfriendly, just indifferent.

"Good morning. I'm looking for Jeff Cory."

"He's not here, dear."

"Are you expecting him back soon?" Isabelle smiled.

The woman said nothing for a moment, sizing her up. "I didn't get your name."

"Oh, it's Isabelle Jacob. I wanted to talk to him about an old case of his." She saw by the woman's face that she was getting nowhere.

"And who do you work for, Ms. Jacob?"

"It's a matter of personal interest actually," Isabelle fibbed, handing her a card with her name and numbers to her direct line at the paper and her cellular. "I'd really appreciate if you could give him this when he gets back."

"He's fishing up north for a few days," she said. "But I'll be sure to give him this when he returns."

"Thank you," Isabelle said and returned to her car. She started it up and drove away, all under the watchful eye of an unsmiling Mrs. Cory, who stood by the counter behind her front window.

Driving back towards Descarie, Isabelle was kicking herself for having been out-maneuvered on the doorstep. Her demeanour must have given her away immediately, and she was angry with herself for having driven across town and then squandered her one chance at Cory. She should have had a better story prepared, she told herself, shaking her head as she took in the sights of the working-class neighbourhood. As she passed a snow-swept, graffiti-sprayed basketball court, Isabelle suddenly remembered why it all seemed so familiar. She stopped at a four-way intersection and guessed at a right turn, then a left. A few moments later she was in front of the housing project where Josée Vachon lived. She pulled over and shut off the engine, looking at the familiar unit and trying to determine if anyone was home. After a brief internal debate, she decided it was worth a shot, got out of the car and crossed the street. She paused briefly at the door before knocking.

A few seconds later, a haggard-looking Josée Vachon, in the same tattered mauve housecoat, opened the door. "Ah, c'est toi," she said, with a slight cackle. She removed the cigarette from her mouth long enough to cough. "What do you want?"

"I was wondering if I could talk to you – just for a moment."

Vachon looked at her with red-rimmed eyes and took a long drag on her cigarette, expelling a foul mixture of stale tobacco and alcohol.

Isabelle shivered, rubbing her hands together. "It's cold out here," she said.

"Hmm," Vachon said, putting the cigarette back between her lips and swinging the door a little wider. "What the hell? Nobody comes to see me anymore."

Isabelle followed her into the front porch.

"Never mind your shoes," she said, continuing down the dark hall to the kitchen. Isabelle followed. "Coffee?"

"Yes, please."

Vachon poured the coffee and sat at the kitchen table, where a tin of tobacco sat open, next to a box of filters and a rolling machine. Isabelle sat across from her, where she had been at their first meeting. The same pictures were displayed on the side table in the adjacent dining room.

"I interrupted," Isabelle said, pointing to the tobacco tin. "I'm sorry, I should have called, but I was in the neighbourhood."

"Who can afford cigarettes these days?" Vachon laughed, causing a short spurt of coughing. "So what did you want to talk about?"

"You don't have any recent pictures of your son?" Isabelle observed, glancing at the side table.

Vachon pushed the rolling machine to the side and swept away little bits of tobacco. "I got plenty. Those are just the baby pictures over there." Vachon lit another cigarette.

"I'm still interested in Bruno," Isabelle said. "For the story I told you about when I was here before. I was hoping we could try again."

"You don't have the lawyer with you this time?" Vachon said.

"No. His client's trial is over. He was convicted of murder."

"That much I know. Maybe someday I'll get a chance to thank him for ridding us of that selfish bastard who took my daughter."

"You were upset when I asked you about Bruno at our last visit. Why, Mrs. Vachon?"

"Was I? I don't really remember. I don't see my Bruno very often these days. Like I said, nobody bothers to come see an old woman like me anymore. Enjoy your youth and your beauty, my dear." She sucked deeply on her cigarette.

"Is he in Montreal?" Isabelle asked innocently. "Maybe I could see him, talk to him myself."

"You'll do no such thing." Vachon shook her head. "I don't know why you came back, but there's nothing else to say. I'm sorry your friend lost his trial–" Vachon was interrupted by the doorbell. She looked down the hall. "If that's those Goddamned Jehovah's Witnesses again, I'm going to send them straight to hell. That's the third time this week." She got up and padded down the hall towards the door.

Isabelle heard the door open and the exchange of voices. She glanced over at the side table and got up to have a closer look at Bruno's baby picture. She remembered it from before – a chubby little baby in a sailor's outfit, with the hospital bracelet inset below. As she picked it up, the frame slipped out of her hand and fell onto the carpeted floor. She glanced towards the front door and saw that Vachon was fully engaged in a tirade against the two unsuspecting Jehovahs. Isabelle reached down and was relieved to see that the glass had not broken, but when she picked it up, the backing came loose and the picture and the bracelet slipped out.

"Shit," she said quietly, trying to replace the picture in the centre of the cardboard insert before retrieving the bracelet from the floor. As she placed the bracelet in the little cardboard rectangle cut out to accommodate it, she realized she had replaced it backwards. She took note of the doctor's name, and one other that didn't register, as she hurried to pop it back into the frame. She heard the sound of the door creaking shut and Vachon's last warning to the Jehovahs and she quickly popped the little clasps on the wooden frame back in place to secure the backing. As Vachon returned to the kitchen, Isabelle was setting the picture back on the side table. "He's so cute."

"Yes, he is," Vachon said icily, looking at the picture, then at Isabelle, who was smiling a little too brightly. "Now, if you wouldn't mind, I've got things to do."

"Of course," Isabelle said, fishing out a card and handing it to Vachon. "If you change your mind, give me a call."

"Hmm," Vachon said, as she followed Isabelle back down the hall.

After she had closed the door behind her, Vachon returned to the dining room and picked up the picture. She flipped it over and looked at the backing, which was securely in place. As she turned it face up to return it to the table, she put a worried finger over her top lip. The bracelet in the frame was upside down.

thirty-two

Isabelle sat in the corner of the hotel bar, sipping her wine. She checked her watch again before picking up her phone. It was after five and even if his trial hadn't wrapped up yet, court would surely be adjourned for the day. She was anxious to talk to him, in part to tell him the good news that Desjardin's office had returned her call half an hour ago to arrange a meeting, but mostly because she missed him. She smiled expectantly as she punched in the number to Verdun's cell phone, but after a few rings, her smile faded, and before long, she was listening to the impersonal greeting on his voice mail.

"Hi, it's me," she said after the beep sounded. "I was hoping to talk to you, but I guess you're still in court. The bad news is I'm stuck here until tomorrow – my morning interview got bumped to tomorrow afternoon so I won't be back much before early evening. The good news is I got you an interview with Desja–" Her phone beeped with a call on another line. Isabelle cursed silently and double clicked to hang it up and return to the message, which was still running.

"Sorry about that," she said quickly. "Damn call-waiting. Where was I? The meeting with Desjardins. I hope you don't mind that I called, but I figured you had your hands full with the trial and all. Anyway, I spoke to him less than an hour ago. He wanted to meet you today but I said you were in court. Then he offered to meet me this afternoon but I explained I was in Montreal until the weekend. He seemed pretty keen. Anyway, I'm rambling and I'm going to run out of time, so just call his assistant Nathalie and she'll set up a time for tomorrow afternoon. I'm going to surprise Dad tonight and take him out to dinner but I'll have my phone so call me. I love you. Bye."

She took a deep breath after she hung up, followed by a sip of wine, then checked her messages, fumbling in her purse as she listened to the message from her garage. They must have been the ones that interrupted her message, and had been persistent enough to call back and leave a message asking ask her to arrange a maintenance visit for her car. Where was her room card? She hung up the phone and looked in all of the recesses of her little purse but came up empty. She was always losing things – it was terribly careless of her, she thought. It must have fallen out in the car, but she wasn't going back down to the bowels of the parking garage again. They'd have another at the front desk. Finishing her wine, she gathered her things and decided to return to her room and freshen up before the short walk to her father's house. As she approached the front desk, she smiled pleasantly at the young man behind the counter and asked for another room key.

"Certainly," he said, reaching into a drawer for a spare. "Uh, I'm supposed to ask you for some identification," he said, as if it troubled him greatly to have to do it.

"Sure." Isabelle obliged, showing her driver's licence.

"Thank you. There you are. Oh, wait," he called as she turned to leave. "There's a message here for you, Ms. Jacob." He passed her an envelope.

"Oh? Thank you." She took the envelope and tore it open as she moved towards the elevators and stepped into an upward-bound car as she read the note.

"Floor?" asked a man who followed her in and pressed the button for the eleventh floor.

Isabelle stood there in silence, her eyes locked on the note, re-reading it.

"Floor?" he repeated politely, as the doors slid shut and the car began its ascent.

"What? Oh, I'm sorry," she said. "Seven please, thanks."

"Long day, huh?" The man smiled.

"Yes," she said, returning to the note. It was a handwritten scrawl from Josée Vachon, asking to meet at a downtown bar at six. Isabelle was puzzled as to why Vachon would feel like talking when she'd brushed Isabelle off that very morning. It was also a little odd that she would have come across town to leave a note instead of calling. But as she stepped out onto her floor, her doubts were replaced with an eager anticipation that the meeting might actually yield some results and this so far useless trip would be worthwhile after all. She didn't have much time though. As she unlocked her room and headed for the bathroom, she tossed her open purse onto the bed, not noticing that her little phone had bounced out and come to rest just out of sight under the bed-skirt.

Verdun dropped his overstuffed briefcase onto the floor by his desk and fell back wearily into his chair. He was completely drained. After a full day in court that had gone until after five, he had spent another hour and a half in a meeting with his client over a last-minute offer by the Crown to plead guilty to a lesser offence. It was a reasonable offer, and he had told his client as much. But as difficult as it was to refuse, they had both been buoyed by the direction the trial seemed to be taking as it wound its way to a conclusion. No doubt the prosecutor had felt the same, triggering the offer that was beyond consideration just a few hours earlier. In the end, his client had opted to see the trial through to its natural conclusion. Verdun only hoped they had read the judge correctly – never an easy thing to do in any circumstance. In any event, the trial had been adjourned until Monday due to a scheduling conflict, so he would have a chance to take a breather tomorrow and recharge his batteries before the final push.

Now, approaching seven in the evening, the office was almost completely dark. The staff had cleared out long ago, and while Smythe or one of the associates might well return later, they were nowhere to be seen for now. He loosened his collar and punched the numbers into his desk phone to access his cellular's voice mail, touching the hands-free button and skipping through several messages, including one from Robert Desjardins' assistant, before hearing the familiar sound of her voice. Verdun leaned back in his chair and turned up the volume, smiling in admiration at her tenacity – she was still working on Josée Vachon! He was even more impressed by the news of her success in getting a meeting with Desjardins, but disappointed when he realized she was probably at dinner by now with her father. He would wait a little before calling, so as not to interrupt. As he sat back in his chair and her words resonated in his head, he caught sight of his tweed jacket hanging on the coat rack next to the door, the glint of his Bar Association lapel pin reflecting the overhead light. He had worn that jacket into the office this morning for the first time since the night of Jean Martin's death. He got up and removed the pin and brought it back to his desk, looking at the logo of the scales of justice on a blue-black background. His face clouded as he considered its similarity to another logo – that of the Department of Justice, except for the colours. He quickly re-entered the access codes to his voice mail and turned up the volume, skipping through to Isabelle's message. He froze in his chair as he heard her voice again, interrupted as it had been by the call-waiting: *The good news is I got you an interview with Desja...*

A series of thoughts and images flooded his brain, from his recent meeting with Malcolm McGavin, whose face had shown great surprise on hearing Verdun's plans to enlist the help of Bob Desjardins in getting to the bottom of Martin's death, to Isabelle's cousin's theory that the death threat on Verdun's mirror could well have been the work of someone protecting a highly-placed informant. Last of all, and most vivid, was the expression on Jean Martin's anguished face as he uncurled a finger towards Verdun's lapel and uttered his final breath, along with what he had understood to be "déjà" at the time but now took on a very different meaning.

Verdun grabbed the receiver from his desk phone and called Isabelle's cell number. His anxiety mounted as it rang over and over, and in desperation, he finally gave up. He called her hotel and tried her room number, but to no avail. She was probably in a restaurant and had turned off her cell phone as a courtesy, he tried to reassure himself, as he sat on the edge of his chair. But why was the damn phone ringing then? Didn't it tell you the customer was unavailable when the phone was off? His heart rate increased again, but he fought off panic by trying to reason things out. What had she told him? She had visited Josée Vachon. So what? he told himself. They had been there together months ago. As for Desjardins, it was unthinkable that such a senior bureaucrat could be involved in protecting a murdering thug like Bruno Jacques – wasn't it? Besides, what was he going to do?

"Oh my God," he said aloud as he recalled her saying that she had told Desjardins where she would be until the weekend. *He offered to meet me this afternoon but I explained I was in Montreal until the weekend. He seemed pretty keen.*

He remembered the message from Desjardins' assistant and hurriedly dialed it up. *Mr. Desjardins asked me to advise you that he will not be able to meet with you Friday after all. Please call to re-schedule for Monday. I will try to contact your office as well to ensure you get this message.*

Verdun realized Isabelle must have given numbers for both his cell and office. He looked at his watch and tore through his day-timer for Julie's home number.

"Hello," she answered on the second ring.

"Julie. It's Peter. Did you talk to anyone from Robert Desjardins' office today?"

"Yes, actually, his assistant called about an appointment tomorrow. He's had to re-schedule to Monday."

"Did she say why?" he asked.

"A prior meeting he had overlooked – something like that–"

"Where? Did she say where the meeting was?" he said abruptly.

"No. What's the matter?"

"I need to find out where Desjardins is going to be tomorrow. It's to do with.... It's just very important that I find out where he's going to be."

"I used to work with one of the assistants in the office when I was with Justice. I could try calling her."

"You could?"

"Yeah, we still do lunch from time to time."

"Could you call her tonight?"

"I can try if you really think it's necessary."

"I wouldn't ask you normally, but it really is important."

"Are you all right, Peter? You don't sound yourself."

"Can you call?" he said urgently.

"Where are you?"

"I'm at the office."

"Let me call her and I'll get right back to you."

"Thanks." He rang off and paced back and forth in front of his desk. His mind was abuzz with possibilities. Should he call the police? What would he tell them? He didn't know what was happening himself. He dialed Isabelle's number on his cell phone again, tapping his fingers on the corner of the desk as it rang incessantly. He abandoned it after twenty or more rings and swore as he tossed the phone onto the desk. The office phone rang and he snatched it up. It was Julie.

"I talked to my friend. She said Desjardins is unavailable all day. She made me swear secrecy but I convinced her to give me his schedule. He's got a meeting with the minister first thing in the morning and then he's got an out-of-town meeting in the afternoon. A last-minute thing."

"Did she say who the meeting was with?"

"She didn't know who he was meeting, but he's booked on the eleven o'clock train to Montreal."

Verdun froze as the destination sank in and another apparent coincidence joined a long string of others.

"Peter?"

"Yeah, I'm here. Listen, Julie, thanks so much for doing that. I really appreciate it." His mind was racing. "Oh, and as for tomorrow, I won't be in. I've got some things I've got to do–"

"But your trial?"

"Adjourned until Monday," Verdun said, in as carefree a tone as he could muster.

"You're sure everything's all right? You don't need me to–"

"Everything's fine. I'm sorry to have bothered you at home. You can reach me on my cell tomorrow if need be. Have a good night, and thanks again."

He hung up before she could ask again what was wrong. Now

he was really shaken. He thought of calling the police again, but they would think his story was the product of a conspiracy theorist. He debated jumping in his car and driving to Montreal, but what would he do when he got there? There was no point sitting outside her hotel room door. He slapped his forehead – her father. He would call her father! He entered his computer password and waited impatiently for it to come to life. What was his name, damn it! Gerald? Gerard? No, it was Georges. He entered the first and last names into an online directory and was soon looking at a list of names and numbers.

"Shit," he swore. Without an address, it was a waste of time. For all he knew the home number was unlisted anyway. He picked up the phone to dial the police but put it back down. There was only one link he was sure of, and that was Desjardins. When his train pulled into town tomorrow, he would have to be there.

Isabelle had the sensation she was falling, or spinning. She awoke abruptly and opened her eyes to dim light and a throbbing in her temples. Her first instinct was to feel her head for bumps, but found her hands were restrained behind her back. She sat up and looked around. She was sitting on a pile of burlap bags containing something soft. She tried to stand but realized her feet were also bound with tape of some kind. Her head ached and she felt very woozy. She shut out the wave of fear building up inside her, directing her energy to remembering how she had come to be here. As the fog lifted from her brain, she remembered leaving the hotel and walking to the address in the note, a bar not fifteen minutes from her hotel but on the edge of a less than desirable part of downtown. She had ordered a drink and taken a seat in the corner. From there, things became foggy again. She hadn't felt well, she knew that much. In fact, she'd felt decidedly ill all of a sudden. She strained to recall what had happened next, and saw a face emerge. It was the friendly face of a woman, the concern in her eyes obvious. She had offered help. Isabelle remembered leaning on her just to walk out the door. A different one than she had used to enter. The woman was saying something. A cab – she was putting her in a cab and sending her back to her hotel. But how would she know which hotel? No, it wasn't a cab. It was a van. A big, black van. The door had closed and enveloped her in darkness – a darkness she had welcomed, as it had stopped the awful, disorienting dizziness.

She had been drugged. Drugged and brought to this place, wherever that was. Now the fear crashed over her, as she tried to call out but could manage only a hoarse croak. "Hello?" she called into the half-light.

Nothing.

She tried to reposition herself on the bags, her back aching now, as well as her head. She ended up half sitting, half lying, tears rolling down her cheeks as she sobbed quietly.

Verdun had checked into Isabelle's hotel the previous night around nine. Before leaving Ottawa, he had passed by her house and retrieved her father's home number. He had tried not to betray his alarm as her father confirmed his worst fears, that no, he had not heard from her though she had mentioned earlier in the week that they might spend some time together before she returned to Ottawa.

"You know what she's like, Peter. She's always dashing off to meet a source at the last minute," he said.

"I haven't checked my messages again," Verdun lied. "She must have called back when I was out."

After changing and shoving a few things into a bag, he drove at breakneck speed to Montreal. He confirmed at the front desk that Isabelle was not in her room before heading out to the east-end to try Josée Vachon. But finding no one there, he had little choice but to return to his room and wait for the next morning. He spent an awful night, lying on the bed, thinking of what he should do. He must have fallen asleep at some point, because he awoke at seven, still dressed, and bolted out of bed. He called the train station and confirmed the arrival times, then showered and headed downstairs to the restaurant to force down some food while he waited for the shift change. He sat in the lobby, pretending to read a paper and watching as new faces appeared behind the desk.

At five after eight, he approached the front desk and smiled at the young man behind the counter. "I was wondering if you could help me. My name is Peter Verdun, room 1407," he said, handing him a business card. "I was supposed to meet a client here yesterday evening – a guest here at the hotel as well – but I arrived late and I've left her cell number back at the office. She wouldn't have left a message here for me by any chance? Her name is Isabelle Jacob."

"Let me check, Mr. Verdun," he said politely, tapping keys on the keyboard behind the counter. "No, there's no message here." He checked the slots behind him and returned shaking his head.

"You wouldn't have seen her here in the lobby last evening, would you? She's tall, dark hair. Very attractive," he said.

"I think she was here, now that you mention it. I remember giving her a message."

"A phone message?" Verdun smiled.

"No, an envelope."

"Oh yes, that would be from the office. Of course. Delivered by a tall, blond man, right?"

"No, he had dark hair, I think." The young man saw enough surprise in Verdun's eyes to sense that perhaps he should stop there.

"Dark hair. Yes, of course," Verdun said. "Well, perhaps I could leave her a message apologizing for missing our appointment and asking her to call my office to re-schedule at her convenience."

"Certainly, Mr. Verdun."

"Thank you."

Verdun crossed the lobby towards the elevators to the parking garage. As he descended to his car, he had a sense that the message had a lot to do with Isabelle's disappearance. But what incentive would have drawn her into danger? He had to find Josée Vachon before that train came in.

Verdun knocked on the door repeatedly and with enough force to wake the dead. As he considered whether to sneak around the back or just force the front door, he heard the sound of footsteps.

"If you're the friggin' Jehovah's Witnesses, you'd better run!" a raspy voice called out from behind the door.

"Mrs. Vachon. It's Peter Verdun. I need to talk to you about Isabelle Jacob. I know she came to see you yesterday."

She opened the door a crack. "So what if she did?"

"She's gone missing. Let me in."

"I'm not letting you in, and what do you mean, missing?"

"Mrs. Vachon, please. She's in danger."

Vachon sighed. "Come in before you wake everyone else in the neighbourhood enjoying a grasse matinée. Coffee?" she asked.

"I don't have time for coffee. What did you talk about yesterday?"

"Nothing really. She said she was in the neighbourhood–"

"Mrs. Vachon, please."

"She was talking about her story and whether I wanted to talk to her about my son. I said I didn't and that was it."

"And afterwards?"

"What afterwards? That was it, I told you."

"So you had nothing to do with her disappearance from her hotel last night, just a few hours after her visit with you?"

"I don't know what you're talking about."

"Did you send her a note?"

"Send what note where?"

"Did you have someone deliver a message to her hotel?"

"No," she said, breaking away from him and shuffling down the hall to the kitchen. "I'm having coffee."

"Mrs. Vachon." He followed her down the hall. "You don't seem to understand. Isabelle is in grave danger. If you don't tell me what you know, I'll have no choice but to go to the police."

"Ha!" she cackled, pouring her coffee. "That's a laugh. I haven't done anything. Call whoever you like."

"Did you call anyone yesterday, Mrs. Vachon?"

She frowned. "Who would I call?"

"Did you call your son Bruno and tell him that Isabelle was asking about him?" For the first time Verdun noticed an unfamiliar expression on Vachon's face. Part surprise, but part fear. He seized on it before it faded completely. "You know what kind of danger she's in, and that she's innocent in all of this. She's just trying to write a story."

"She's not in any danger from Bruno. My son would never hurt a woman."

"So you did call him?"

"It doesn't matter. I want you to leave."

"I'll leave all right. I'll go straight to the police, and if anything happens to Isabelle, they'll come straight here."

"You have no idea who you're dealing with, do you?"

"Tell me."

Vachon shook her head.

"Tell me where to find Bruno."

She laughed again. "I'm his mother and I only see him a couple of times a year."

"You got him a message yesterday." He crossed the kitchen and stood over her.

"You'd never get to him," she said, sipping her coffee.

Verdun noticed a large hardcover book on the counter, with the name of a Catholic saint on the cover and a coat of arms. A year was written in the top right-hand corner. He picked it up. "Is he in here? Can I at least see a picture of him?"

"Give me that," she said, grabbing at the book. He held it out of her reach and opened it to the graduating class. The pictures were arranged alphabetically.

"Oh, go ahead, but don't say I didn't warn you. You don't know what you're getting into."

Verdun found him, the corner of the page with his picture having been turned down. The picture was of a thickset youth with long dark hair and a moustache, sporting a Montreal Canadiens T-shirt.

"Here," she said, reaching into a drawer and pulling out a 4x6 in a frame and handing it to Verdun, her motherly pride getting the better of her. The smiling man standing next to his gleaming motorcycle shared little in common with the earlier picture, other than being adorned with a Canadiens jacket.

"He likes the Canadiens, I see."

"They're his religion," she said. "Growing up, that's all he wanted to be. If only..." She stopped as she noticed Verdun's expression as he squinted to focus on the gold chain around the neck of the man in the picture. He followed it to its lowest point, hanging in the "v" of the open shirt.

"What is it?" she asked.

Verdun paused to consider its relative importance before putting the picture down and checking his watch. "It won't matter unless I make my next appointment," he said, looking at Vachon. He hadn't noticed how pathetic she looked as she stood there in her tattered housecoat, a cigarette dangling from her bloodless lips. If he wasn't so worried about Isabelle, he might have felt sorry for her.

thirty-three

Verdun was at the train station a full hour before the train's scheduled arrival and, after making a careful assessment of all possible options, chose a short-term, metered parking spot just ahead of the waiting taxis. He assumed that Desjardins would either be met outside the station, or he would take a cab. He put in money for the maximum allotted time of thirty minutes and headed inside the station to confirm the arrival time. The train was running a few minutes ahead of schedule, so he bought a coffee and sat in the waiting area, sipping it and thinking of Isabelle. He wondered what they had done with her, and had to close his mind to the worst scenarios. He felt inside his coat pocket for the bowie knife he had brought with him from home. He had stopped by his house and found it in an old camping kit he had stored away in the basement. He had debated trying to buy a gun last night, but he didn't have the first clue how to go about getting one on the street. He looked at his watch and, realizing he was nearing the end of his meter time, returned outside to the car. He fed the meter again and was about to return to the terminal when something occurred to him. He had been assuming that if Desjardins didn't take a cab, he would be picked up at the curb. He realized now that if someone met him inside, following them in his car could be problematic. What if the other vehicle was parked on the other side of the lot, out of his line of sight? As he debated what to do, he heard a long blast of a horn, indicating the train's arrival.

He jumped out of the car and made his way over to the entrance, looking through the glass doors. A few minutes after the train stopped, people started getting off. Verdun scanned the mix of passengers and greeters for the face he had memorized from the picture. As the seconds passed, his eyes darted feverishly over the crowd, with still no sign of Robert Desjardins. He swore under his breath. There! He was coming straight towards him, dressed in a camel-coloured overcoat and towing a rolling overnight bag. He was alone. Verdun returned across the street to his car and started it up, keeping watch in his side mirror as Desjardins hailed a cab. Verdun breathed a sigh of relief as he pulled away from the curb and slid in behind a blue taxi with Desjardins in the back. He followed as the driver left the station and turned right into traffic. Squeezed out by a young man in a beat-up van, Verdun lost sight of the cab momentarily. But he regained his breath as the van took the next right and he saw the cab in his sights, with only a little Honda separating them. As the lights changed, the cab scooted through a stale yellow and Verdun veered to the right and around the Honda as it slowed. Ignoring the red light, Verdun gunned his way through the intersection. Fortunately no one had started moving across in front of him, though he was fully prepared to drive right through them if it meant keeping up with that taxi.

Before he knew it, they were on Sherbrooke Street. Verdun slowed to allow not more than two cars in between him and the taxi, and as they came up to the Ritz-Carlton, the cab's indicator light came on. Verdun looked for places to stop, but everything was taken. He pulled into an open space that was the entrance to a store across the street from the hotel and put on his indicator light, adjusting the side mirror to see Desjardins getting out of the cab and entering the hotel. Verdun tugged on a baseball hat to go with his sunglasses, put his hazard lights on and got out of the truck.

"Hey you! What do you think you're doing? You can't park there!"

Verdun wheeled around to see the proprietor of the store standing on the doorstep, shaking his fist at him. "I just have to stop in over here. I'll be two seconds," he replied.

"No, no, no!" The man was having none of it, but Verdun didn't care. He turned to cross the street, but as he did, he saw Desjardins coming back out through the hotel's front door without his bag. He watched him turn down a side street.

Verdun rushed back to his truck, almost running over the store proprietor. "Relax, I'm going already," he said, hopping back in and looking over his shoulder. Desjardins was getting into a dark sedan and heading off down the side street. Traffic was stopped all around Verdun. He put on his indicator and looked at the nearest driver, who refused to make eye contact but edged forward to ensure Verdun's path was blocked.

"Fuck you, too," Verdun said aloud, slamming his truck into gear and jolting it forward, smashing into the front fender of the car. As Verdun backed up a few feet and prepared to do the same thing, the other driver recoiled in horror and moved his car into reverse, tapping the car behind him. A flurry of horns began sounding, and in the confusion, Verdun nudged across in front of the damaged car before butting his way across the other lane, cutting off a terrified-looking woman in the process. A few seconds later, he had made it back to the side street, and he sped off in hot pursuit, the car horns ringing out in unison behind him.

Reaching a T at the end of the street, Verdun looked quickly right, then left at a dead end. He sped off to the right and, after a bend to the left, saw a stretch of straight road with a line of cars at the end, stopped at a red light. As he came up at the back of the line, he made out the sedan at its head, just as the light turned green. He breathed a sigh of relief and continued with the flow of traffic, checking his rear-view mirror for any sign of the police but saw nothing. The sedan's occupants would have missed the sights and sounds of the traffic melée he had left in his wake.

He kept a safe distance, and there was enough traffic that he felt he had probably been unnoticed so far. As they drove farther east, the traffic thinned and he had to fall back for fear of coming up too close behind them. The weather had begun to turn from overcast to light flurries, and the farther east they went, the darker the sky became. Verdun switched on his wipers and strained his eyes to keep a clear view of the sedan.

As they reached the outskirts of an industrial area, the sedan made a right onto a small street leading down to some depots and warehouses. Verdun pulled over to the side of the road and watched the sedan follow the slowly dipping road into a little valley. It pulled up at the side of an old warehouse with rusted steel siding and an unrecognizable logo on the side. From his vantage point, Verdun could see two figures emerge. Desjardins' camel coat was clearly recognizable as he got out of the passenger side. The driver was dressed in black and was shorter but stockier. The flurries were picking up and the visibility deteriorating. He watched them go up a long staircase and after the man in black unlocked it, they both went through a door.

Verdun jumped out of the truck and began striding down the road towards the warehouse. Within minutes he was at the foot of the stairs. He walked slowly and quietly up the steps and tried the door at the top. It was unlocked. He held his breath and turned the knob, slipping inside and closing it behind him as gently as he could. His heart was racing as he took in his surroundings. He was in a small, dirty and dimly lit office that overlooked a great expanse of open space below. Some large wooden crates were piled up at the far end of the warehouse floor.

Through the office window, he saw two figures below, crossing the warehouse floor. He watched from above as they reached the far end and what looked like a series of inner offices, some with windows and some without. As they went through a door into one of the windowless ones, Verdun made for the door on the far side of the office. It led out onto an elevated steel platform crossing the top of the warehouse. From there another set of stairs descended to floor level.

He looked at the closed door at the other end, then at the stairs. Once he was on those stairs, he would be completely exposed until he reached the floor. And there wasn't much cover down there either. His heart pumping with adrenalin, he headed for the stairs and went down them as quickly and quietly as he could. At the bottom, he hugged the side wall all the way to the rear of the warehouse and crept up outside the door he had seen the two men pass through only minutes before. He leaned close and heard something from within. It was a muffled sound. It sounded like...crying.

Isabelle was in there, he knew it. He heard a man's voice, giving some command, and put his hand on the door handle just as the unmistakable feeling of cold steel behind his right ear made him freeze like a statue.

"You must be the lawyer," a voice growled from very close to his ear. Verdun was grabbed by the scruff of his neck and hurled against the door with overwhelming force, knocking it open before he tumbled onto the floor like a rag doll.

Lying on his back, Verdun looked up to see Desjardins, still in his overcoat, standing over Isabelle, who was sitting on a chair, looking very tired and scared, but showing no obvious signs of other injury.

"Here's your boyfriend now," Desjardins said, smiling. "Come to rescue his damsel in distress." He laughed. "Saves us having to chase you down later."

"What are you doing with her?" Verdun asked, his anger rising.

"Well, I was going to use her as bait for you. But now that you've saved me the trouble…"

Verdun turned to look at the other man, who loomed over him. He was built like an ox, an assessment confirmed by the effortless way he had just tossed Verdun through the air.

"Bruno Jacques? Or is it Vachon?"

"Keep your fucking mouth shut," the man said and promptly kicked Verdun in the ribs.

"Stop it," Isabelle cried out in a strangled voice.

"You're not going to get away with it," Verdun said, through gritted teeth. "We're not the only ones who know."

"Save it," Desjardins said. "You don't know shit. And in a few minutes it won't matter anyway."

"You're going to murder us in cold blood?"

"No, he is." He pointed at the other man, whose expression didn't change as he glared back at Verdun.

"You going to kill her too?" Verdun said, nodding at Isabelle. "Your mother said you'd never hurt a woman."

"I knew it." Desjardins shook his head. "I knew nothing could keep that drunken sow from flapping her–"

"Hey!" the other man shouted. "Don't talk about her like that."

Desjardins swore quietly and turned to Verdun. "It doesn't matter. Whatever she told you will go with you to your grave. Serves you right for being so God-damned nosy, both of you."

Isabelle straightened on her chair, as if she'd just come awake. "You're Bruno *Desjardins*," she said, looking at the other man with pleading eyes.

There was a silence as the man averted his gaze, and Verdun looked from Desjardins to Bruno, and back. "You're his *father*?" he asked Desjardins, who said nothing.

Instead, he pulled a second chair next to Isabelle's and ordered Verdun onto it. "Go make sure no one's around," he said to Bruno, as he slipped on a leather glove, pulled a small handgun out of his pocket and pointed it at the two seated prisoners.

As Bruno left to investigate, Verdun took hold of Isabelle's hand. "Are you all right?" he whispered. She nodded but was clearly distraught. He squeezed her hand tightly, before turning to Desjardins again. "Do you honestly think you're going to murder a lawyer and a crime reporter and walk away?"

"Like I said, I'm not going to murder anyone. That's not my job."

"Your job? What about your job? What happened to the prosecutor who wasn't afraid of anyone? You're an ADM, for Christ's sake."

"Don't be naïve. After a few years of playing it straight I got tired. It starts with a favour here, a plea bargain there. Then there's a little payoff, then a bigger one…"

"But Bruno…"

"I lost track of Bruno a long time ago. Josée was different back then. We were in love but…it doesn't matter." Desjardins shook his head. "When I was on the anti-gang task force we would set up moles through intermediaries. Bruno was our star, but I'd never been face to face. It wasn't until years later that I found out. By then he was our most valuable source…my own flesh and blood."

"So you were lining your pockets with bribe money and advancing your career running informants."

"Taking the money was against the rules, but the work we accomplished was second to none."

"And when you found out about Bruno? You didn't try to get him out of it?"

Desjardins said nothing, so Verdun continued. "You didn't want anyone to find out, did you? Wouldn't exactly paint you as a good parent now, would it? To the point of screwing up your promotion track maybe."

"He was dead to me as a son from the moment he first turned to crime twenty years ago. Besides, money can fix anything." Desjardins laughed, catching himself as Bruno returned from his reconnaissance. Verdun sensed anger in Bruno's appraisal of Desjardins and wondered how much he had heard.

"All clear?" Desjardins asked, to which Bruno nodded.

Desjardins stepped away as Bruno moved closer, his gun raised.

"Wait, I have to know. Did you kill Jean-Christophe Malle?"

Bruno paused, lowering the gun and approaching Verdun. "Slitting that bastard's throat was the best thing I ever did," he said almost triumphantly.

"But how? And why after so long?"

"The last stretch I did in Kingston I got pretty good at the internet. One of the other cons taught me how to find people. I had no idea how easy it was. I tracked down that piece of shit Malle the day after what would have been Annie's thirtieth birthday. A few months later I got out and made paying him a personal visit my first priority."

"But how did you get a passport?"

"Connections." He gestured to Desjardins.

"Come on," Desjardins said irritably. "We don't have all day."

"You know it's only a matter of time, don't you?" Verdun said.

Bruno looked at him with a puzzled expression.

"You left a piece of jewellery at the crime scene. Your beloved Canadians pendant." From Bruno's reaction, Verdun could tell he had hit the mark.

"How the fuck–"

"It was found at the crime scene."

"He's bullshitting you," Desjardins interrupted. "They convicted that poor chump from Foreign Affairs."

"Not for long," Verdun lied. "After I saw your mother's pictures of you in your hockey get-up, I faxed a copy to the

French. All they have to do is compare your DNA with something from the scene – a hair, whatever."

Bruno looked at Desjardins, who shook his head. "That stupid bitch. I told her not to–"

"I told you not to talk about Maman like that," Bruno growled, turning to Desjardins.

"You think he's going to help you out, Bruno?" Verdun said, gesturing at Desjardins. "You're already a liability to him. I'm surprised he hasn't gotten rid of you already."

"Shut up," Bruno shouted, waving the gun at Verdun.

"Don't do it. Think, Bruno, think. And what about your mother?"

"I said shut up!" Bruno barked, hammering Verdun on the side of the head with his big fist, knocking him off the chair and onto the ground.

"He's trying to mess with your head," Desjardins said. "There's no DNA from the scene. This guy doesn't know anything. Go on, get it over with!"

"Is he going to make you kill her too, Bruno?" Verdun said, looking at Isabelle and ignoring the ringing in his ear. "You're no better than Malle."

"Shut up," Bruno screamed, with a ferocity that shook the room.

He stood over Verdun for several seconds with the gun pointed at his head, just staring at him as Verdun waited for the end.

"Go on, kill him," Desjardins shouted.

"Why don't you do it, you're such a big man?" Bruno said, lowering the gun as a shot rang out, its echo reverberating in the small office. Isabelle screamed as she felt the warmth of spattered blood on her face and saw the gun slip out of Bruno's hand as he collapsed in front of her. Desjardins lowered his still smoking gun and walked towards the slumped-over form as Verdun grabbed Isabelle and pulled her back into the corner of the room. As Bruno's torso toppled backwards, Desjardins looked at him in disgust and kicked the gun away.

"You're just like your mother. Born under a bad star. I should have done this as soon as I found out..." He turned to look at

Verdun and Isabelle in the corner and took a step towards them, slowly raising the gun. "As for you, you fucking smart-ass," he growled, pointing the gun at Verdun, then, thinking better of it, he directed it to Isabelle. "You're going to watch your girlfriend die first."

"No!" Verdun shouted, lunging in front of Isabelle and bracing himself for the impact of the bullet as a second shot rang out, then a third. He felt nothing, and looked up to see Desjardins' lifeless form crash to the ground, revealing Bruno's outstretched arm and the glint of a shining gun barrel in his hand. Verdun and Isabelle sat frozen in the corner as the arm went limp and fell to the ground and the gun clunked against the floor.

Verdun slowly got up and moved towards Bruno, stepping over Desjardins' contorted body, his head oozing blood into a growing pool on the floor. Verdun approached Bruno carefully, picking up the gun and staying out of his reach. Bruno's shirt was soaked in blood from the wound to his chest, and a red line flowed out of the side of his mouth.

"Maman," he whispered, as Verdun drew closer. "Tell Maman I'm...." He was labouring to get the rest out. "I'm sorry."

As Verdun watched Bruno's eyes glaze over and his head loll to one side, he looked down at the small leather holster strapped to his right ankle. As Isabelle came up behind him, Verdun turned to look at her. "How did you know?"

For a moment she just stood there, looking uncomprehendingly at Bruno's lifeless body.

"That he was Desjardins' son?" he added, standing up.

"The baby bracelet," she said, her eyes still on Bruno. "It fell out of the frame at Vachon's house yesterday, and I saw two names on the back. I thought the second one was the doctor's. I didn't make the connection then..."

Verdun held her in his arms. They were both still shaking. "Come on," Verdun said, gently moving her towards the door. "Let's get out of here."

thirty-four

"You sure there's enough wood for the whole night?" Isabelle called out, surveying the pile of logs by the hearth with a critical eye. "The temperature's supposed to drop tonight."

"There's more out back," Verdun replied, then appeared from the kitchen with a couple of mugs. "Hot toddies."

"What?" she said as she took a mug of the steaming liquid and sat on the couch in front of the fire.

"You know. A hot drink...with booze in it," he said, sitting next to her and raising his mug. "Cheers."

"That doesn't really sound like much of a recipe." She smiled and took a sip.

"All right, I confess. I have no idea what a hot toddy is, but it sounded good."

"I think you're on the right track. It is good."

As they sat sipping the hot drinks and listening to the crackle of the fire, Verdun couldn't help thinking he had outdone himself in finding this place. He had been looking for something within an hour's drive of his parents' home in Halifax, and someone suggested Mahone Bay. Some internet research and a few phone calls later, he was on the phone with the agency, trying to book the place for the Christmas holidays. He ended up in a bidding war with an American couple, but settled it by agreeing to pay a premium and to wait until the 27th for the keys. He and Isabelle spent Christmas Eve and Boxing Day at his parents' place and were now enjoying the picturesque little town, as well as the maze of cross-country ski trails all around the farmhouse.

They had enjoyed themselves so much in fact, that they had almost forgotten about their awful ordeal just a few weeks before – almost.

While the violent encounter with Desjardins and Jacques would always be with them to some degree, as would the image of a dying Jean Martin, the whole experience did have at least one positive result. In the days following that fateful afternoon in Montreal, a flurry of interviews, meetings and legal motions on both sides of the Atlantic took place. Once apprised of the connection between Bruno Jacques and Jean-Christophe Malle, the Department of Justice moved mountains to get an expedited analysis of Jacques' DNA, confirming within days that it matched a sample found at the crime scene. As for Jacques' connection to Robert Desjardins, Verdun and Isabelle were surprised to discover that an RCMP investigation into Desjardins' connection to alleged improprieties in the informant program had been ongoing for months; the case against him had already begun to build. Upon learning of the paternal connection, every detail of both men's lives came under the microscope, and would remain there until the complex puzzle was finally put together.

Armed with this new evidence of Karl Roy's innocence, the Canadian government intervened vigorously on his behalf, and within a week of Desjardins' and Jacques' deaths, Roy's conviction was reversed and all charges against him dropped. He was released from custody and promptly returned home, a free man. Steps towards a formal apology were in the works, and the subject of compensation had already been broached, along with an assurance that these remedies would be both swift and considerable.

With the miscarriage of justice reversed, the focus quickly turned to Desjardins' role in Roy's extradition. It was soon clear that he had used personal connections to senior people in both Justice and Foreign Affairs to influence the minister's decision to extradite, to the now obvious consternation of the officials charged with handling the file, whose recommendation to refuse the extradition request had not been followed. It was also clear that the fallout from the case would send shock waves through both departments, the impact of which would be felt for some time to come.

The sudden scrutiny applied to Desjardins' past also confirmed his brief and star-crossed liaison with a young Josée Vachon, though it was easy to see how it had never surfaced, given the lengths he had gone to distance himself from her and the child their encounter produced. Desjardins had paid for her silence initially and then simply refused to talk to her ever again. Attempts from a teenaged – and already troubled – Bruno were similarly stonewalled, with Desjardins having married and begun a family that he had no wish to disturb with loose ends from his past. As a result, it was likely that Desjardins had no idea who Bruno Jacques was when he first came into contact with his informant file some years later. Once Bruno made him aware of their biological bond, though, it was clear that the former had exercised considerable leverage over Desjardins, forcing him into decisions that were of strategic benefit to the Rollers, to the detriment of their enemies. Desjardins had also authorized a series of offshore payments that had been one of the triggers for the RCMP investigation, but whether the investigation would ever have connected Desjardins to Bruno Jacques was unknown. As for the connection to Jean-Christophe Malle, the authorities were still trying to figure out under what identity Bruno had entered France, but they assumed it was with the benefit of a passport forged by someone in Montreal with ties to Bruno's gang.

Josée Vachon was interviewed at length for her role in Isabelle's kidnapping, but she would likely not face criminal charges, given it was not clear she fully understood the consequences of telling her son about Isabelle's inquiries. This was surely of little consequence to a woman who had lived to see the second of her two children's lives end in tragedy. The fact that he had died at the hand of the man who had rejected her so completely so long ago must only have made it worse. As he thought about it now, Verdun had nothing but pity for Vachon, and the image of the two dead men lying not five feet from each other, as incongruous in death as they had been in life, sent a chill down his spine.

"What time's dinner?" Isabelle asked, offering him a welcome escape from his morbid thoughts.

"Reservation's for eight," he said, getting up to poke a wayward log back into the centre of the hearth. He had reserved a table at an oceanfront inn, in nearby Chester.

"I'm going to run a bath and get out of these clothes," she said, referring to her ski suit. They had just skied ten kilometres of a trail that followed the shoreline. Verdun watched her leave, noting that she looked as good, if not better, in gore-tex as in evening wear.

"You could come and help, if you like," she added, pausing at the bottom of the stairs.

"Be right there," he said, downing the rest of his drink and deciding to give her a few minutes before joining her. As he sat there enjoying the heat from the fireplace, his mind returned to Karl Roy and how mesmerized he had seemed by the sudden turn of events. He was understandably overwhelmed when Verdun visited him after his return home. Still trying to work out how he felt about the government's role in the unfortunate series of events, he seemed sure about only one thing – the gratitude he felt towards Verdun and Isabelle. And while the whole incident would leave an indelible mark on Roy, Verdun was confident he would be able to get on with his life from here on in.

But it wasn't only Karl Roy who would be permanently affected by the case, as Verdun had already known for some time. He listened to Isabelle's footsteps upstairs and waited for the sound of running water before going over to check in the drawer of the antique bureau for the little black box he had concealed there. He had known how important Isabelle had become to him well before she came into harm's way, but nearly losing her had made that fact all the more evident. After Roy's release had been secured, the very next item on his to-do list was a trip to Jim Smythe's jeweller. He flipped open the lid of the box and the solitaire diamond sparkled in the last of the afternoon sunshine streaming in through the picture window. He snapped it shut and tucked the box away in its hiding spot, where it would stay until they returned from dinner to the fireside, to bring in the New Year together with a bottle of Veuve Cliquot he had picked up in Halifax.

As he pushed the drawer shut, Verdun smiled. He would have good news for Margaret Smythe when they got back to Ottawa.